Small Town Taxi

by

Harriet Rogers

If you want to know what is really happening, ask the taxi driver.

This book is dedicated to professional drivers everywhere.

This book is a work of fiction. The names, characters, places and incidents are products of the writer's imagination or have been used fictitiously and are not to be construed as real. Any resemblance to persons, living or dead, or to actual events, locales or organizations is entirely coincidental.

Chapter One

When she shot my front seat, I thought about getting a different job, but it was the passenger side and empty, so I didn't update my resume. I was surrounded by guys in blue uniforms with guns pointing at my cab. I was inside.

I'm not asking for sympathy here, but I want to go on record that this situation wasn't helping me be the best taxi hack ever. Prior to the bullet flying around my cab, I had been thinking about two things. One was the taxi business. The other was Jon Stevens, a lieutenant in the local police force and a person of interest in my strictly fantasy love life.

A small-town taxi is a vehicle with built-in entertainment. I should know. My name is Honey Walker and I drive for Cool Rides Cab Company in Northampton, Massachusetts.

I love driving taxi, I love moving people and I love the people I work with. Driving taxi was what I was meant to do. Most of my life, I've been a ditz at earning a living and a massive disappointment to my parents and society at large. The phrase that continues to pop up is "does not live up to potential." When I dropped out of college to pursue my own direction, my parents told me not to come home until I had a diploma

1

in hand or a job that would help add to their retirement. I developed an aversion to their attempt at control of my life. Any control over my out of control life was going to be my own.

So here I was trying to live up to my potential as a cabby. My potential seemed like it might be short-lived.

I arrived in Northampton at age twenty-one. That was four years ago and I was on a quest to find something that I could do well enough to earn a living. But even on a quest, nature calls. I found Northampton when I got off the interstate for a bathroom break and I decided to stay. Right now, I wasn't sure staying was a good idea but there wasn't a lot of choice.

People use taxis for lots of reasons. We get calls from the cops telling us not to pick up a guy on whatever street. Contact central immediately if the escapee calls for a ride. I once delivered their escapee to the front door of the police station after he asked me to transport him across the state line, as fast as possible. Neither the cops nor the prisoner paid or tipped so I never did that again. This morning's fare wasn't an escapee—yet—but she definitely fell into the "shouldn't have" category, as in "shouldn't have picked her up."

She'd called for a ride to the courthouse. I figured her for a lawyer or a thief. She had that arrogant, self-assured walk that reminded the rest of us we weren't her. Might mean a big tip. She waited at a mini-mall in front of a hair salon, hair freshly styled, short in back, long in front. You don't get that good a cut if you don't tip well, so I just assumed. Hindsight is wonderful but it rarely solves problems. I should have noticed that the salon was next to a bait, tackle, and gun shop.

She got in the back seat before I could open either passenger door. In a small-town taxi, where someone chooses to sit in the car frequently defines their purpose and their character. If they sit in the front seat, they want to talk, be friends, get cheap therapy. The back seat is the power seat. The driver is separated and is in the service of the client. This passenger oozed lawyer. Power seat, power clothing, briefcase, nice shoes—really nice shoes—red leather, four-inch spikes, with gold trim. Flashy, but you need to be noticed in a courtroom. I always thought if Marcia Clark had owned a better wardrobe, O.J. would have been in the slammer sooner.

"So, where'd you get the shoes?" I asked, figuring she'd want to share sources. She must be a shoe girl— look at what she was wearing.

"Just drive," she snapped.

"Yeah, okay," I grumbled. What kind of woman wears shoes like that and won't talk about them?

We pulled up to the courthouse. "Wait for me," she ordered.

"There's a 10-dollar wait fee." I hated waiting and I'm not good at following orders.

"Fine." She stalked off up the sidewalk, those four-inch heels drumming like Charlie Watts playing *Honky-Tonk Woman*.

Pulling into the no-parking zone, I down-buttoned the windows to let in a breeze and turned off the engine. I adjusted the band in my excessively curly blond hair. With the air-conditioner off, it was about ninety degrees in the sun. If the police noticed me, I could smile and hope my melting mascara didn't make me look like a terrorist raccoon. Then I could move to a legal spot.

Ten minutes later she flew out the side exit five feet from where I'd parked.

"Drive," she screamed and slammed into the backseat.

Rule one of taxi driving: Never drive when someone is yelling at you. Then I caught the black metal shape of a gun in my peripheral vision. I felt something small, round and cold against my neck. I had never had a gun actually touch me. I didn't react well.

I yanked the steering wheel to the left and mashed my foot to the floor. The taxi leaped forward, right into the police car in front of me. The impact threw my passenger forward, whacking her head against the front seat. The gun went flying, landed with a thump, and shot the front passenger seat.

"Shit!" I threw it into reverse, twisting the wheel the other direction. I hadn't noticed the car behind me. A blue wave of cops flooded out of the courthouse and surrounded the taxi. They had guns, big guns. I felt like they were all pointed at me. Right now, in the moment, I tried to focus on surviving the lunatic behind me.

"Oops," I whispered and slid down the seat, wishing I were a lot more invisible.

All four doors to my car opened at the same time and cops grabbed whatever they could get their hands on. That would be me, my fare, and *her* gun, which they handled with a lot more care than they handled either of us. We were cuffed, stuffed and driven over to the police station in the injured cop car. My fare maintained her silence while I stammered and stuttered about my innocence of whatever they thought I had done in the last five years.

In thirty seconds, we pulled up to the police station. Northampton is not a big town. But there were rules about how to safely transport dangerous prisoners—as if one of us might try to escape with at least a million cops surrounding us—so there I was in handcuffs. I was pretty sure I had a lawyer sitting next to me, but she was as mute as a dead fish. They hauled us out and dragged us inside. My father taught me when a situation gets bad, tomorrow is a new day and life always gets better with the passage of time. I wasn't sure he was right about this particular time slot. The next day I might wake up in a jail cell.

Attitude goes with driving a taxi. In this town, there are women, men and others who can stop traffic with their appearance. We have gender combinations that turn visitors into rubbernecking idiots. Me, I'm the girl who makes the phrase "they all look alike" a reality. When I turned seven, I became a tomboy and wanted to look tough. Hoping a scar running down my cheek would create the desired fashion statement, I used one of my mother's matched set of bone handled steak knives to make myself into Scarface. Creating long-lasting damage to facial skin takes a lot of effort. I ended up with a scab that itched like hell for a week and no scar. As a teenager, I considered a tattoo of a feather drifting down on my small but expanding chest. Tattoos hurt. I'm about to turn twenty-five and I remain free of "distinguishing marks." A nose job for me would be to add an inch and a bump. You could find my doppelganger walking down almost any street in London. Blond hair, blue eyes, 5 feet 6 inches tall, yada, yada, yada. It lets me be anonymous when I want to be. Which can be convenient…or not. Right now, it was hard to tell.

Northampton is a city with a funky outlook, bizarre history and politics on every side of every spectrum. Close to the interstate, it's a prime setting for everything from gourmet dining and till-you-drop shopping to drug running and money laundering. It has a courthouse because it's the county seat, which is convenient for the drug runners and money launderers. Since the police force, the local legal establishment and the whole legal system partly depend on the existence of the dirty money and criminal activities, it all forms a nice circular economic interdependence with the courthouse at its center.

The front half of this historic building is made up of huge gray stone blocks and dates back to the 1800s. The addition they slapped on looks like an 18-wheeler hauled in a prefab, postmodern trailer park. Given an uptick in the crime rate over the last decade, the addition was sorely needed.

The population here is a mix of sane and crazy, rich and homeless, ultra-conservative and flaming liberal, and lots of other, more mysterious lifestyles. Our mayor of the moment is a liberal white guy. Our previous mayor was a liberal gay woman. The City has generated publicity for everything from being the best small arts town, to having the largest gay population outside San Francisco, to being a major stop on the north/south drug running corridor. One of our city councilors looks like King Kong and dresses like Marilyn Monroe. Northampton wears the sophisticated glamour of a big city, but the functional underwear of its agricultural, blue-collar origins sometimes rides up its butt crack and shows over the top of the tailored Armani slacks. I fit right in and I had started thinking of this small city as home. It seemed laid back, crime free, and interesting in a weird way. Until now. Now it was exhibiting some of the problems that have been plaguing small towns throughout the country. Police forces were suddenly facing an uptick in violent crime, mostly involving drugs, especially opioids.

But cops are cops everywhere, and none of them like to see anyone except them using, carrying or even thinking about guns.

Half an hour after a bullet drilled my passenger seat, I was in interrogation thinking that, even with its odd construction, the courthouse seemed dignified compared with the cop house, which has been called one of the worst organizational disasters in the city's history. Outside, it's a flat-topped, utilitarian brick building. Inside, it's a rat maze. Trying to find a way out would be time-consuming and pointless. The cops know where they are, and they know where you are. The City is putting up a new building to house the boys and girls in blue, but the old one is still in use and I was somewhere deep inside.

My hands were stuffed under my butt to be sure they weren't shaking. An over-weight, cheerful cop was beginning the interrogation.

"You could be in a lot of trouble here, Miss," he mumbled.

"Hey, I had a gun in my face. I saved you guys a high-speed chase down Main Street. How was I supposed to know what my fare was up to?"

More realistically, I'd had a gun in my back and no way to get out of the parking space without a tank.

This guy was a sergeant. A gun in the courthouse should merit someone higher up the food chain. They were probably deciding who got the short straw and had to sort out my part in the fiasco.

After ten minutes, there was a tap on the door and Lieutenant Jon Stevens poked his head in. I know Jon. He's outrageously good-looking with tight buns and a fabulous smile. He wasn't smiling now, and neither was I, but it was hard for me to keep my heart rate from picking up a little when he came in. My hands, released from under my backside, had stopped shaking, I wasn't in tears and I hadn't thrown-up. Circumstances considered, I thought those were accomplishments worthy of praise. The sergeant left.

"You still drive for Cool Rides?" Jon stood over me, looking impatient. I wasn't intimidated by his scowl, and my eyes were just below belt level. His face wasn't what I was staring at.

"Was that a question? Or are you introducing me?" I snapped, trying to brazen my way through a real police interrogation.

His bright blue eyes stared at me for so long I looked down to make sure my shirt was buttoned and I didn't have any blood dripping down my front. "What?" I jutted my chin forward.

"Did you know the woman?"

"Lady Red Shoes?"

"No," he said. "The woman in pink lace underwear. Who did you think I meant?"

The image of pink lace underwear and the Lieutenant might have been appealing—a straight woman's wet dream. And in this city, a lot of guys might be interested as well. But Jon was in super cop mode, a man of authority. His attitude pissed me off. Have I mentioned that I have some control issues?

"She was a fare," I said. "And I didn't get paid. And I didn't get my wait charge. And the boss is going to be pissed when he sees the dent in the car." I was beginning to wail.

"Jesus Christ, spare me. We got a guy in the hospital getting a bullet out of his ass cheeks and his lawyer-wife who put it there is in holding. I don't give a rat's ass about your cash flow."

He turned away but was still standing with his rear end at eye level. I had to admit it was a fine-looking backside. He gazed down at his feet. My gaze followed, down to his size ten shoes, authoritatively planted in front of me.

He looked at the ceiling. I looked at the ceiling. Nothing there either.

He stalked over to the door, knocked once and said to the sergeant, "Cut her loose."

"Can I have my cab back?"

"Yeah, we got the bullet out. Good luck with the boss."

I dragged through the warren of the cop house. I didn't want to face Willie, my boss. I did want to know the story on the lady lawyer. I wanted to collect my fare and, mostly, I wanted to know where she got those shoes.

Northampton is an almost typical small New England town. When Eisenhower became president, he decided America needed an autobahn. The interstate highway system is America's autobahn and Northampton is on the right side of the interstate. What the president, ex general, meant to be an efficient way to move troops has become a way to move merchandise from fresh produce to crack cocaine. Traffic from larger cities to the south is extensive and Northampton residents think of themselves as only one step from the Big Apple. We are the Little Apple, maybe even the Medium-Sized Apple.

My curiosity sometimes gets me into trouble. I figured if I dealt with my boss first, I could come back to the holding cells later and visit the shoes. I called in and talked fast. I wanted to explain the situation before he started yelling.

"How bad?" I could feel Willie seething over the cell phone. Word about the accident had gotten back to Cool Rides before I did. It was better to tell him about the dent rather than show up pretending I hadn't noticed it, and that I hadn't spent the morning running fares, but sitting in the police station admiring the Lieutenant's backside.

"We just got a scratch. And the cop car isn't too horrible. The civilian car is kind of dented."

"If the cab can be driven, get your ass back here." He didn't ask whether I was hurt or even alive.

I flipped the phone closed and started the car. It was late in the morning and I'd missed half a day's worth of pickups as well as my morning caffeine and sugar fix. I sighed and headed back to the office to face the music.

The crew was standing in front of the garage, next to our fleet of cars, when I drove up. The Cool Rides Company is like that TV show from the '70s with Judd Hirsch and Danny DeVito. Except the cars are more like *The Italian Job*. We don't have Mini Coopers, but the Scion XB has personality. Think a chopped British taxicab. Or a Mini on steroids. There were five of them lined up next to the glass wall that made up the front of the office. All in perfect clean condition, different colors, with creative graphics adorning their sides and cute names printed on the fenders. My personal favorite was the flame job with yellow taxi checkerboard inside the flames. "Cool Rides, the Best Ride Ever" was printed across the doors. They were all washed, waxed, and vacuumed. And now there was mine. The dented fenders would have fit in fine with any other cab company. At Cool Rides, it looked like it had been through a junkyard slalom. I didn't mention the bullet hole in the seat. It hardly showed.

Willie avoided looking directly at the car. I knew he wanted to kick my ass around the parking lot. But he had the personality of a golden retriever trying to pass as a Rottweiler. His curly white hair fell in uncontrolled splendor, his gray eyes were kind. He wasn't the hard-ass he thought he should be.

Andrew, one of the other drivers, stepped forward as I pulled to a stop.

"Wow! Hey, boss, do you think the car is embarrassed? He fidgeted and danced around the car. "Maybe we should hide it around back." He shuffled up the other side and almost stopped in front of me. He couldn't actually stand still, but he gave it his best effort, drumming a loose finger on his leg, tapping a free toe, bobbing his head to music I could never hear. Being around Andrew was like being around a small explosive device. He jittered away, bouncing like an overheated electron, polishing a nonexistent spot on one of the cars with his shirttail.

Mona, our dispatcher, gave me a look that would level Muhammad's mountain. Her soft sultry voice came out of a 5-foot-2-inch body as wide as a linebacker's. Short dark hair and smile lines framed a deceptively cheerful face. Her outlook, however, resembled the attack dog her boss wanted to be, and she protected him like one. Her dark eyes told me not to mess with him. He was in a pile of hurt. I wanted to say "Hey, me too," but, in a rare moment of self-control, I kept my mouth shut.

"So, what did she do?" Andrew wanted to know.

"She shot her husband. In the courtroom…and in the buttocks." I glanced at Willie to see if I was getting sympathy. "And caused general mayhem." I paused. "While I was waiting for her." Not even a flicker of compassion. He was busy feeling the pain of the car by osmosis.

"Wow, how'd she get a gun past the checkpoint?" Andrew was leaning over rubbing the dent in the front fender while his feet beat a little pattern on the ground.

"She's a lawyer. They don't always search them." I'm a good judge of clothing, and her suit had lawyer written all over it. Too bad I wasn't as good a judge of character. My front seat might not have a bullet hole in it.

∂∾∾

Since I didn't get any sympathy at Cool Rides, I decided to see how hard it would be to see Lady Red

Shoes. Maybe if I collected the fare and wait fee, Willie would forgive my accident. And what the hell was this woman doing shooting someone in the backside, in the courthouse, in broad daylight?

Andrew, also our resident body man, had taken my car into the garage to assess the damage, remove the dents, and apply first aid. I walked to the police station only to find my favorite red shoes had been released on bail. Her husband with the bullet in his butt refused to press charges, and that lowered the violation—and thus the bail—significantly. The cops were left with illegal discharge of a firearm. She had a permit for it. Being a lawyer, I'm sure she knew how to get out of jail faster than a master Monopoly player. I might have to find my own pair of red spikes.

As I was walking up Main Street, my cell phone buzzed.

"You got a ride." It was Mona's sultry voice.

I hustled back to the garage and Mona handed me a slip with name, address and phone number.

"Another fare to the courthouse. Take the same cab. The boss said it's drivable, so it might as well be you that drives it. He figures to limit the damage to one vehicle." Mona gave me her look again, the one that made towering mountain men into insignificant mole holes.

"Hey, none of it was my fault. You can even ask Lieutenant Jon. He's the one who cut me loose."

"You got a private audience with Lieutenant Jon?" Mona's expression changed to jealous. "Details when you get back," she demanded. Most of the women who knew Jon, even from a distance, harbored some fantasy about him.

"What's the story on this fare?" I asked, glancing at the slip. "I don't think I want to be hauled in front of Jon again quite this soon. He was a tad grouchy about my last appearance."

"She has a tracking bracelet and she's wearing it, so they know she's coming. Pickup is Hamp Heights."

I groaned. "A tracking bracelet? Why? And why are you giving her to me?"

"Everyone else is out."

I looked at the parking lot. My car had been moved back from the garage. It was alone in the lot. Slightly smushed but still cute.

"Okay." I shuffled off, trying to look dejected.

"Pitiful doesn't look good on you," Mona yelled after me. She was right. It was a lousy fashion statement.

Hamp Heights was Northampton's version of a housing project. It started as low-income but luxurious apartments in the '70s and hasn't aged well. It was the dead toy, dead plants, lots of trash school of landscaping. Unfortunately, the buildings were brick and solid enough to withstand any destructive force of nature. They would stand forever or until a new generation of urban planners bulldozed them into a pile of rubble. They were currently mostly subsidized housing. I spent a short time there when I first worked driving cab. When I decided that taxi hack was my life's calling, I settled in and found a real apartment within walking distance of work.

I've never had a problem with any of the fares I pick up at Hamp Heights, but they don't tip and they always keep me waiting while they dig up enough change to pay the ten-dollar fee. I stopped at the apartment number on my fare slip. A car of undetermined make and color was on four cement blocks next to the curb. It had no wheels, doors or hood. Half a child's bike lay by the step. Hanging by a single hinge, the screen door creaked and banged erratically against the doorframe in the wind.

The person who slammed it open was over six feet of mocha-brown woman in two feet of sequined red spandex. The door flew off its remaining hinge and landed in the dead landscape, crushing any plants brave enough to challenge the inhabitants. After clattering down the steps in her six-inch black and silver spike heels, my fare yanked open the back door of my cab before I could get out and open it for her.

She wedged into my car, ducking her head to fit. Her Afro added another two inches and grazed the ceiling. I didn't mention the seat belt issue. We aren't supposed to go anywhere with a passenger until they fasten it. I decided not to argue with someone who had just ripped a screen door out of a brick wall. Then I noticed the tracking bracelet. Not a good fashion statement unless you're a card-carrying member of the criminal sisterhood, and it did not go with her spiky, silver-sequined shoes. But her fingernails did. They were black and silver and had to be 2 inches long and curved like the talons of the raptors in Jurassic Park.

"Nice nails." I said.

"Yeah, you gotta be real careful pickin' your nose." She growled and slumped back in the seat, yanking up her spandex top, which shifted as she slid down. Her attitude told me she probably wasn't good woman-friend material. I could deal with that. But

15

those fingernails must be good for something and I wanted to know what.

When we got to the courthouse, my favorite Lieutenant was waiting at the entrance. I hopped out of the cab and opened the door. When my fare took her time getting out, I offered my hand to move her along.

"Time is money, ma'am," I grumbled.

She stared at me until I withdrew my hand. Then she shifted her gaze to Jon.

"Fine." I scowled at him. "A gentleman would be helping out."

He stepped forward, smiling broadly, and offered his hand. She exited gracefully, batting mascara-coated eyelashes.

"Pick her up in an hour." Jon leaned over and flipped a curl of hair out of my face. His eyes darkened slightly.

Jon and I have history. When I first came to Northampton, I was basically homeless. But I was young, foolish, and on an adventure. My parents had booted me out of the nest, expecting I would go to college, have a four-point GPA, and find a respectable husband. They were anxious to get on with their lives. I worked jobs from waitressing to night shift at the local pickle factory. Finally, uninspired by school, work, or husband material, I developed my own plan, leaving the chosen educational institution well before graduation exercises.

I redefined the diagnosis of attention deficit disorder to wanderlust and bought a beater car. I headed from the Midwest to the East coast and turned north, landing in Northampton because it was right off the interstate and I needed a bathroom break.

The first person I talked to was dressed in recycled specials from his battered Reeboks to his artfully faded and torn blue jeans. He pointed me to the Goodwill store and gave me a prioritized list of public bathrooms starting with Starbuck's and ending with McDonalds. He instructed me about where the homeless shelter was, that it closed for the summer, and where to get free food. My car was almost out of gas, my stomach and my wallet were empty, and the adventure was beginning to feel lonely. Northampton spoke to me. It loudly said free food, shelter in cold weather and lots of entry level—read: minimum wage—jobs. I decided to stay.

I was spending nights in my car or on park benches and days filling out job applications. Officer Jon Stevens found me sleeping on my bench one night when he was walking patrol. He suggested it wasn't safe for a woman to spend nights on benches, even in Northampton. I suggested it was none of his business where I spent my nights. He started lecturing me on lifestyle, and I started telling him what I thought of his profession. I think I used the word pig a few times. I might have used a few more inflammatory words as well. And maybe I poked him in the ribs, or maybe it was more than a poke. Jon used his handcuffs and I spent the night in protective custody. I yelled about lack of a charge, and he coolly explained about assault on an officer and my personal safety and did I really want him to charge me? It would be a hell of a lot more obvious, I told him, if I had actually assaulted him. And the only person I wasn't safe from was him.

"You are an obtuse asshole," I hissed at him.

"Obtuse? Nice word from someone sleeping on benches," he replied calmly.

We were both sure who was in charge. Unfortunately, we both thought it was not the other person. I had my civil rights. But he had handcuffs.

We were inches apart and I wasn't going to let this control freak tell me how to live. His blue eyes were narrowed and his mouth had a grim set to it. Then I noticed just how blue those eyes were, and how they were focused on my mouth. My brain took a slight detour into some sort of romantic fantasy. But my adventure was mine and mine alone. So I ended up spending the night compliments of the City.

Jon was young, serious and idealistic. I was young, rebellious and a little crazy. I couldn't believe he was arresting me. In retrospect, I still can't believe he arrested me. But maybe I have a better understanding of how frightened I really was. I had no place to go, no one to fall back on unless I called my less than sympathetic parents. Maybe Jon knew that and dealt with me the best way he could by letting me lash out at him. What I learned was there is no sound quite like the soul crushing slamming of a jail cell door.

After my night of incarceration, Jon dragged me out to his patrol car.

"Wait a minute." I pulled back, dug in my heels and brought us to a sudden halt. "Where are you taking me?"

"Somewhere safer than a park bench," he muttered, and grabbed my arm again, propelling me forward.

Now my curiosity raised its cute, oversized head and went to war with my need to be in charge. I really wanted to gain control over this man but, even more, I wanted to know what he considered safe and acceptable for someone sleeping on a bench.

He delivered me to Willie at the Cool Rides garage and told him I needed a job. I got close to his cop's face and told him I could handle my own life, so he should back his obtuse self off.

I've been working for Cool Rides ever since. Everyone on the force knows about Jon hosting my overnight. One of my female cop friends told me Jon also spent that night at the holding cells. Mostly checking up on me. It was a rocky beginning to a relationship that has since mostly consisted of circling each other like dogs with our hackles up. I stay busy with my job, and I guess he does, too. We've both grown up some in five years. Maybe Jon more than me. We have agreed to disagree about who is in charge of my life and who has control issues. He denies the control compulsion and calls it "looking out for the public safety."

Since that first encounter, Jon has used his brains to work his way up the promotional ladder to lieutenant. Recently I discovered my grandparents had left me a small inheritance and I used it to buy a tiny percent of Cool Rides Taxi Company. My thirtieth birthday wasn't all that far off and was approaching like a freight train. Willie had offered me a ten percent share of the company. Now I was committed to a new life of small business ownership. Jon was committed to being part of a community. He passed his thirtieth birthday without turning into an unrecognizable monster. We keep an eye on each other without much close contact. Until now.

Jon sees life as a puzzle. Which is probably why he's a good cop. I see life as my personal entertainment. I'm never disappointed. But I want to be in charge of my life and I keep my distance from Jon because I'm not sure I could handle whatever it is he might offer. He's an in-control kind of guy and I'm an out-of-control kind of woman. But that doesn't mean I'm not tempted. He does have dimples when he is willing to smile and the nicest ass I've ever wanted to run my fingers over. And then I remember he is a cop and, for me, that comes with some automatic issues.

My dream is to own the taxi company outright when Willy retires. I actually asked a few banker friends what they thought of a loan possibility. They laughed for longer than I thought was polite.

A month after I had talked to them, I was sitting uptown next to the taxi sipping my five-dollar oversize, excessively whipped mocha. Two guys who looked like they had just walked off the set of Godfather V approached me.

"So, we hear you wanna buy a taxi company." He sounded like he looked.

"Huh?" I said with all the intelligence I could muster.

"The Cool Rides Cab Company. We could help you buy it. We hear you might need some cash to make the deal."

"Who are you?"

"We're like, ah…bankers. We make loans."

"What bank do you work for?"

"You wouldn't know it. It's from some distance away. Not your concern. We just give you money. You do us a few favors."

"I don't know. Loans usually have a contract. Who are you again?" I smiled sweetly and played as dumb as I felt.

The two guys left. I never saw them again, but I wondered if I had let an opportunity go by that I should have paid attention to.

Right now, I called into Cool Rides. Mona told me to come back, do a quick cleaning of the cab and pick up more fare slips.

"You got two short hauls to and from the impound lot. Fit them in before you go back to the courthouse."

"Yes, ma'am." I trotted back out the door. We get a lot of business from impound. The first fare had driven his car through a row of newspaper vending machines and snapped off a fire hydrant. The resulting papier-mâché made the following day's front page featuring the ruptured hydrant with a newspaper draped over it. The caption read, "Local man makes editorial statement." Between towing fees, damages and cab rides, his "statement" cost him $500. He didn't tip.

I ran him home and motored sedately to the other end of impound. This driver had "become unconscious" outside a bar, in a handicapped space. This city takes its handicap spaces seriously and he woke up, still in the car, in the impound lot. He had been towed and ticketed to the tune of $250. When I dropped him off, his wife screamed I should have brought home the car and left him impounded. But she paid, no tip.

The impound pickups are mostly idiots, but they're our idiots and the Cool Rides staff treats them with the respect they deserve.

An hour later, I swung back around to the courthouse. Lieutenant Jon and my glittering fare were waiting. He handed me twenty dollars and helped Madam Amazon into the car. No tip, which would make it harder to pay my rent or buy those sexy shoes I could use to walk all over him. And, possibly, someday—in my dreams—some sexy undies. Tips pay the rent and the fun money.

"Okay, lady, let's hustle," the spandex wonder said. "I got appointments to keep." I was pretty sure I knew what appointments she needed to keep but I wasn't wasting time passing judgment. Everybody's life is their own and mine needed to move fast enough to collect enough fares to buy my dream shoes.

I zipped off toward Hampshire Heights. It was an easy drive with no back streets to negotiate, built close to the highway for easy access—and because no developer would put luxury houses in that location. Halfway there, I heard a siren wailing up close and personal. I rear-viewed it and saw an unmarked police car on my rear bumper. The siren blasted, the cop bubble flashed and headlights blinked. I pulled over. If I had been speeding it couldn't have been much over the limit. I plastered a smile on my face, prepared to bat my eyelashes and blame my fare. Oh, officer, I just was so upset by the funny bracelet she's wearing, I was completely distracted. Then I remembered when she'd come out of the courthouse, the bracelet had been removed.

I lowered my window and there was Jon. What had a lieutenant done to pull traffic duty? I didn't know the punishment routine in the Northampton Police Department, but this seemed a bit extreme. He knelt by my window and looked over to my passenger. His head was at window height and the temptation to run my fingers through his soft-looking, slightly long, brown hair was intense.

"God, I'm glad I caught up with you, both of you." He leaned his head on the door and relaxed slightly.

"What's going on?" My plastered smile faded. My eyes closed and I tipped my head back against the seat. "I know I wasn't speeding very much."

Jon had ignored my fluttering eyelashes, so I figured either I was off my game or whatever had happened was serious.

"There's been a shooting at the Heights," he said low enough that my backseat passenger couldn't hear. "Stay behind me and pull in when I stop."

Chapter Two

I obediently did as instructed. Jon's cop face was in don't ask and I won't tell anyway mode.

"What? What's goin' on now? I shudda' told you not to speed. If we get a ticket, I ain't payin'. That's on you."

This from the lady with the full appointment book. I nodded and kept my mouth shut.

When we arrived at the Heights, police cars were scattered around the parking area. Yellow crime-scene tape circled the small dirt yard and an ambulance was backed up to the only apartment without a screen door. A metal gurney was being rolled out. Jon had barely gotten out of his car when my lady of the ankle bracelet shrieked and launched herself out of my cab and up the cracked cement sidewalk. One of the uniforms ran over to keep her outside the police tape. It was like trying to stop a charging buffalo.

She made it as far as the sheet-draped gurney. Holding off the police officer with a stiff arm, she whipped the covering off the body with her other hand. She yelped, grabbed the dead guy by the throat, lifting him, one-handed, off the metal slab. This all took less than thirty seconds and, although the body wasn't that of a large man, the feat was still impressive. She caught the cops completely off-guard.

"You good-for-nothin' cocksucker! What've you done? What'm I gonna do now? Huh?" she screeched, throwing the body to the ground. She marched back to my taxi. Why couldn't she march to someone else's car? I noticed the police ranks parted to give her easy access. Even men with guns know when to give a woman her space.

"Take me back downtown," she demanded and glowered.

I looked at the nearest police officer and lifted my hands in a "what now?" gesture. He trotted to where Jon and several officers were watching the EMTs reload the body onto the gurney. As the officer waved his hand in my direction everyone stared at me. Jon hung his head in a frustrated way. Hey, I thought, I didn't cause any of this.

He walked over to my cab and leaned down to the open window.

"I got no reason to hold her. Take her where she wants to go. But—" he pointed at her— "don't go far. I will want to talk to you."

My spandex Wonder Woman slumped in the backseat and scowled. Hoping Jon didn't see what her middle finger did, I eased out and then floored it, ready to drop my very pissed-off passenger anywhere, fast. I like to know what's going on, but I draw the line at dead bodies. For once, I didn't think about who was going to pay the fare.

She directed me to an ornate in-town Victorian with a wrap-around porch. There was a set of white wicker furniture on the porch and two signs close to the sidewalk. One sign was for a dentist. The other said "Susan Young, Attorney at Law" in gold letters across a black background. Classy sign. My passenger might need someone with class. I wasn't sure why she needed a lawyer, but some guidance with her wardrobe might help her stay out of trouble.

I didn't volunteer to assist her out of the car this time. As my fare fumbled with the door, who should walk up to the house, briefcase in hand, but Lady Red Shoes. Didn't shooting someone in the courthouse constitute grounds for not being allowed to practice law? How about stiffing a cabdriver? That was definitely cause for disbarment. I jumped out of my cab and reached her before the Amazon could.

"Hi, remember me?" I stood between her and the building and got up close and personal. Little is more personal to a cabdriver than collecting a legitimate fare. This woman was a lawyer and she owed me money. She was at the top of my "I hope you die after you pay me" list. If the apocalypse came, I wanted her right up front.

The Amazon approached from behind. We had her sandwiched. The only question was which one of us wanted her more. It was the principle more than the $20 she owed me. Cabbies can't afford to let the world think they can be taken advantage of. Anyway, not on my watch, and not with my cab company. I wanted that fare. I didn't know what Amazon might want, other than a new ankle bracelet, maybe gold with some cute beads this time.

Lady Red Shoes looked over her shoulder and saw the Amazon closing in from behind. She turned back to me and realized I was blocking her way.

"You owe me, lady."

Amazon crowded closer. "I got a problem, too."

"I'm sure we can settle this," she replied, facing me first. "What do I owe you?" She was dressed in a dark pantsuit and looked lawyerlike and intimidating. She had the posture down: arrogant, aggressive, clenching the briefcase like it was a permanent part of her body. I always have trouble figuring out what to do with my hands which are usually out, upturned, asking for money. I stuffed them into my pockets and stood fast. I admired the chutzpah it took to walk into a courthouse and unload a bullet into someone's rear end. It was creepy that Amazon, who had recently dealt with a body full of bullet holes, was meeting a woman who had just drilled bullet holes into her own husband's still alive body. I decided to get my fare money and not worry about Amazon and Susan Young.

"Ten dollars for the ride and ten for the wait. And any tip you might want to use to make up for the trauma."

Lady Red Shoes, whom I assumed was the Susan Young, attorney at law, referenced on the sign, reached into her oversized designer bag and rummaged around. We all stepped up onto the porch where she sat down to give herself better access to the cavernous interior of the bag. She pulled out a notebook, a set of keys, brass knuckles, pepper spray, a hardcover law book, a trashy paperback and a gun.

The Amazon paced and fidgeted and muttered, back and forth across the porch. I couldn't hear the whole conversation, but the gist of it was her stupid dog of a husband and, by the way, her pimp and currently a major source of income, had fucked up again. My problems seemed trivial by comparison. I had a pissed-off boss and a short fare till. She had a dead body in her life.

"Oh, fuck," Lady Red Shoes said and emptied her purse onto the wicker chair next to her. A piece of paper fluttered to the floor from the pile of purse detritus. I glanced down. It wasn't a grocery list. It was a list of taxi companies from the area, written in careful block letters. There were six other companies on the list, but Cool Rides was highlighted in yellow, with three checkmarks next to it. If she liked us best, I didn't return the sentiment.

"How much do I owe you again?" She snatched the taxi list off the floor and stuffed it back in her purse.

"Are you giving me danger compensation? How about material damages? Emotional distress? To both me and my boss. He gets very emotional about the cars. And I haven't told him about the bullet hole yet."

"Look, I'm really sorry about that stuff at the courthouse. I got crazy when I heard my husband had surfaced. I needed to make a clear statement about how I felt about the fucker." Her defiance didn't back up the apology. I didn't care about her marital problems. I cared about my bottom line.

"Next time don't take a taxi to do it. Walk! It's good for your health. And mine." I huffed a bit. "Twenty dollars. And you can take us off that list."

She looked at me with an odd expression, somewhere between anger and guilt. She should have felt guilty. She tried to burn a taxi driver. And she shot her husband.

"That's what you owe me. Fare plus wait fee."

"Right." Her attention had shifted to Amazon, who was becoming increasingly agitated. Susan Young, attorney at law, gave me a twenty-dollar bill.

"Keep it," she said. I stared at it, trying not to grumble about tips.

"Thanks loads." I shuffled toward the steps leading me back to my taxi. I had my money, but my curiosity was gaining ground. What did Amazon want with a lawyer? And what did she know about the dead body? And who was the dead body? And...I pulled a wallet out of my bag, leaned against the doorjamb and stuffed in the twenty. I was just short of being rude when Susan turned and asked what else I needed.

I turned to Amazon. "You gonna need a ride home?"

She slumped into the wicker swing that faced the chairs. The swing groaned and Amazon sniffled. She looked like a stray puppy, a very tall stray puppy.

"I guess. I'm not sure I can go back there." She whimpered a little. I had just seen her throw a body to the ground one-handed, and now she was whimpering. It was strange. I continued to lean, looking away from the lawyer lady.

I sighed. I knew what it was like to be alone, but I'd been lucky. Willie had taken me under his wing, stuck me in a taxi, handed me an address and told me to drive. I'd considered him an angel of major proportions when he let me sleep on the couch in the office for six months while I saved up enough to even get into subsidized housing and, soon thereafter, my own apartment. For the first week of my employment, I lived off stale bread and a jar of mayonnaise some previous driver had left in the office fridge. I don't recommend it as a long-term diet, but it did let me save my fares and, realistically, it was probably just as good for me as any of the fast food offered on the strip. The reality was Willie was desperate for drivers. I had a valid driver's license and no felony convictions. Turned out I was good at it.

I sank onto the chair next to Amazon. Susan sat opposite us. That was a good sign. Lawyers usually don't promote comfort and sympathy. They always try to stay in charge. Amazon didn't need any more intimidation. She had been flying on anger since the dead body. Now that her adrenaline had evaporated, she slumped, and her eyes drooped.

Susan leaned toward Amazon. She had an almost sympathetic expression.

"What brings you here, Belle?"

Belle? I looked at Amazon. I had trouble making the name fit.

Belle sniffed. She pulled herself up straight and raised her chin. I was impressed and reassessed my opinion. She could have class, even in spandex glitter.

"Horace is dead," she said without any of the anger she'd had when she confronted dead Horace.

"What!?" Susan slid off her chair and sat on the other side of Belle. "Oh, Belle, I'm so sorry."

Belle put her hand over Susan's. "Oh, he was never much to me but a pimp. I didn't waste any like on him. So, don't you."

Susan sat back. "You didn't kill him, did you?" She glanced at me. "Do we need privacy? Let's go inside."

There was an irony to someone, who had just been in police custody for shooting someone in the very public courthouse, asking for privacy. But I stood up and leaned against the porch railing figuring Belle could ask me to leave if she wanted me to. She might need a friend more than she needed a lawyer. The lawyer in question gave me an odd look when I followed them inside. I figured Belle might be turning into girlfriend material and I didn't think Susan qualified for that position for anyone.

Belle smiled sadly. "Naw. Not that there weren't times I wanted to. But I've got an alibi even the cops won't break. I was in court witnessing against some idiot who beat up a friend of mine. They even gave me a tracker bracelet when he threatened to kidnap me. Anyway, I heard a few of the cops talking about that Scarpelli guy out of Springfield, from the crime family, and that scared me. He's got a nasty rep for disappearing people who turn up in pieces later. I don't really need a lawyer but I think I need some place to stay for a while. I thought you might have a safe-house where you send clients."

I stared at her. She was still using inner-city slang, but the accent was straight out of the British upper class. How weird was that? My native tongue crossed with the Queen's English.

All I was sure of was her profession. She was a prostitute. Horace was her pimp and possibly her husband. And who the hell was Scarpelli? Susan had looked startled at the mention of his name.

Belle continued. "I'm not particularly sad to see Horace gone. He was a mean fucker. The only reason he didn't whack me around is that I'm big. And he wasn't." The refined accent remained. Maybe it was her first language.

Right now, Susan was the friend Belle needed, but lawyers can be anyone's best friend until the law locks the client up forever. Then they would be on to their next best friend and the first someone, who had paid them a small fortune, would be out of luck.

Susan looked intently at Belle. "What did the police say about Scarpelli?"

"Not much." Belle rose and started pacing around the office. She walked with a new grace. No more stomping, striding or slouching. Her posture said, I'm in charge of myself. Regal. Okay, African Queen, I thought. Either way, no one would mess with her. She wasn't overweight but she was tall and well built. She projected self-assurance.

"What worries me is who did kill Horace. The police will be as tight as their sphincters about giving me information. Horace knew the Scarpellis, but I never met any of them personally. If someone is gunning for me, I want to know. And I have to find some place to stay off their radar. Most of my friends are in the business so the Scarpellis know them. I need someone they wouldn't think of." Suddenly she turned to me with a new expression on her face.

"No," I blurted. "I don't even know you. One minute you're a pissed-off Amazon and the next you're a British...princess."

"Ah," she said. "The accent? I'm bilingual."

Maybe bipolar too, I thought. Did I want to be roomies with a pissed-off royal hooker possibly being stalked by a deranged mafia killer? The police did have a body and they might want to know why it was a dead one. My apartment only had one bed. And a fold-out sofa. A short fold-out sofa.

Susan brightened and looked at me. "It would only be for a few days. Until I can find out what the police know and what kind of problems Belle has."

She turned to Belle. "If I'm your attorney, your location would be privileged. We would be the only ones who know where she is."

Belle looked at me speculatively. "Who would think I'd be staying with my taxi driver? And I could pay you some rent money." Her gaze traveled down to my sneaker-clad feet. "Enough for a new pair of shoes."

I was thinking about how to say no when my cell phone rang. When had I become her taxi driver? I did need some new shoes, and she probably knew where to get the best shoes at the best price.

"Cool Rides, Honey Walker," I answered in my most professional voice.

"You got an airport," Mona purred into the phone. "Pick up at Smith's Funeral Home ASAP. She's a special consideration."

"I'm on it." I answered loud enough both Susan and Belle could hear and understand I had a job to do.

"Just a few days," Susan said. She put her hand on my shoulder, possibly trying to look sincere. "We would both owe you."

I could see having a lawyer indebted to me might be helpful in future life experiences. But a prostitute? Why would I want that? Of course, she did have fabulous taste in footwear and probably a few sources for them I had never heard of. And fingernails to die for I thought, looking at my own blunt cut, slightly ragged, never manicured, ones. Maybe she would turn out to be girlfriend material after all.

Right now, I needed to get my airport fare. "Okay," I blurted. Crap. I needed to slow down. "Just stay here until I get back from this fare. It should be about two hours." Special consideration meant extra time while I parked, accompanied the fare into the airport and through security. It usually involved a wheelchair.

"Thank you," Belle said with the grace of royalty. I felt, but resisted, an urge to curtsey.

As I headed out to the car, I wondered what I had gotten myself into.

I pulled up to the funeral home and found an elderly woman sitting in a cast-iron chair by the door. She was short with curly white hair and nicely built for her age. She wore an old-lady big print dress and cross trainers on her feet. A plain cardboard box sat next to her. The man standing behind her must have been the funeral-home director because he was dressed completely in black except for his white shirt. She looked happy with the world and was ignoring him completely.

I hopped out of the cab and grabbed her box. The funeral-home director melted away.

"Whoa!" I said. "What's in here?" The box was small and heavy for its size.

"Oh, that's my dearly departed husband. And a right big one he was, too. I'm going to scatter his ashes." She smiled beatifically. "Do you need some assistance? I was always able to move him by myself. Of course, I never tried doing it with anyone helping. That would be a threesome, wouldn't it?" She beamed at me.

"I think I can handle it. Do you want him in the backseat?"

"No, no. I do believe I'd prefer him right here on my lap. That will be a nice reversal of position, won't it? I didn't let him get on top all that often."

"Umm …" I fastened her seat belt and eased her husband on top of her. She seemed oddly cheerful about the purpose of her trip.

When we got to the airport, I parked in short-term, helped the widow into the shuttle, and heaved the box onto the rack. It settled like a sandbag. I hoped the old man was well wrapped. When we pulled up in front of the terminal, I hustled inside and snagged a wheelchair.

The shuttle driver helped Granny off and got her settled into the wheelchair. I thanked God for accessibility as I staggered back from the shuttle with the box of Granddad. Placing him gently on Granny's lap, I slung my handbag over my shoulder, shoved through the automatic doors and we were off toward the long line at check-in. The airport was crowded. Security was tight but not restrictive. I could take my fare as far as final check in. An airline employee would take over from there.

"Oh, what a cute little dog." Granny noticed the drug-sniffing beagle pacing the walkway with its handler. As we passed it, I heard the dog sneeze. And sneeze. And sneeze. I turned around and noticed a thin gray line between Grandma, Granddad and the dog. The dog was following the trail. I leaned over and pushed the torn corner back into the box. Digging in my oversize bag while I picked up the pace to get to the wheelchair line, I came up with the standard solution to everything. Duct tape. I tore off a piece, slapped it on Granddad's escape hole and took off in a hurry. The dog stopped sneezing, threw back his head and howled.

"What the hell?" His handler stared at the trail of ash ending in the middle of the walkway, a good 20 feet from us. I was trying not to watch the beagle when I noticed the ride around vacuum making its hourly sweep of the main concourse. It rumbled from one end of the terminal to the other, making a graceful arc at the far end to turn back and follow our trail past the cute beagle and the hordes of people waiting at security. It roared by, sucking up dust and stray bits of human remains inadvertently scattered on the wall-to-wall carpet. Pieces of Granddad were whisked away with dust and grit from around the world. Now he would be mixing with a lot of interesting international stories and characters. Who knew, maybe there was some space dust mixed in on that carpet.

"Is there a problem?" Granny noticed me staring at the giant vacuum.

"Oh, no. I just wonder how they keep this place clean. With so many people and all." A little bit of Granddad wouldn't make it to his final resting place. Most of him would be spread to the wind. And the wind would spread him across the planet. And some of him would end up in the same place vacuum cleaners and everything else go sooner or later. The dump.

I turned Granny over to a young female airline agent in a crisp blue uniform.

"Hope Granddad enjoys the new location," I said.

The agent looked around for Granddad. I patted the cardboard box. "Granddad," I added.

"Oh, my mother just told me where to scatter her."
The agent smiled.

Grandma asked, "Oh really? Where, dear?"

"The casino. She's there every weekend. Loves it.
Wants to play the slots for all eternity."

"Oh, how wonderful," Grandma replied, smiling
conspiratorially. I suspected she had visited the casino
herself more than once.

I left them chatting happily. People skills. Some
got it, some don't. Taxi drivers have it or they'll go
crazy. And broke. No people skills, no tips. No tips, no
shoes. I grinned at the $125 Granny had slipped me.
Twenty-five-dollar tip. Those hot red shoes were
getting closer to my feet. Maybe my rent would be on
time, too.

I trotted back to my ride and hot-pedaled up the
turnpike back to Belle. I wanted some answers to at
least a million questions.

When I pulled up in front of Susan Young's
office, I recognized the unmarked cop car parked at the
curb. There were lots of possibilities. Susan had
discharged a weapon in a courtroom. She had
wounded someone, even if it was her asshole husband
or, possibly, her husband's asshole. I wasn't sure of
the exact location of the bullet. Belle was a hooker.
Belle was married, apparently to another asshole, but
a dead asshole. I shouldn't be surprised to see the cops
visiting Susan's office, especially with Belle inside. If
it was Jon, I knew he would give me a hard time about
letting Belle stay with me.

I strode up the sidewalk. At least I tried to stride
because I thought it would give me an air of authority.
I should have known better than to think Jon would see

me as authoritative. He was leaning against the open door and looked like he had been waiting a while. Looking good was part of what Jon did.

He knew how long a trip to the airport would take, but he didn't know I had taken Granny and Grandpa, inside and to security. That had added at least forty minutes.

"Where've you been? And what are you thinking, getting involved in a police investigation? You're a taxi driver, for Christ's sake. I told you to drop her off, not take up house-keeping with her."

"Hi, to you too, Lieutenant…Jonny, and how did you know I was going to be here?" He hated to be called Jonny. I think it made him feel too young or immature or less authoritative. I didn't care how he felt as long as he was distracted. I wanted some answers from Belle or Susan. Jon would clam up the minute I started asking questions about an open investigation. And Belle and Susan wouldn't be as willing to talk with Jon hanging on their every word.

So we had a brief staring contest. Nose to nose. Scowl to scowl. Suddenly he grinned and ran a finger down my cheek. I tried to swat his hand away, but he was faster, grabbed my hand and held it. His eyes got a little more intense.

"Wouldn't want you getting injured in the line of duty. And Willie told me where you would be. Remember, you always call in your location." He kept grinning. I felt my heat rising. I started to lean forward, rethought that idea and jerked away from his grasp. I felt suddenly rebellious. Of course, before that very second, I had been considering saying no to Belle. Now I might have to insist she stay with me.

"I just offered Belle a place to stay. It's not like I'm interfering. I'm hardly ever home anyway. I mean, between my job and my fabulous social life."

Jon frowned. "I don't know what's going on with this yet. I don't need a civilian wandering around where I might have to worry... What social life?"

"I'm flattered you're worried about me. Now that you've rescued the maiden in distress, you want to go beat your chest?"

Jon eyed my chest speculatively.

"Don't even think about it." I backed up another step.

"You're not a maiden...are you?" He realized we had an audience. Belle and Susan were watching our little interaction with fascination.

"I don't want any more casualties. Too much paperwork." He stuffed his hands into his pockets.

"You're telling me you don't want Belle to stay with me because there might be danger. Where do you want her to stay? And how much danger are we talking here? This is Northampton, not some inner city, crime ridden, drive-by shoot-out, gang infested ghetto. I think you're exaggerating reality."

"Jesus." Jon shook his head as if to clear away some fuzz. "This is a murder investigation. A person got killed."

Belle mumbled under her breath.

"What?" Jon turned toward her.

She returned his stare. "I just said I wasn't sure Horace could be considered a person. And we don't know whoever did him is looking at anyone else. I just need a place to regroup. I didn't like the man, but I did know him intimately, and staying where we lived together is just creepy. Okay? Besides, you probably still have all that yellow tape stuff strung around like Christmas lights. It'll kill business." Belle paused, remembering Jon was a cop. She was using her high-class accent but still managed to convey a lot of defiance. "And there must be more evidence you can find," she finished.

"Okay, I know you can't go back there. Maybe we could set up some sort of surveillance wherever you end up." Jon sighed and turned to me. "I can reroute a squad car by Honey's apartment every hour or so."

I thought about the possibility of Belle staying at a motel but realized Jon wasn't about to send her off to somewhere she might continue her profession. It probably wouldn't work to turn tricks off my sofa bed. And I was fairly certain the police department didn't have the funds to pay for a motel.

He turned back to Belle. "But your 'business' is over. Nothing happens out of Honey's apartment." Jon, the Lieutenant, was with us in full force. I decided I had asserted my independence from his control enough. What Belle decided to do was now her choice.

We went back and forth for a few more minutes. Jon was not happy about Susan or Belle. Susan had just given the legal system the finger when she shot her husband in the lower right cheek in the middle of the most secure place in town. Lawyers have a way of working that system the rest of us pay them dearly for. When it involves their own behavior, they can slip through like eels. Susan stayed surprisingly silent, but she had made bail and walked, and that had to irk the hell out of Jon. At least she had missed that vital hole that made her husband what he apparently was.

Belle baited Jon for a while about her profession, wondering aloud how she would make a living now. He gritted his teeth and didn't say much. We finally settled on me not taking the taxi home and Belle and Susan not telling anyone about where Belle was staying. Jon would check on us in the evening when he could. I figured he would also send a squad car around with or without our approval. This plan was going to try my already minimal social life and I really, really hoped it wouldn't last long.

In the meantime, Mona called.

"You got a pickup at the train station. You remember to pack your mace this morning? I still don't know why you won't get a gun."

"So I won't shoot myself." I had reluctantly put the mace canister in my oversize bag that morning, hoping I wouldn't spray my face. Weapons are an "oops" kind of situation for me. I headed south on the interstate.

Chapter Three

The train station was in Springfield, twenty minutes south of Northampton. Springfield was a city with a history of politicians who somehow managed to avoid indictment. Their style of leadership has induced a lack of confidence from the general population. Violence was not unheard of. Thus the mace in my bag. The Springfield cabbies were probably the toughest in the state. And there were places that even they wouldn't go in that town, no matter what they were packing. A cabbie had been shot there recently, so everyone was a little on edge.

Once upon a time, the train station was one of those fabulous Grand Central-like structures. They took out the Grand and the Central until it looked more like the servant's entrance to the castle. It was a wall of spectacular oversized stone blocks with a door that looked like you were going into the neighborhood Laundromat. We just called it The Station. Rumor was it would be rebuilt soon.

It's not in a great neighborhood, but the city has a lot of cops on patrol in that area. And hanging flower baskets. And extra lighting. If they didn't, Amtrak might whip right on through and forget to stop. Politicians would have to leap from a moving train. To avoid this embarrassing possibility, they keep it safe enough for most passengers to make it from the train to a waiting taxi. Passengers do not linger. Taxis, however, have no choice.

I pulled up to the station in time for the 11 o'clock arrivals. Of course the train was late. There were three other taxis waiting. Two locals and one from Holyoke. The crime rate in that city, which lay about halfway between Springfield and Northampton, didn't even get mentioned anymore. Holyoke was synonymous with the phrase "steer clear."

The other drivers were out of their cars, smoking or leaning against fenders. Cool Rides drivers aren't allowed to smoke around the car or eat or drink or have sex or do anything except be nice to customers and drive. I decided to stay in my cab.

I was watching two cabbies in front of me when a parking-enforcement officer pulled up in her gas-powered three-wheeler. She parked on the sidewalk, hopped out and rushed into the building. Based on her posture, my guess was bathroom break. One cabby grunted and chomped down harder on his soggy, smoking, smelly cigar.

The sound of an incoming train triggered a Pavlovian reaction in the cabbies. It means money and money means food and rent and clothes and a life. Cabbies here are extremely protective of their turf.

The first passenger came out of the station lugging a huge suitcase. The second cabby in line opened his back door and trunk. The passenger steered her overstuffed baggage toward him.

The first cab in line was a Springfield Cab, and the driver looked like he was moonlighting from a local semipro hockey team. He was huge and tough and he viewed this fare as his. Unless you've been called ahead and are doing a by-appointment, there is a protocol for fetching fares. First cab in line gets first guy off train. And the big guy wanted that fare.

I sank below window level so as not to get involved. My hand inched over toward my bag and the mace. Thoughts of guns danced in my head. But then thoughts of what might happen if I had a gun in my possession and even the mace seemed like overkill.

The drivers were in each other's faces with lots of hand waving, loud voices and creative language. The Springfield driver had a gun and was holding it in the air, pointing at the sky. The other driver had his hand on the one tucked in his pants. He was smaller than the Springfield driver but he looked like a pissed-off weasel. He wasn't going to give an inch even if cabbie number one outweighed him by about 80 pounds. The passenger loaded her luggage in the second cab and slammed the trunk. The sound set off a fight-or-flight reaction and both drivers chose the fight option. Another gun came out, and one of them started firing off rounds. I felt a bullet hit the passenger side of my car. The second two shots connected with the parking cart, which started spurting gas from its now-ruptured tank. One last round was fired off and the second driver dived over the hood of his cab, threw his gun onto the seat and took off, triumphantly, with the fare. Not to be left behind, the local tossed his cigar over his shoulder and pursued. The last I saw of them, they'd run a red light and were flying down the road playing bumper car.

I once saw a program on the Discovery Channel where someone set out to prove that, contrary to urban myth, a gas tank ruptured by a bullet would not explode. They couldn't get theirs to explode, but then again, they didn't have a lit cigar.

The bullets had stopped flying and I wasn't real close to the leaking gas tank, so I slunk out to view the damage to my cab.

I was leaning over the hole when my fare appeared.

"Whatcha' doin'?"

I looked up at a young man wearing a black T-shirt that said "My bad ass misses your bad ass" in white letters. I wondered what his parents thought of his college career. Whipping a tissue out of my pocket, I pretended to polish the front fender, strategically placing myself between my passenger and the telltale mark.

"Oh, just taking off a spot of mud." I opened the door for him.

"Thanks." He slid in.

I got in the driver's side, made sure his seat belt was fastened and fastened my own. As I pulled out, there was a loud kawhump. The parking-enforcement cart rose gracefully in the air, sparks erupting from the gas tank. It flipped onto its side, wheels spinning madly, looking like a giant cockroach someone hadn't completely squashed. I guess the cigar wasn't as soggy as it looked.

"Holy shit!" My passenger craned his neck to see the smoking ruin.

I nailed the accelerator, heading back to the interstate. The meter maid ran out of the building waving madly. I sped up.

About five miles up the interstate, we passed a taxi on the side of the road. It had a flat tire and two windows with what might have been bullet holes in them and no driver. I ducked and sped up. When you see a burned-out vehicle on the highway in New York City, it's probably an illegal cab with a stolen fare. Cabbies can be really sensitive when it comes to fares.

Once past the larger cities, the scenery turned into pastoral farmland, green forest interspersed with corn, potatoes and squash. It was like entering a different country when you headed north. By the time you got to Northampton, the insanity and violence of the bigger cities faded to invisibility. That didn't mean it didn't exist. It was just more difficult to see. I suspected Lieutenant Jon Stevens saw it all too often. Since taxi drivers pick up a cross section of the population, I probably had seen the players from the more violent culture to the south but if I was driving someone to a drug deal or an assassination, I didn't want to know.

I dropped off my passenger and headed into town.

I was driving down Main Street when I spotted Jon. He was wearing a suit and tie so I assumed he was taking a work break. I pulled over and stopped. As he strolled up to the window, his eyes were riveted on the passenger-side fender.

"What's that?" he asked. He knelt and traced a finger over the hole. "Looks like a bullet hole."

"What?" I smiled innocently.

"You've been in Springfield again, huh?"

"Train station."

"Drug deal?" He raised an eyebrow in question.

"Cabbie wars."

"Ah. Those cabbies can be temperamental."

"Need a ride? No charge." I leaned over and pushed the door open.

"Is this a bribe?" He got in anyway. "I need to talk to you."

"Uh-oh." I had almost forgotten he was a cop.

"Springfield called." He leaned back and clicked his seat belt. "They seem to think there was a Cool Rides cab at the scene of severe damage to a city vehicle."

I smiled sweetly at him. "We have five cabs." One of the good things about our cabs is they are very recognizable. Sometimes that's also a bad thing.

"A woman was driving." He tapped his fingers on the dash and stared into my eyes. "How many women drive for Cool Rides?"

I sighed. "Just me."

"They also were curious what a Cool Rides driver might know about a taxi deserted on the highway. Tires shot out, two windows. You're a scary person."

"What? Hey, I just drive."

"And I'm sure you do a fine job of that. It's the extracurricular stuff that worries me." He leaned over close to me and ran a finger down my cheek. "Maybe a bit of ash from some sort of fire on your face right there."

I shrugged. "Well then, hold onto your seat, stud muffin. I'll get you back to the cop house in record time."

A smile played across Jon's mouth. I purposefully screeched away from the curb and was at the police station in about three minutes. Jon stepped out and knelt next to the open window. He glanced at the bullet hole again.

47

"Don't get that fixed. It may be evidence." His eyes darkened. "Stud muffin? I like that."

"Like my boss can let it alone." I breathed out. "I haven't told him about it yet."

"The stud muffin?"

"The bullet hole!"

Jon tapped the door. "I work until eight tonight. Stop by and give me a statement…please." He said the last word with reluctance, so I nodded in agreement. He sauntered into the cop house, and I watched him and his fine butt disappear inside. Umm. Resistance to whatever I was resisting might be fading.

I swung the cab back around to the Cool Rides office. We had agreed I would stop by and talk about the Springfield shooting incident, so that would take care of his evening checkup. I was viewing Jon as less of a cop and more of a friend as I got to know him. I wasn't sure I wanted him around my apartment, even with Belle as a chaperone. She was, after all, of a special sexual persuasion. Mostly it was all right anywhere, anytime, with anyone. And probably better if money changed hands.

I ran two more short hauls. One was an older lady who needed batteries for her flashlights. It took her a half an hour in Radio Shack to match batteries to flashlights. When she was done, the clerk looked like he'd been staring into a thousand-watt bulb. It was an eight-dollar fare and a ten-dollar wait fee. She gave me $25. Sometimes, life is good. I could feel those shoes on my feet. The ones with the sequined heels I had seen in one of the uptown stores. Where do people wear these shoes? Who cares? I just wanted them to be on my feet or in my closet. I had visions of my slut-shoe-clad foot draped over Jon's shoulder.

After I dropped off the flashlight lady, Mona called me with a couple of old geezers who had been out shopping for gifts for their girlfriends who shared a birthday. How sweet was that, I thought, noting the address. It was the local hard-core porn shop. I pulled up to the back of the building where the hidden entrance opened onto the parking lot. One of the old guys had a walker with a convenient basket attached to the front. It was full to overflowing with bags and boxes. They started pulling crotch-less panties, silk handcuffs, and dildos that belonged on an elephant out of the shopping bags along with some hard-core videos.

"What ya think, lady? You being a woman and all. Should we start with Debbie Does Dallas or Deep Throat? What would get you most riled up? At our age, we only get one shot at this." He looked me up and down with a grin as I loaded his walker into the back of the cab.

The other one smirked as he tossed his cane in with the walker. "Unless we get one of them four-hour erections. Did we get any of that Viagra stuff?"

"Naw, they don't sell that in this store. I think we gotta go to the grocery store."

I wasn't going to redirect their search for Viagra. They had to be 80 years old. The Hardy Boys in their golden years. Or, possibly, Tweedledum and Tweedledee. Now I knew why the entrance to the porn store was well hidden.

I pulled over fast and left them at the retirement complex. When had 80 become the new 30? I was approaching the latter and I didn't want to think about any age after that.

I dropped the cab off at the office and reluctantly headed over to the cop station on foot. It was 6 o'clock and I was sleepy, hungry, and grumpy, three of the seven dwarves rolled into one.

Having given Belle a key to my apartment, I wanted to get there before she got too comfortable. I agreed to let her sleep on my couch, but I wanted to be sure she was the only one sleeping on it.

I stopped at the front desk and picked up the phone to communicate with the cop behind the bulletproof glass. He looked like a big blue fish stuck in a small glass bowl.

He buzzed me in and I wound my way around the desks and cubicles to find Jon's office. Jon rose when I paused at the door and motioned me to a chair in the corner. He came around and sat on the edge of his desk facing me. That was a good sign. I squirmed anyway and he grinned. I shifted my butt deeper into the visitor's chair and looked at my feet. When I raised my eyes, his grin had widened. The fact that it made him more attractive pissed me off. My automatic reaction to authority was a mix of intimidation, defiance and a little respect. Jon wore his authority easily and well. That I almost really liked him only made it worse.

"Captain Donnelly called from the Springfield police. It seems you may have witnessed, or been involved in, the destruction of city property. Namely a parking-enforcement vehicle. It exploded and had to be towed away. What would you know about this? And, Honey, let me remind you I am a cop. Don't even think about lying. Or omitting anything pertinent. I have a lot on my watch right now and I need cooperation from Springfield."

"Hey, all I was doing was picking up a fare. I brought him back here. The cabbies down there are crazy. I don't know how they survive. Most of their fares would be just as happy to shoot them. And down there they shoot to kill," I said. "I might have to start packing a weapon." I knew I would never carry a gun but I wasn't sure if Jon knew that. My rule of thumb is to tell the police as little as possible so I dropped the subject of weaponry.

"God prevent that. You don't need a weapon to cause mayhem. Just tell me what happened."

I told him the story of the two cabs playing bumper car and the lighted cigar-gasoline-bullet hole combination. Jon shook his head. I had been running into some bizarre situations recently, but none of them were my fault. Some people call this attitude denial. I knew I was an accident waiting for a catalyst.

"Okay, I'll call Springfield and clear that up. I don't suppose you got a cab number, license plate or any kind of ID on the two cabs?"

"One was local Springfield and the other was from Holyoke. I just kept my head down. And one of those bullets hit my car too. If you find them, I want to sue." Jon had already seen that bullet mark on my car.

"If anyone finds them, and it won't be me, they won't have two bricks to rub together. Their sorry asses will be behind bars."

Jon stood up and I followed. "So, can I go now? I really need to get home and eat." And check up on Belle.

"Come on, I'll give you a ride. We can pick up a pizza on the way. I want to talk to Belle about her future plans, arrange an interview. See what she might know about the husband, Horace, and what activities might have contributed to his having a hole in his head." Jon rested a hand on my back and steered me out of the cop maze.

I wanted to know Belle's plans too. I sincerely hoped they didn't include turning tricks out of my apartment. I wondered what other job skills she had.

When Jon and I got to the apartment, pizza in hand, Belle was there and had made herself at home. Which was nice because, apparently, being at home included cooking, grocery shopping, and cleaning. My tiny place was spotless, and the fridge was stocked with soda, orange juice, eggs, cheese, and salad makings.

"I'll make a salad to go with it." She jumped up when she spied the pizza and headed into the kitchen.

I worked to close my mouth. Jon smiled. Maybe a roomie wasn't such a bad idea after all.

When we had settled into the pizza, Jon started the conversation in typical cop fashion, with blunt force trauma.

"How are you planning to make a living, Belle? Now that Horace is gone. And when can you come into the station for an interview?"

Belle swallowed hard. She was probably telling the truth about not liking Horace, but he was a major part of her life, and having someone close to her shot dead had to make rational planning difficult. Her solution was to live with me. How rational was that? For either of us.

"I don't know. Maybe I'll go back to college, do some post-grad work. I could add some real diversity to their classes, a few reality checks, the wisdom of age."

I looked over at her. Post-grad meant she was a grad of some college somewhere.

"Huh, a former prostitute in classes with impressionable young ladies from rich families, rich, full-tuition-paying families. It is former, isn't it?" Jon raised an eyebrow at her.

"Oh yeah, I've learned ho'ing ain't no life. I got better endeavors to pursue. Maybe work part time and do school the rest."

Jon just nodded. They arranged to meet the next day.

Chapter Four

The next morning I headed to the taxi garage, and Belle went to face Jon and the cop station. I hadn't learned much more about her. No girl talk. No revelations about Horace or life in the trade. That was okay with me. I hadn't decided how close I wanted to get to Belle and her problems. They could be pretty overwhelming. She could be overwhelming even without any problems. I might be willing to get some shoe advice from her. And how did she keep those nails so long and perfect? And what did a prostitute do with 2-inch nails? She had some skills I might lack. Not my job skills, but there were lots of other areas of expertise I was willing to learn about. I could see some crossover potential from her former job to my... whatever, my thoughts drifted to Jon.

The only time Cool Rides had ever picked up Belle was when I transported her from the courthouse. I had seen her riding in another company's cabs. Mostly heading south on the interstate. I hadn't asked why she never called us.

When I got to the garage, the parking lot was filled with a bizarre collection of cars and people. I skirted the crowd and went around and through the back door.

"What's with the misfits?" I asked Mona.

"We have five cars and three drivers. I ran an ad for new drivers."

She held up a stack of applications.

"We have interviews every 15 minutes starting right now. Since you're officially management, you get to help."

I liked the idea of being recognized as management even though my share was tiny. Then we looked out the window at the line of people scrambling to establish a pecking order. I sighed and understood the downside of being in charge.

A guy with arms bulging out of a black T-shirt that declared "FUCK You" to the world made it almost to the front of the line and shoved a small blond person of indeterminable gender backward into the bosom of a well-endowed woman where he/she was swallowed by oversized breasts.

An elderly lady, whose white hair looked like a light bulb sitting on her shoulders, stood at the head of the line brandishing a heavy cane. Even Mr. FUCK You wasn't getting by her.

She backed in the door, waving her cane, and hobbled to the visitor's chair. She put one hand in her lap and she primped her hair which had frizzed a bit more in the fight to get through the door and now looked like a dandelion gone to seed. She stared blankly at the wall.

"You must be Margaret Snazhour." Mona looked up and blinked at the whiteness.

At the sound of a voice, Margaret Snazhour refocused her gaze.

"I'm here to be a taxi driver. What do I have to do to become one?"

"You need a valid driver's license. And you can't have any felonies on your record." Mona paused.

Margaret Snazhour stared at a point closer to Mona. She was zeroing in.

"Do you have any felonies on your record?" I asked.

Margaret smiled serenely. "Not yet. Do you think I need one?" She glanced around to see if a new felony might pop up.

"We'll call you." Mona helped Margaret to the door and yelled "Edwardo Szezmecki, you're up next."

Mr. FUCK You sauntered in. He might help with our need for big guys to go into the rougher parts of Springfield but I wasn't sure about his intellectual capacity. He did have to find Springfield before he could brave the combat zones.

"Do you have a dress code? 'Cause I don't need nobody telling me how to dress. I need to let the assholes I pick up know who they're dealing with. I want 'em to see these." He flexed, watching his biceps wiggle. "What kind of weapons do we carry? Does the company supply a gun?"

"We'll call you," said Mona.

Stewart Slipslit, the blond, gender-ambiguous person, came next.

"Do you have any driving experience?" Mona asked.

"I've always wanted to drive. I just worship Dale Earnhardt, Jr. I bet I could make those cars do things you never dreamed of. I could make Jr. do things he's never dreamed of." She/he smiled. "And I've only been busted once. It's still pending. I would never have solicited such a brute. God! He was so ugly. I'm going to fight this charge like horse cocky. Does the company provide legal counsel?"

"You get the next one." Mona handed me the clipboard and fled to the bathroom.

"Bobby DeBenny, come on down," I yelled. A man and a woman fought to get inside, Keystone Cops making a big entrance through a small door.

"Which one of you is Bobby DeBenny?"

"I am," replied the woman.

"I was born first." The guy shoved her backward and slammed the door.

"We're twins. But I'm better for this job. Robert—that's me—and Roberta. That's her." He waved dismissively.

We ended the interviews with only one application not in the wastebasket.

We had gone through a guy who wanted to know if our insurance covered him if he accidentally ran over his neighbor. "Who, by the way, is boffing my wife," he said and asked if the company provided personal-injury lawyers.

Mona almost beheaded a large, muscular man who asked if he had to take orders from a fat old lady like her or did we have a real man in charge somewhere.

When the last applicant came in, he seemed sort of close to almost normal.

"Got any driving experience?" Mona inquired.

"God is my guide. I trust he will steer for me. Can I offer you some literature?"

We really needed drivers.

The rest of my day was made up of short-haul fares which meant a lot of driving and not a lot of income. Fortunately I got a couple of good tips.

I picked up a British woman at the downtown hotel where shopping, coffee, entertainment, drug dealers, and casual prostitutes are all within an easy walk. There are at least two coffee shops on each block to reboot energy levels continuously. Good shopping, good food, and good everything else.

She wanted to go to the mall outside Holyoke, twenty miles south on the interstate. I sighed. We motored off to the acres of concrete.

Like malls around the country, this one has killed the inner city as a shopping district. That's why cabbies going into downtown Holyoke carry at least a can of mace. But the mall is an easy run off the interstate, and the likelihood of car or driver returning with bullet holes is slim.

When I picked her up later, she smiled a well-sated woman smile and handed me a fat tip.

The next fare was the Smoker. Mostly we ran errands for him. Today he wanted a ride downtown.

His living space reflected his belief that it is dangerous to be more than six inches from some form of nicotine. Cigarettes were stacked against the wall in cartons, boxes, and individual packs. Loose singles were everywhere. He was planning ahead for the apocalypse in case it didn't include smokes. Lately he had added nicotine patches. This was not an effort to cut back on his smoking. He had two patches on his arm and a lighted cigarette.

I staggered back from the secondhand smoke, held my breath and bolted outside to suck clean air.

I stashed his walker in back and checked his seat belt. When he died, it wouldn't be from putting his head through my windshield. After dropping him off, I rolled down windows and turned the air conditioner on high. He didn't smoke in the cab, but I still did a two-exit run down the interstate to deodorize the cab. Fortunately, he tipped really well.

The last fare was a regular in need of toilet paper. I grabbed a six-pack from the fast-mart and delivered to their door.

"Ah do appreciate this. We was usin' coffee filters 'cause we run out of everything else. Kinda rough on the rear, if ya know what ah mean."

I snatched the 10-dollar bill plus a fiver for the toilet paper and scurried to the cab.

When I dragged myself home, Belle was in the kitchen cooking. Jon was leaning back in a chair, flipping through television channels. I liked the cooking concept as long as someone else was doing it. Maybe I liked seeing Jon there too. He was growing on me.

During the morning, Jon had had a formal interview with Belle in a formal interview room with a recorder running. Which accomplished nothing.

Right now, he was rolling something around in his brain and had decided to join us for dinner.

I was curious why Belle never used Cool Rides unless the police made the phone call, so I switched my focus to her. No other cab company in town had cars as nice as ours. And the other company's drivers…ugh.

Belle served dinner on the kitchen table which was actually in my living room which would also be the guest bedroom.

"So, Belle," I said, "why don't you use Cool Rides when you go to Springfield or Holyoke?"

Jon came back from outer space and his attention shifted to Belle. He watched her like a retriever eyeing a tennis ball.

"Horace made the arrangements. I figured he had an agreement and he usually came with me to the drop off. He said he wanted to check out the clientele, make sure they wouldn't give me any grief. But he never came inside. They could have been space aliens for all he knew. And, Honey, those other drivers? They're huge. I never had one that didn't scare me just to look at him. I always thought they were packin', too. They sat like they had a lump up their butts. I would have used Cool Rides but Horace said your boss wasn't accommodating enough."

"Yeah, since the shootout at the train station, he's been taking all the Springfield and Holyoke calls himself or letting Andrew do it. We really need to get some new drivers." I rested my head on my hand. I was ready for bed.

"I thought you had enough." Jon looked at me. "What about that big guy? He would have been good for those runs, maybe even for late-night bar runs."

"Willie avoids bar runs. Doesn't want barf in the cars. And the big guy got a less stressful job as a guard up at county jail. We're down to two drivers plus Willie."

Belle looked at me speculatively. "So, what's it pay?"

I stared at her, thinking about the day of interviews we'd had. Well, she beat any of them. As long as she wasn't using the car for her own business ventures, Willie might not hold her previous job experience against her. She would be good company when business was slow. She had lots of people experience. Taxi driving is a service job—and she'd been in a service profession—sort of.

"I've been thinking about a career change. I need to lower my stress level. Men have expectations when they're paying. Besides, I'm tired of having strange things stuffed in my mouth." She sighed. "And in other places."

I gulped and coughed.

"How often you been busted?" Jon knew the rules for driving a cab in Northampton.

"Me?" Belle shook her head indignantly. "Never. No, uh-uh, not ever. Not even a parking ticket. I'm smarter than the law."

Jon knew better than to start a pissing contest with Belle. "I mean you can't have a record if you want to get a taxi-driving license. They run your background through the police database before they even look at you."

"Nothing in their precious database about me. You want me to put something in there?" She smiled wickedly at Jon.

"Then what was the tracking bracelet for?" I asked.

"I was a witness. And we won't go there. Suffice it to say I will pass the felony check with flying colors." Belle adopted her British accent. I was

61

beginning to enjoy the way she played with her language skills.

"Tell me more about Horace and the other cab companies." Jon wanted to pull on that string for a while.

I wanted to know more about the tracking bracelet, but Belle had decided to stop talking. The conversation continued, mostly from Jon's side. He kept trying to get information from Belle who clearly wasn't ready to implicate herself or anybody else, living or dead, in illegal activity. She smiled her best "kiss my butt, copper" smile and kept silent.

I was moving around the kitchen and I noticed Jon's eyes following me. He finally stood up. "I'm going home. Long day tomorrow, researching local taxi companies." He stretched his hands over his head. My libido kicked me in the stomach a little. Jon was a very attractive man. "Honey, could I see you outside?" he said.

"Yeah, sure." Whatever he wanted, spying on Belle wasn't on my agenda. I stepped into the hall, pulled the door closed and turned toward Jon.

"Honey, I…" Jon was suddenly close. I looked up and our eyes met. My world narrowed to a tight focus on his face. He reached out, gently sliding his hand behind my head. The kiss started out gentle and ended with my toes curled in knots. This man knew how to kiss. He leaned back, his attention seemed to narrow to my mouth. I blinked, wide eyed.

"Honey, I..." he repeated, running his finger down my cheek and his thumb over my lips. Now I was awake. His eyes were dark and unreadable. Of course, the hallway was also dark and unreadable. I hadn't seen Jon tongue-tied before. It was an odd sensation and I wasn't sure how I felt about it.

"Be careful." He held my face with both hands, kissed me softly on the forehead. "Jesus!" he mumbled and was off down the stairs. What kind of goodnight was that? What did he do when he wanted to stay? If that was just a "thanks for supper, dear," what was his seduction arsenal? I staggered a little and went back inside to Belle.

Belle eyed me with the disdain of experience. "Man, that is one hot behind. Too bad he's a cop. And get rid of the shit-eating grin."

"Wait a minute. What's wrong with being a cop?" I hadn't realized how big my smile was. I tried to frown.

"Honey, what's not wrong with being a cop?"

"He's a good guy." I didn't have much invested in Jon, but I could see potential and I didn't want my temporary roomie dissing him. "He could say the same kind of stuff about you and your profession."

"Anyway, I'm thinking about changing it. Self-employment sucks. Horace considered me an independent contractor so he didn't give bennies, and who can afford health insurance these days?"

She wanted out of the Jon discussion, clearly. I wasn't sure how I felt about Jon the cop myself, but my reasons were different from hers. The pull was getting stronger. My libido had kicked up a notch, and my curiosity about what could happen was rising faster than a teenage boy's hard-on. Jon and I would have some major control issues. Like who would be in charge of my life. When he had arrested me, in another lifetime, it was clear he had standards of behavior I might not share.

"Tell me more about this taxi-driving job possibility," Belle said, finishing the dishes.

"Come down in the morning and meet Willie and Mona. If you're still serious, Willie will give you a driving test. See if you're any good." I knew Willie's driving tests. You needed near-worshipful reverence for the car. No on and off the gas, no sudden braking, no tailgating, no speeding. Well, no getting caught. Willie broke the speed limit. Actually, he destroyed it, especially on longer runs. But he never got caught. He had tried to pass his sixth sense about cops and radar on to me but, mostly, I memorized where the speed traps were and I slowed down when I came to those places. I hadn't been nailed yet.

After Belle figured out the change in pay scale from her previous employment, I didn't think she would be interested in taxi driving no matter what the bennies were.

Chapter Five

I opened my eyes to daylight and coffee. Coffee? Oh yeah, Belle. I staggered into the kitchen/ living/dining/guest bedroom, resenting the intrusion into my space. Then I saw the kitchen table. Apparently my mother and Belle shared the belief that breakfast is the most important meal of the day. Grabbing a toasted sesame bagel smeared with garden-crunchy cream cheese, I tried to remember the last time I used my toaster. I was surprised it worked. How about that? I had a working toaster. How domestic. The fresh-ground coffee was a mystery since I was sure I didn't have a coffee grinder. Even the coffee pot was a surprise.

"Jeez, what do I owe you for all this food? And where did you find a coffee pot?"

"Consider it rent. The pot was in a bag behind a box labeled kitchen junk." Belle had, apparently, explored my tiny kitchen. I wasn't sure how I felt about that until I tasted the coffee she poured into one of the free ceramic mugs from the Cool Rides closet of promotional junk. Advertising companies sent samples of stuff we could use to get people to use Cool Rides. What we needed was more drivers for the customers we already had.

"I need to go to the office with you today, Mom. Take-your-girl-to-work day. Remember that idea? Wonder what my clients would have thought of me taking a kid to work. Anyway, I need to impress your boss with my skills and abilities." She didn't specify which skills and abilities.

"You'll have to impress Mona first. Then you'll need to get Willie to let you near a car. He's very protective. Then you go to City Hall and apply for a taxi ID and license," I mumbled around my last bite of bagel. "Yeah, I'll take you in. They need people right now, and I actually think you might make a good driver."

She would fit the Cool Rides driver profile— because we didn't have a driver profile. People tried it and we waited to see if they stuck around. If they didn't get freaked out by the insanity of the population they served, they might stay. We went through a lot of drivers.

She raised an eyebrow. "Why, thanks. I think."

When we were tanked on coffee and bagels, we headed, on foot, to the office. I was in my usual driving uniform of black jeans, T-shirt and sneakers. Belle was in her own professional outfit of spandex black pants, gold-sequined glitter top and 4-inch spiked fire-engine red heels.

Northampton is a city of believers. We buy into all the major religions and most of the minor ones. Even non-believing is a belief system in Northampton. People here pay attention to their convictions. As we passed one of the many churches in town, the sound of singing drifted out the open windows. Belle stopped. She stared at the church. It was one of those New England Postcard Moments: white spire reaching into a clear blue sky, the sound of music coming out of the arched windows. And Belle, in her special spandex and really special shoes, heading up the sidewalk toward the church. That would change it to a Northampton moment.

"It's nice to listen," I called after her, "but we should probably get to the office."

"We gotta go in. I know that song." Belle stared at the open door.

"Well, I guess…" I followed her up the steps. It was choir practice so the pews were empty, but I knew they were okay with an audience. I'd stopped in to listen before. I squeezed by Belle and paused at the back, ready for a quick escape. When the music stopped, so did my belief in the Almighty.

I slid into the last row of seats. Belle ignored me, walked to the front row and sat down. The choir began a song and stumbled on the first few bars. Belle, in her glittered glory, might have distracted them.

At the first pause in the singing, Belle suddenly rose. "No, no, no. That part needs a solo. It needs some love. The guy is asking God to save his soul, so you better put yours into it. Like this."

And she began to sing. Her voice pulled the heart right out of the song. The minister's mouth dropped open and his eyes bugged out. The choir stared until Belle raised her arms and said, "Now you come in and give me some support here."

She brought her arms down with a flourish and they followed her. At the end of the stanza, she lowered her voice into a hum and ended with "amen."

"Well, won't you join us?" The minister was ready to adopt Belle no matter what her fashion statement or personal beliefs.

"Oh, I gotta run right now. Job interview. But I could come back if you have another rehearsal later."

The reverend grabbed a schedule off the table and thrust it at her.

"I didn't know you were religious," I said as Belle clattered down the sidewalk.

"Oh, I ain't religious. I just like good music. Gospel is good music. My momma took me to church. I sang in the choir until I was 16 and found other outlets."

I wanted to ask more about Belle's other outlets, but we had arrived at Cool Rides.

Mona was standing out front, overflowing her tank top and tapping her toe. Our visit to church had made us 15 minutes late. My shift started at 9:00 every morning, Monday through Friday, sometimes Saturday and Sunday. Maybe having a new driver possibility in tow would make up for the 15 minutes.

"You got a Holyoke pickup as soon as you can get there." Mona never wasted time with small talk like Good morning when a fare was involved.

"Good morning to you, too. This is Belle. She's interested in driving for us." I gave Belle a little goose to push her into Mona's sphere of focus.

"Unnh!" Belle gave me a dirty look. "Pleased to meet you, I'm sure." She used her most sophisticated accent.

Mona looked her over carefully. "Don't I know you from somewhere?"

Uh-oh. Mona kept careful tabs on the competition. She might have seen Belle in the other company's cars. It wasn't my business to bring up an applicant's previous profession. Mona's attitude about

68

sex for hire might be different from mine. She would not tolerate it coming back on the company. Or spilling over into the backseat.

"You ever done any professional driving?" Mona's eyes moved over Belle's eye-popping outfit. I thought about Mr. FUCK You. We needed drivers and we needed them fast. It was more about attitude than fashion anyway.

"I have been in a car in a professional capacity."

"Well, someone has to pick up this guy in Holyoke. Gimme your driver's license and I'll run it up to City Hall. You gonna save me some time and let me know if you got any problems that might show up on the police records, right?"

"Ma'am, I ain't ever been in that kind of trouble." Belle had reverted to her street talk as she handed over her license. Mona gave her an odd look. "And I know Holyoke like the back of my beautiful butt," she said to me. "I can get you anywhere in that uuugly city."

"You can't drive the cab until you have the taxi license." Mona glanced at the Massachusetts driver's license. "Jacobsen? Where's that come from?"

"South African. My mother was a cleaning lady from Jo'burg. My father was an American diplomat. Boy, did they have nothing in common. Produced me, and there ain't nothing common there."

"You can navigate while I drive," I said. "I'll split the tip with you if you get me where we need to be." I didn't know interior Holyoke because Willie never let me drive there. He thought it was too dangerous for a woman. I thought it was too dangerous for anyone. I used the GPS when I needed to, but it couldn't read socioeconomic deprivation from outer space.

"Where's Willie?" I looked at Mona.

"He went to the train station. After your last pickup there, he decided not to let you draw any more fire."

"Nice of him to care."

"Not you. The car. He found the bullet hole."

"Oh, yeah." I hadn't mentioned the shot that connected with the car. "He hasn't fixed it, has he?" I remembered Jon had asked me not to touch it. There was still a bullet hole in the passenger seat, but the bullet itself had been taken as evidence. No need to remind anyone about that.

Mona sighed. "No, he figured, why bother? You'd just add something new if he went to the trouble. Andrew is on his way to the airport. You're all I got. So, get going." She handed me the slip with pickup address, drop-off and cell-phone number. No name.

We headed to the car. I slid behind the wheel. Belle ducked into the passenger seat. I showed her how to enter the pickup address into the GPS and off we went.

"The GPS is going to tell me the fastest route, but it won't know shortcuts. And it won't tell me where the high-crime areas are. If you know a better way, tell me."

Shortcuts were important. The more fares you crammed into a working day, the faster you got new, sexier undies. My underwear drawer needed even more help than my shoe closet. I didn't really have a shoe closet.

We were approaching the first Holyoke exit when Belle said, "Go to the next exit. I know a way to get there faster. This is the exit wussy people use. We gonna do the drug runner's route."

"What?" Too late. I was past the exit my GPS had told me to take.

"Please execute a legal U-turn as soon as possible." The soft feminine computer voice pleaded with me. She obviously knew this shortcut was going to cause me some grief. Maybe they did program in social conditions.

"Recalculating route," the voice whispered. It had given up on the U-turn concept.

"Yeah, yeah, see? You got a built-in wuss in this here car. I went this way a couple of times with Horace. Came back this way, too. You just gotta drive right through. Don't stop for nuthin'. Anyone step out in front of the car, just go around. Or through if you gotta. But don't stop."

"What about stop signs? Or stoplights?"

"Honey, don't nobody care in this neighborhood. You just slow down enough not to get broadsided by some other fool running the light from the other direction."

"Shit," I said. "Why don't you just shoot me?"

"'Cause I left my gun in Horace's place and I'm not going back there just yet. 'Sides, I wouldn't shoot you. I'd shoot whoever is shooting at you 'cause they might hit me by mistake."

"It wouldn't be a mistake. Next time the GPS wins. It knows better."

Belle grunted and looked sulky. "I ain't sayin' nuthin' more. You can find your own way to whatzit street."

71

"Oh no, no, no. You got us into this place. You better get me out of here." I slammed the brakes with both feet as a guy the size of a football field stepped in front of the cab. His pants were drooping and dirty, his shirt was long-sleeved despite the hot summer weather, and he was waving a greasy rag at my windshield. I managed to stop a good six inches from his shinbone.

As he started to run the rag over the front window, Belle jumped out and screamed, "Get out of our way, muthafucka. I'm on a mission here and I don't need no slowing down." She was almost as tall as the window washer and a hell of lot more vocal. She shoved her middle finger over the hood and into his face. He slunk back to the curb.

"Huh." She lowered herself back into the car and fastened the seat belt. "Drive on," she said, adopting her alternate linguistic personality.

I had to smile. We didn't have any more dents or bullet holes in the car...yet.

"Thanks, I guess." I looked at Belle who looked pleased with herself. Maybe this was a good time to satisfy some of my curiosity.

"What did Horace do when he came down to Holyoke with you?"

She stared at me for 10 seconds, which is a long time when you're on the receiving end of a stare.

She hmphed again then turned her head and most of the rest of her body toward the window.

Okay, that seemed to be a dead end. There was plenty more I was curious about with Belle. Like the language thing.

"Why do you talk like royalty sometimes and gutter talk other times?"

Belle turned back toward me. This was safe territory for discussion.

"It's like any language," she told me. "Once you know the basics, different dialects are easy. You instinctively know when to use what." She paused. "Like right now, I'm talking to you in American English."

She was right. I hadn't even noticed the transition.

"But that guy back there? He needed something more direct, though it would have been interesting if I'd used the more complex cadence of the Queen's English." She grinned.

I felt like I might have just broken through a communications barrier, so I said, "I don't mean to pry, Belle, but come on. I'm going to be pretty close to you for a while. I'd like to know if the shooters are looking for anyone who knew Horace or what he did when he was in Holyoke. Or if they're targeting you."

"Yeah, well, I don't know what that creep did. I just did my job, which, as you know, would be done with some privacy. Horace didn't hang around while I was working. I never did threesomes and nothing kinky."

"Did he get a ride back with you?"

"Sometimes. Sometimes not."

"You think he had a side business that someone didn't like?"

"How the hell would I know? What I know right now is you should be driving and I'm gonna navigate." She pronounced it naveegate. "And you should be

73

hangin' a left here. Now." She waved abruptly at the upcoming corner.

I screeched around the turn and almost clipped a black Lincoln Town Car parked by the curb. The driver was leaning against the front fender, smoking a cigarette. He jumped out of my way, dropping the butt as he scrambled. He was making a properly pissed-off gesture with his hand when he saw Belle. His expression changed from anger to surprise. I saw all this in milliseconds, but the expression was hard to miss.

"I guess these cars don't handle the corners all that well, huh?" Belle looked back over her shoulder and hunched down in the seat.

"Someone you know?" I asked.

The driver got into his car fast and screeched out to follow us.

"Please take a right at the next intersection." The computer voice took me off guard. I did as requested, and the computer said, "You have arrived." I jammed on the brakes.

We were in front of the Holyoke police station and I pulled into visitor's parking. The Lincoln Town Car barreled by us and the passenger-side window rolled down. A large man leaned out. His face was dark, his hair slicked back. Even at thirty miles an hour, the wind didn't put one hair on his head out of place.

He stared at Belle. She pretended not to notice, but she turned away and tried to get smaller. Not easy. The town car disappeared around a corner.

"This is where we're picking up?" Belle looked at the massive brick building. If it was supposed to intimidate, it succeeded.

"Mona didn't say anything about cops." Maybe because Mona didn't know Belle had an allergy to them.

"This is the address on the fare slip. Why don't you go in and tell the desk sergeant the Cool Rides taxi is here? I'll stay and guard the car." I turned the key and took it out of the ignition. Picking up at a police station isn't unusual for taxi drivers. People making use of the short-stay option in the holding cells have often had their cars towed, confiscated or wrecked. I once spent an hour driving a guy around from the police station to the bank to the registry to the parking clerk and finally to the tow lot. He'd been driving drunk on an expired registration with four overdue parking tickets, and he stuck his fist in the face of the cop who stopped him. Including my fare, the previous evening had cost him $500 in cash. Lots of stops at the ATM. He didn't tip, but I made a good hourly wage.

"Number one," said Belle, "I don't do police stations. Number two, which of us do you think is going to guard anything against anyone better here, you or me?" She drew herself up until her head touched the roof. She had a point, but I had the car keys.

We had reached a standoff when the fare sauntered out of the station house. It was Jon. I shouldn't have been surprised. Due to the drug trade along the interstate corridor, there was a lot of back-and-forth between the Northampton cops and the Holyoke station.

"Hello, ladies." His smile made me grit my teeth and grip the steering wheel harder. It also made my heartbeat pick up just a bit and caused some muscle contraction a little lower down. I sighed. Jon did that to me and when he smiled, he did it even more.

Chapter Six

"Belle," Jon greeted her. "How's it going?"

Mona must have told someone in the cop house that Belle was going to be with me. And that someone knew Jon. That someone had radioed him at the Holyoke station, telling him Belle and I were together. Any of the Holyoke or Northampton cruisers could have transported Jon home. Sometimes people trapped in cars together get more talking done than hours of formal intimidation can achieve, and Jon had gotten nada so far from Belle. This was his innovative approach to interrogation.

"Hey, I could drive like a NASCAR guy if you coppers could admit I don't got any felonies." She was back in her streetwise hooker character.

"The application is being processed as we speak." Jon showed her his smile and almost batted his eyelashes. I imagine few women are immune to Jon when he turns on the charm. "You have a good teacher." The information about Belle's application must have been radioed to him. He turned his smile on me.

"Uugh. I don't need teachin'. I could drive you guys into the ground. Just gimme a car." Apparently, Belle was one of the immune few.

I eased the car away from the curb.

"Fasten your seat belt, please." I imitated the computer.

"So, has Willie met Belle yet?" Jon asked as he clicked himself in.

"Nope." Belle turned in her seat. "But what's not to love? He gonna turn me loose on all this here people movin'."

I drove up the ramp onto the interstate toward Northampton and glanced in the mirror to check traffic. What I saw was big, square, and black. Shit! The Lincoln Town Car was right behind me.

"Hey, Belle, check your side mirror. That anybody you know?"

Jon jerked around in his seat to see what I was talking about. Belle had sunk down in the passenger seat and was trying to make herself as invisible as someone over six feet with a full afro could. Even with the seat belt strangling her, her hair stuck up above the headrest. I would have laughed, but the car behind us was too sinister. Whoever was in it had no way of knowing we had a police officer with us. It would be more likely we had an overnighter from the drunk tank and were an easy mark if they had some business with one of us. Like Belle.

"Shit, that's one of Scarpelli's goons." Jon turned around. "Belle, if you got information, now's the time to tell me. Just how bad might these guys want to talk to you?"

"I don't know what they want. Why you pickin' on me? You the cop. Maybe it's you that pissed them off. Maybe we should just shove you out the door and see if they stop."

Jon wasn't happy with the answer. I kept driving as fast as my little car could handle. We were on the interstate in two lanes of traffic. It was light traffic with cars moving at the speed limit or faster, but I really didn't want to go over 90 in a car that weighs, maybe a couple thousand pounds, while I was playing dodge-em with one that was at least double that. The Town Car was right on my bumper. There was no way I was going to outrun it. The car was going 90 and my mind was doing warp speed when I saw two 18-wheelers blocking both lanes ahead of us. I had to slow down.

The Lincoln pulled up beside us. The tinted window rolled down slowly. Like someone right out of the Godfather movies, the guy in the passenger seat raised one hand and made a gun shape with his thumb and finger. Then he pretended to pull the trigger. It might have been a cliché but it was very effective as an intimidation tactic.

Jon lowered his window, leaning his hand on the edge. He was holding his badge. It's hard to have an effective conversation with someone in another car at high speeds, but Jon was doing a good job of it. He held up the badge where they couldn't mistake it, and the big black car dropped back out of sight. I saw it pulling off the exit. Another crisis averted. How many more before Belle wanted to talk? And was she the target? And what did she know? I hated not knowing things.

I pulled off at the first Northampton exit. "Where do you want me to drop you?" I asked Jon.

"I'll go to Cool Rides with you." He leaned his head back against the seat, his eyes closed. He had moved from adrenaline-pumping confrontation to comatose in minutes. Of course, I had too, but I probably didn't do it as often. And I didn't carry a weapon or a badge. I would never need to make the split-second decisions that Jon's profession required.

"Belle," he said, "if you tell me what you know, they might decide it's better to ignore you. If they think you're a loose end, they'll keep coming after you. You're putting yourself in more danger by not talking to me."

Belle leaned her head against the window. We pulled in front of the Cool Rides garage. I parked and we all sat for a minute. Belle turned to Jon.

"I don't know what all Horace was into." She paused and sighed. "But I can make some experienced guesses and give you some leads."

Jon looked at her funny and I realized she had switched back to her kiss-the-queen accent.

"She's bilingual," I said. Maybe her reality was in between. Jon's reality seemed to be 'take whatever comes at you and deal with it.' He got out of the car, opened Belle's door and put out his hand. She took it and rose with that dignity she did so well. Another technique I might study.

"Let's go inside and talk," he said. I followed them, feeling like the odd one out. Given our company, being odd fit in.

Chapter Seven

Jon got three chairs from around the office. Apparently he wanted me to join them, and I figured I had a right to know what Belle said. She was living with me and I didn't want to be blindsided by some goon who was looking for her and found me instead.

"I just have suspicions." Belle slumped in the chair. "I won't testify in court. And I don't have any proof, but I might point you in a direction. I guess I owe Horace that much. It just never seemed like he was into the dangerous stuff."

"You don't owe Horace," Jon said. "But I'll take whatever you can give me. It might keep some trouble away from you, too."

"Do I get any protection out of this deal?" Belle looked at Jon. I thought about my little apartment. Did I get protection? Did I need it?

After 40 minutes of talk, Jon had learned almost nothing about Horace's death but quite a lot about the transportation of various illegal substances up the interstate. According to Belle, Horace had been in regular contact with some oversize guys she thought worked for both Scarpelli and one of the other taxi companies in the area. This was probably of more interest to a vice cop than to homicide, but in a police department the size of Northampton's, everyone worked on everything. And it did create some motives for Horace's untimely trip to Neverland. Belle had also heard some vague rumblings about discontent in the Scarpelli family.

"Horace talked a lot but didn't say much. He used that Larry's Limo company and acted real nervous around the drivers. Who wouldn't be? They were some scary guys."

Belle stretched her arms over her head. Her large, very visible breasts rose. I watched Jon's eyes follow. He looked down at the table and smiled, shaking his head. Maybe Belle's sexuality was natural, but maybe it was a little overdone. And maybe I could take a few lessons from her. So much to learn, so little time. Whatever I learned, I wondered if Jon might be appreciating it in the near future.

"I need something to drink. What you got around here that's cold?" Belle glanced at the Coke machine on the far side of the room. "That monster needs quarters, I bet." She rummaged in her bag and came up with two quarters. I stuck my hand and then my head into my own oversize bag. No matter how much I tried to contain it, the loose change always found its way to the bottom. I came up with two more. Jon produced two out of his pocket. How do men cram all the necessities of life into their pockets? Belle collected the quarters and headed off. Jon did carry a gun and it wasn't in his pocket.

She put in the required six quarters and pressed a button. Nothing happened.

"Open the door," I said.

She gave the door a yank, but the machine had changed its mind and stayed obstinately closed. Belle moved to the side. She gave it a shove and pulled on the door again. She grabbed the machine with both hands and started shaking it.

"It's not nice to mess with Belle, you fucking machine," she said, shoving it harder. I guessed her adrenaline was still running high.

"Don't do that!" I said. "It reacts badly to violence."

She gave it one last shove. The door sprang open, crashing against the wall. Soda cans cascaded onto the floor, rolling around erratically.

"Cool!" Belle looked satisfied with the havoc. "Want one?"

"I expect every one of those cans to be put back," I heard Mona growl from the inner office. I think she owns a share in Coke. She's very protective of the ancient machine.

Belle leaned over and picked up a can of Diet Coke.

"Don't—" I managed to gurgle out before, carefully pointing it away from herself, she pulled the tab open. Jon, who had cop reflexes, jumped out of the line of fire. Soda sprayed over the floor, the table, and the other soda cans, and splattered against my hair, down my clean white T-shirt and onto my jeans. "—do that." I was head-to-toe sticky.

"Oops," Belle said, giggling. She turned to Mona. "Got any towels?"

"Enough for the floor. Blondie needs a shower."

I looked down at my clothes. Clean this morning, laundry by nightfall. Shit. Another stellar evening at the Laundromat.

"And don't forget you have an airport this afternoon." Mona surveyed the disaster. "I expect that mess cleaned up by anyone who might want a job here in the future." She stared pointedly at Belle.

"Does that mean my application went through?" Belle pumped the air with her fist.

"Never had them process one that quickly before." Mona glanced over at Jon who was studying the floor. It certainly warranted a good looking over. "Give me a photo and I'll have it laminated. I need twenty-five bucks to give to City Hall," she said, her attention back on Belle.

Belle started rummaging in her bag again.

"I guess I'll go home and change," I muttered to myself. No one else seemed to be paying any attention to my problems.

"I'll go with you." Ah, except Jon. "It's on my way to the station. Sticky is cute on you." He was looking at my wet T-shirt, about chest level. His eyes darkened a bit. Grinning, he let his eyes travel upward. He ran a thumb over the drops on my cheek and then ran it down, gently caressing my lips. The grin disappeared and his nostrils flared a little. My apartment wasn't exactly on the way to the station.

"Whoa, do we need a bed in here?" said Belle, smirking.

I narrowed my eyes at him, but I didn't object to Jon's company. I wasn't about to stay and help Belle clean the floor.

Opening the door, Jon held it for me with his hand resting on my back. I swung my bag over my shoulder and sashayed out, trying hard to maintain some dignity and maybe add the sexy walk Belle did so well.

Jon held my arm as we started walking. "I don't like the Scarpelli's involvement in all this. Maybe you should rethink this sleeping arrangement with Belle. She could stay in a motel somewhere."

"You think that finger-gun thing was because of Belle? I, uh, kind of came close to hitting their car before I picked you up." I didn't think they would have gone after me if I had been alone. But I really didn't want Jon telling me what I should, or shouldn't, do.

"You sideswiped them?" Jon laughed out loud. "I like that you made the Scarpelli gang jump a little, but I don't think they would have followed you for that. It is Holyoke. Either they recognized Belle or something else is going on." We started up the hill toward my apartment. I lived a few blocks from work and around a few corners from the police station, the Laundromat and the bakery. In Northampton, everything was around the corner. My apartment was on the second floor, above a deli.

I stopped to get food to keep my stomach quiet during the airport run. The teenager behind the counter didn't comment on the stripe of soda down my front. He had a pierced lip, nose, eyebrow, and ears, a tattoo running the length of his arm, and a purple and green Mohawk, so his fashion statement trumped mine.

Jon grabbed the bags and followed me up the staircase. I knew he was trying to get more information about Belle. I didn't have any, but it's always good to make a man carry groceries. I reached into my bag for keys. There was a little hook on one end of my oversized, overstuffed bag for keys. Were they ever there? Not in my lifetime. I pulled my head out of the bag to avoid tripping on the last stair and stopped. The door to my apartment was open, swinging in the breeze. The frame was shattered where the lock had been.

Chapter Eight

Jon was following me, but he hadn't had his head in a bag. He stepped around, shoving me behind him, and drew his gun. He held his hand up to tell me to stay put. Dream on, Jon. My space, my business. I was right in back of him.

Then I saw the inside of my space. Oh God, oh Christ, oh shit! They'd trashed it. Jon crouched low, gun in front of him. He moved around the open door and slid behind the upended sofa. I peered around the broken door jamb. He rose and was in the bedroom in one stride. Long strides, small space. It took less than 30 seconds to be certain no one was inside. My dishes were broken and scattered on top of a mound of what food had been in the fridge. A pair of my sexiest silk panties were hung like a potholder over the stove. They had ketchup dripping down the front.

"Honey, I told you to stay outside." Jon paused, surveying the damage. "I'm really sorry. Looks like you and Belle need new living arrangements."

I had saved every penny I made for a year to get this place. I spent six months on Willie's couch at the office the cab company and lived in subsidized housing for six months after that. Whoever "they" were, they had no right. It was broad daylight next to one of the busiest stores in town. Somebody must have seen them. Part of me wanted revenge. The rest of me wanted to hide somewhere safe. Shit! I sniffed and hiccupped and leaned against Jon.

Jon had his cell phone out.

"Who are you calling?" I started pacing, which probably seemed silly in the small space left without trash. But it worked off some of my anger.

"I'm getting some crime-scene guys over here." He held the phone to his ear with one hand and reached out with his other arm to pull me back against him. I wanted to cry. I wanted to curse. I just laid my head on his chest and closed my eyes.

"Tonight, you can stay at my place. We can't clean this up until the crime scene is processed anyway. You don't want to stay in this stuff. And you really do need a shower." Jon dropped the phone into his pocket. I backed up a step.

"I have a job. I have an afternoon airport run. I promised Mona. I've got a job to do. I don't know what time I'll get back. I can't just pick up and move. I have a life." I knew I couldn't stay in this mess, and I knew they had to go over it before it was cleaned up. Reality just hadn't quite made it from my brain to my mouth. I gave myself a mental "shut up."

"And what about Belle?" What about Belle? When had she become my responsibility? And when had I become Jon's responsibility?

"I have a whole house. I'm sure we can fit Belle in somewhere." Jon tightened his arm around me.

"Your house? How many bedrooms? How many bathrooms? Who else lives there? I don't know enough about you to move in. And Belle! She'll go through the roof. She can barely be in the same room with a cop."

"Calm down." Jon held my hand and started to massage it. "Belle is going to like my kitchen a lot better than yours. I have three bedrooms and two bathrooms. I just want to get a handle on where Scarpelli comes into this. Belle didn't shoot Horace and he didn't shoot himself. Honey, a guy is dead. Someone killed him. And Belle is a witness, even if she doesn't know to what. I need to keep an eye on you because…" He stopped talking and looked at me. "I'm not sure why." He ran his hand up my arm. I was considering my response when the thumping of feet on the stairs told us the crime scene was about to be investigated. Jon went to the door. I stood there like an idiot, rubbing my arm.

"I need to pack a few things," I mumbled. I hoped I had a few things left to pack. Taxi drivers frequently carry oversize bags as standard equipment. I kept one handy in case I didn't want to drive home between late night drop-offs and early pick-ups. Belle, in her previous profession, had kept the same kind of bag.

I looked disconsolately at the toothpaste. It had been used to spell out shit happens on the floor. Or maybe slut opens.

"What do you think that says?" I asked Jon.

Jon looked down. "Slap happy?"

"Slut shopping?" I giggled, beginning to melt down.

"I have toothpaste in both guest rooms," Jon said. "Let's go back to the garage and run it by Belle. You can follow me home with a taxi and leave for the airport from my house. And I have a really nice shower," Jon said. He kissed my forehead and steered me out the door. I leaned on him to avoid shaking. Shaking would not be good.

Maybe Belle would be fine as long as she didn't have to go back to Hampshire Heights. Gunshots were part of everyday living in Hamp Heights, and the cops wouldn't get called until it was too late to catch the shooter if they got called at all.

When we got to Cool Rides, Willie, Belle and Mona were sitting around the table. Belle was humming. From the tune and from Willie's expression, I guessed she was relating her impromptu performance in the chapel. Mona was smiling. Well, maybe.

Belle nudged Willie. "Come on, sing it." She stood up and waved her hands in the air, and they harmonized the chorus. Holy cow, I thought, she might convince them to join her for choir practice. Jon applauded. I had other stuff on my mind. Like Jon's house and the bedrooms in Jon's house. There was a new body in the morgue. I didn't want mine or Belle's or anyone's to join it. I was a small-town taxi driver. All I wanted to do was move people from where they were to where they needed to be. Guns and bodies were not on my agenda.

Jon explained what had happened to my apartment and what we, or at least Jon, had decided to do about it. Belle grinned. Apparently her cop phobia wasn't real deep.

"A real kitchen? When can we go shopping? Let's see now, I'm going to need..." She started a list of groceries. "What kind of cookware did you say you had? Oh, sorry about your apartment. I know a good cleaning service if you need it." She walked off talking to herself about ingredients and recipes.

"There's a shower in the Cool Rides garage. It's not pretty, but I'll use it," I grumbled. "Maybe I can pick up a few short hauls before the airport and make some money to buy those 'eat me' thongs I saw downtown," I said, looking at Jon. He had his cop face on, but I saw a flicker at the words thong and eat me. I had an interior sigh moment. "I'll head over to your house after my airport."

Jon, blissfully unaware that I knew where he lived, gave me directions, and he and Belle left.

When I walked out of the shower/locker room/changing room, Mona handed me a pickup slip.

"O'Grady's bar, going to Holyoke. You're up. You have plenty of time before the airport."

I headed out, figuring work would take my mind off the reality of my vandalized apartment and the distraction of my growing interest in Jon. Normally I avoid O'Grady's, the local bar most likely to appear in the police report. But most of their incidents take place around closing when the hard-core patrons are tossed out. Since it was early afternoon, I could look the fare over first. If it was a candidate for the barf bag, I'd keep driving and call Mona. She could hand it off to a different cab company. When a fare looks fall-down drunk, we call the competition and pretend we're the pickup. Most of the other companies never say never to a fare.

As I drifted by the entrance to O'Grady's, I noticed a man, mid-thirties, suit and tie, nice haircut. Maybe stopping for a drink after work. I pulled over and he got in.

"Where to?" I asked, punching the GPS on.

"Just get on Route 5. I'll direct you."

Route 5 had been the main road before the interstate was built. Now it's a quiet back road dotted with dead and dying businesses. A lot of life around Northampton, and many small towns, is defined by "before the interstate went in." O'Grady's is about 30 feet from Route 5. I had settled into driving when my passenger said, "Take the next right."

It was a narrow side road. I swung in and there was a house hiding behind the trees on a circular drive.

"Pull in here," he said and leaned back to dig out his wallet. A big guy dressed in a black suit and looking like an undertaker came out of the house and started around the front of the car. That didn't look right to me. Most people who are greeting someone open the passenger door. If they mean to pay for the fare, they lean in the front passenger window. I'd lowered that window in anticipation when the man came out of the house. My passenger had his door open and one foot out. I watched the big guy pass in front of my car. He slid his hand into his jacket. He was around the car and had one hand on my door. By my door, I mean the one he would drag me out of if he intended to shoot me with the gun he now held in his other hand.

I yanked my foot off the brake and smashed it down on the accelerator. The car lurched forward. My passenger hadn't quite cleared the door. His left leg was still in the cab and his right hand was resting on the window. The bozo at my door held on to the handle. He was big enough to stop most people with one hand. A car is not a person. And he was not going to stop 2,000 pounds of steel with 135 pounds of freaked-out woman behind the wheel.

The driveway ran out to the road between two huge pine trees. In another life, I might have thought "Christmas trees." Right now, I was thinking the fastest way out was between those honkin' big, real solid-looking trees. I knew there was room for the car, but the attached bodies hadn't noticed the trees. They were focused on holding onto the car and their guns and staying upright and getting me out of the car. I was focused on making sure they didn't do any of that. They hit the trees going ten miles an hour. That's really slow if you're driving in traffic, but when an unprotected body moving at that speed hits a stationary object, it's plenty fast. The passenger-side door slammed against the tree, closing tightly on the body wedged between it and the car. The guy holding onto the driver's-side door threw out his arm to ward off the collision and ended up looking like Wile E. Coyote in a Road Runner cartoon. I reached the end of the driveway. The backseat passenger was pinned by the door, half out of the car.

"Gaaahhh!" I heard a moan from the backseat. "I think my arm is broken...and my leg."

"Out," I screeched. The guy hurled himself out and lay flat on the ground. I laid rubber. The back door slammed closed with the momentum of my departure.

What the hell did they want? Cabbies never carry much cash. Maybe they didn't know that. I thought about my apartment, thought about calling Jon, then I actually did call him. He wasn't in, said the desk sergeant, and could someone else help me? I decided that no one could help right now and headed back to the safety of the Cool Rides garage before I made any more decisions. I hadn't collected any fare money in advance so my till was going to be short for the day. This didn't bode well for me becoming the best taxi driver in history or the owner of a profitable company. A small business in a small town doesn't usually plan on passengers with guns. I had experienced more guns in the last week than I had in my whole driving career.

I swung out onto the highway. About five minutes down the road my hands started to shake. Shaky hands are not good when applied to a steering wheel. I pulled over and leaned my head back. Shit! I threw the door open and vomited.

Now I had to go back to my apartment and brush my teeth and…no, not to the apartment. I had my toothbrush with me but no toothpaste. I needed strong toothpaste. I let my stomach settle, gripped the steering wheel with white knuckles and headed back home to Cool Rides.

I stopped at the drugstore on the strip. My stomach was woozy, but my head had cleared. I swallowed a few times and went in. Grabbing toothpaste and a bottle of water, I zipped through the checkout without opening my mouth. No need to knock out the salesperson with vomit breath. I drank most of the water and headed back to the garage.

There would be no way to avoid explaining what had happened when Willie saw the car door. I could make up some lie about a hit-and-run, but I knew if Willie didn't figure it out, Jon would. I could lie with the best of them, but Jon had probably had some experience with the best liars in the world. Not having fare money to hand over to Mona would make an explanation mandatory. Fares that fail to pay are a fact of every taxi driver's life. The addition of violence is less frequent but not unusual. If we reported every episode to the police, we'd spend half our waking hours in the cop-house interview room. I'd had enough of that depressing place for a long time. Willie would fix the dent in-house, and the insurance company would never hear about it. But this incident was serious enough to make me think Jon might have to know about it. It involved firearms.

When I pulled in, Willie and Mona were out front washing one of the cars. No one keeps cars as clean as the Cool Rides crew. And now there was mine. Two bullet holes, three dents, and a big smear of dark red-brown stuff down the passenger window. I should be happy there weren't some fingers stuck in the door. Actually, I hadn't checked.

I needed normal fares. I was still shaky from the mugging and didn't want to burst into tears or throw up again.

The damage was clearly in view. Mona and Willie stopped scrubbing and stared at the door.

"I'm okay," I said. "And the door still works, but I could use some of that cleaner." I grabbed the towels and the spray bottle and started working on the brown streak. Jon would have had a fit, but I wasn't going to press charges against those bozos. I never wanted to see them again. So evidence wasn't in my vocabulary at the moment. Drive to the airport were the words I wanted to hear.

"What the hell happened?" Willie knelt in front of the dent in the door. He stroked his hands over the damage like he was feeling a wound in a loved one.

"I'm okay," I repeated.

"We can see that," said Mona. "Don't avoid the question."

"I had a run-in with some thugs. But they look worse than me. They even look worse than the car." And maybe I'll never pick up at O'Grady's again, I thought.

"Nothing could look worse than the car." Willie said.

"Well, yes, these guys do. One of them probably has a broken arm and maybe a leg, too. The other one may have a broken nose...or face...or body. He kind of looked flat, sort of attached to the tree."

"What tree?" Willie finally stood up and noticed me.

"Unh, the ones they ran into, but the car didn't... very much. I mean, just the door. Because it was open. Because he had his arm and leg out the door. Because he was trying to get out...of the door." I stammered to a stop.

"Who?" Willie looked at me like I had an alien sticking out of my head.

"The fare. Can we go inside and discuss this?" My legs felt rubbery and I wanted to sit down. And, after my legs didn't feel like Jell-O, I wanted to be allowed to drive to the airport.

We sat and I explained the disaster in Holyoke. I had no court-worthy evidence this was more than a mugging. I didn't recognize my assailants. We keep $50 in change in the box, and it was reasonable for them to think a driver could have more. Muggings were unusual but still a fact of life in this business. And they hadn't managed to get any of the money I did have. So, realistically, all I could say happened was the display of a firearm.

Willie sat back. "Jon stopped by and told me about the apartment. There's just too much dangerous stuff going on right now. I want you to limit your driving to airport runs with fares we know and car service with our regulars."

I almost hugged him. Local car service was a good deal. We rented the car and driver out for $50 an hour. The customers were mostly older and had given up driving. We would run errands and take them to appointments. Sometimes we took their pets to the vet's office. It was a guaranteed $25 an hour plus tips for the driver. Combined with airport runs, it would be a respectable income. And I wouldn't have to worry about large stupid men with guns.

"Do the seven o'clock run to the airport. That's Professor Brant. He's been out in California, so he'll be tired when he gets in. Let him sleep," Willie said.

"And Iggi Paluska wants his cat taken to the vet tomorrow. You can do that," added Mona.

"Take the pocket limo to the airport," Willie said. We have one cab with extra-dark tinted windows and plush leather seats. It's a Scion and we all know it's not a limousine. Willie says it's a matter of attitude. And the pocket limo has style.

"Aawright!" I pumped a fist and headed to the bathroom with the toothpaste.

"Good idea," said Mona. "Your breath could put another dent in that car."

For the next hour, I calmed and distracted myself by cleaning and detailing cars. Passengers leave gloves, hats and glasses, and the mysterious single shoe that means someone left with one bare foot. I found a state-police evidence envelope once, still full. I had found boxes of condoms, baggies of illegal substances and, once, a two-month-old baby whose mother "just needed a break from the screaming. I knew where to find him when I was ready to pick him up." We told her we charged $50 an hour for use of the cab. She arrived in five minutes and indignantly retrieved her squalling youngster.

As I was finishing vacuuming the last car, Mona came out with a fare slip. "He's going home." She grinned and handed me the yellow Post-it. The name on it was Steinberger. We all knew Mr. Steinberger. He needed a ride either to or from the liquor store. Another windows-down, air-conditioner-on kind of guy, depending on how much he'd consumed before he got picked up.

He looked functional today, but when he leaned over to pick up his bag, he got stuck. I sighed, hopped out and grabbed the first bag.

"It's really heavy," he said.

"Unh, what's in this?" I grunted. There was a cardboard box inside the bag and a plastic bag inside the box.

"Wine."

"I don't know much about wine." I had never seen it packaged in a cardboard box before.

"I call it booze in a box. It's awful."

"Oh," I said. "Good for cooking, I guess."

"Oh, no, we're having dinner guests. I'm serving it to them. I'd never drink this stuff myself."

"They like the cheap stuff?"

"No, but I'll get them blotto on cheap scotch before dinner."

"You don't like these people, do you?"

"Not especially, no."

We finished loading up the five bags of assorted bottles and headed up the hill half a block to his residence.

I helped him unload and waited until he'd made it inside. He'd been known to take a header over a sidewalk crack.

I returned to Cool Rides and finished detailing the mini-limo.

At 6:15, I left for the airport. When I got back, Mona was leaving for the night.

"Take the bang and dent for Iggi Paluska's cat to the vet at 10 tomorrow morning. Then I'll see if we got anything else you can't screw up."

"The bang and dent" was the new name for the car I usually drove. I didn't argue none of the dents were my fault. I just wanted to get over to Jon's house and find a bed.

I knew Jon's house, although Jon didn't know I knew it. Right after he'd busted me and took me to Willie to get a job, I had done a little bit of semi-stalking. I wasn't sure whether I wanted to burn the house down with him in it or knock on the door and ask if he was busy for the evening. Either result would have been his fault because he'd busted me.

The house was a beautiful old Victorian two family side-by-side that needed some fixing up, which Jon was doing on the weekend warrior plan. Apparently he rented out the other side.

I had no doubt Willie or Mona had already told Jon about the incident in Holyoke. He's a cop and he's a guy. I prepared for the control-issue discussion. At the moment, I didn't feel like answering questions or justifying my job or fighting over who was in charge. I just wanted sleep.

The door jerked open before I had a chance to knock. Jon stood there in jeans, open work shirt, and bare feet. My brain said wow, but my libido was like the piece of extra luggage the airline had lost, and I couldn't be bothered to find. My adrenaline had spiked so many times today I was running on zero. Still, my first thought was to reach out and stroke that lovely chest.

Instead, I stepped back defensively. He stepped forward and pulled me into his arms. No questions, no wandering hands. I struggled not to feel needy. I don't like people who are emotional black holes. It isn't always easy for me not to be one of them.

"When did you talk to Willie?" I mumbled into his chest.

"I told him about the apartment. He was upset." He paused.

"At least it wasn't the car," I said.

"And he told me about what happened in Holyoke. To the car. I assume you were in it at the time. We need to talk about you picking up strange men. Didn't your mother tell you not to do that?"

"It's my job. Besides, all men are strange."

"I know."

He wrapped me in big strong arms again. I leaned again. He wasn't taking this lightly, but he wasn't pressuring me. He knew I was going to stick with my job and Cool Rides. He was mixing giving me space and protection at the same time and doing a damn fine job of it. I sort of snuck my hands around his waist and held on for a few more seconds.

My brain began to drift toward off. I was in the arms of one really hot guy and I was so tired I was passing out. He herded me inside and sat me on a sofa that made mine look like a dollhouse miniature.

"Belle made food. Sit, I'll get some." He went into the kitchen.

We were stuffing ourselves with macaroni salad laced with sweet peppers, sweeter onions, bacon and hard-boiled eggs when Belle made her entrance. She was dressed in lavender jeans and a white sparkle top that dipped as low as it could without her boobs overflowing. Her shoes were ankle-breaking tall, and rhinestone earrings whacked her shoulders. She took denim to a whole new level. Boy, did I want to look like that when I grew up.

"Honey, I'm glad you like the food, but if I had a man looking at me like that, it ain't food what I'd be eating." She whirled by in a cloud of perfume. My eyes moved over to Jon. She was right. There was an odd expression on his face. I wasn't sure it was what Belle thought it was, though. More likely he wanted information about the Wile E. Coyote flat guy in Holyoke. The one with the big gun.

"I'm going out," Belle announced.

"Whoa, wait a minute." Jon stood up and tried to tower over her. Given the addition of the spiked heels to Belle's six feet, it was a hopeless effort. "You're here because it's safe. And I don't want you doing anything I have to explain to my boss tomorrow morning. There's a curfew in this house."

"Isn't he just the cutest thing in the world? Darlin', nobody tells Belle when to come home. Even Horace didn't try that." Belle touched Jon on the cheek with one iridescent lavender fingernail and kept walking toward the door. Jon might have admired Belle's swinging rear end, but he seemed more focused on who was in charge. I admired her fingernails. And her toenails. And her shoes. And her ability to stay upright in them.

"Where the hell are you going?" Jon glanced at the handcuffs lying on the counter. Of course, Belle was carrying her big bag and it might have a gun stuffed in somewhere with ammo for added weight. But it was mostly verbal sparring over who might be in charge.

Belle grinned wickedly. "Oh, don't get your thong in a crack. There's a late concert uptown. A friend of mine is singing. I promised her a month ago that I would be her date. She's picking me up and dropping me off." We heard a horn honk outside.

Belle had her hand on the door handle. "And tomorrow morning I'll be leaving early for choir practice." She hummed an Amen as she closed the door behind her. Belle knew how to make an exit. Jon stood with his mouth shut tight, fingers drumming on his nicely muscled thighs. If I could get past the general control issue, I really, really wanted to deal with those thighs.

"Choir? Do they know what they're in for? Jesus. How do I get involved with these people?" He flopped down next to me.

"You're a cop. Same as a taxi driver, strange people go with the territory," I mumbled, yawning, and leaned my head against him. I don't remember falling asleep. I don't remember Belle coming home. I don't remember Jon moving me from the couch to one of the spare bedrooms. But I opened my eyes in a strange bed. One with super high thread-count cotton sheets and huge pillows.

Chapter Nine

I smelled coffee and bacon. Takeout pastry with chocolate or butter or both is my usual breakfast. When I wandered into the kitchen, Jon was standing at the counter drinking coffee and shaking aspirin out of a plastic bottle.

Belle emerged from the bathroom and sauntered into the kitchen. Her makeup was toned down, she was wearing a plain white shirt and black slacks, and her shoes only added an inch to her height. They had some glitter on them, so she still made a little bit of a statement. Jon narrowed his eyes. His fingers toyed with the pair of handcuffs that still lay on the counter.

"Sweetie, how would it look if you tried to stop a woman from her God-given right to worship?" She slid the sugar bowl toward him and moved the cuffs down the counter, out of Jon's reach. "Add some of this to that coffee. It'll sweeten you right on up."

"Black, and you might make me doubt there is a God." he said but didn't pull the handcuffs closer.

Belle swung her butt toward the door. "Siiing, sing out loud." She sang and slammed the door behind her. Jon held his head. He downed the aspirin and took a careful sip of coffee.

"Headache?"

"I didn't sleep well." Maybe because he'd slept alone, I thought to myself, surprised I would even consider it.

"I did, sleep well. Thanks for the bed. Temporarily. I wasn't sure about the sleeping arrangements."

"I have three bedrooms. That's the sleeping arrangement…for the moment. If you want to change that, let me know. I'm a very accommodating guy."

"No 'honey, I have a headache'?" I slid onto the seat across the counter from him.

"Honey, where you're concerned, a bullet in the brain wouldn't slow me down." He focused his blue eyes on mine.

I blinked first.

"So, you want to talk about it?" he asked.

"About your headache? Or slowing you down?"

"Yesterday. The thugs. Remember? You got mugged by two big guys who are paying dearly for underestimating your blind luck." He swallowed the black coffee and winced. Belle had added chicory.

"Oh, those guys. It's a hazard of the job. Willie put me on local car service and known airport for a while. I think I can handle that."

"I want a description."

"Well, local service runs are mostly old people without driver's licenses…" My voice trailed off when I noticed Jon was eyeing the handcuffs again. He looked back at me. I knew I was being snarky but that's how I cope with pressure, and I was feeling the heat of too many weird events in too short a time.

"Just dreaming about you in handcuffs, where at least I could keep some small amount of control over you."

"Are we back to discussing sleeping arrangements?" An image of Jon cuffed to the bed, spread eagle, flitted through my brain.

If looks could kill, his made a gun unnecessary.

"Okay, maybe not." I was having a lot of trouble keeping my snark voice under control. "The pickup looked like a stockbroker. The other guy was an oversize hockey player in a suit...with a gun... pointed at my head. It was hard to concentrate on detail. When I left, he was kind of flat. The stockbroker guy was rolling around on the ground holding his shoulder...or his knee or both. You might want to check the emergency rooms."

Jon stared at me. Then he burst out laughing—his way of coping.

"You are truly a wonder. Let's talk about the house. Where was it?"

"In Holyoke off Route 5. He wouldn't give me an address. I'm driving along and suddenly he said, 'Turn here.'"

"Could you find it again?"

"In a heartbeat."

"We have to go there."

"Right now? I have an airport run in a couple hours."

"Right after your run." His cell phone rang, and he snatched it off the counter where he'd laid it next to the handcuffs.

"Stevens." He listened for ten seconds. "What?" he yelled into the phone. "Yeah, give me the location. I can be there in ten."

I inched closer, hoping to overhear the other end of the conversation. Jon's hand came up and covered my face completely. He straight-armed me, keeping me from getting close enough to hear what was being said on the other end of the line. He snapped the phone closed and moved his hand over to my cheek and down my neck. He pulled me over and kissed me lightly on the lips. Then he kissed me harder and deeper and our tongues got involved.

When we came up for air his eyes were dark and thoughtful. He kissed my nose and said, "You're on your own. I need to get to the station." He went to a small closet just inside the front door and extracted his holster and gun. After checking the gun, he clipped it to his belt and shrugged into a jacket that had been hanging in the closet. He headed toward the door.

"Wait, what's going on? This is Northampton. Are we having a crime wave?" I figured he would pull that need-to-know stuff and stonewall me. I was right. I was still struggling past the kiss when he opened the door and eased out.

"Gotta go. Be sure the door is locked when you leave. I'll call you later about checking out that house." He looked at me. "When I leave, flip the dead bolt. And be careful going out to your car. Don't hang around outside. Okay?" He handed me a key. "This is for the front door."

He was giving me a key to his house! I stared at the key. "What do you need to tell me? On a need-to-know basis, sometimes I need to know."

"No," he replied. His cell phone rang again. He snapped it open and listened.

"Oh, shit. Yeah, okay, I'll tell her. Send someone over to keep an eye out. Thanks." He closed it slowly and looked at me.

"That was Rodriguez at the station. The press has the story. You'll see it in the media anyway." He turned away from me and looked out the window.

"What, what? Did something happen at Cool Rides? Is everyone okay? Where is Belle? What's going on?" I was yelling by this point, and Jon grabbed me by the shoulders.

"Calm down. It's no one you know. I got another body. That crazy lady lawyer lost her husband."

"Oh, no. She didn't shoot him somewhere besides in the butt, did she?"

"She was in court with about 30 other people, including a judge and jury, when he was killed. We have a witness who heard the shots. Didn't see anybody, but at least we have a real time of death. Shit! I don't know what to do with you." He scowled, which seemed to be a common expression for him these days. "I want you to stay in very public places until we figure out what the hell is going on. I know the Scarpellis and their drug transportation business are connected to all this. I need to figure it out before we find any more bodies."

"I have that airport run anyway." There isn't any place with more security these days than an airport. For a taxi driver, airport security can be an inconvenient pain in the backside. Right now, it was fine with me. I just had to pick up the fare and get him there first. And I would have Belle with me since she was still learning about airport runs.

"Then I'll see you tonight. Don't go anywhere there aren't lots of people. Safe rides only, okay?" He pulled me in close and just held me for a long second or two. I could have made it a lot longer, but his duty called. He sighed and was out the door.

"Humph," I answered.

And he left me sitting there, alone, in his house. I had some time before I picked up the airport run. I started with the master bedroom.

His bed was king size. A huge painting of a peach hung on the wall opposite the bed. The peach managed to be erotically, sexually feminine and still look like a peach. His bedroom closet had...my God, the man owned a tuxedo. It was in a clear cleaner's bag so it might have been used recently. Not in Northampton. Now I had to wonder where Jon might have worn a tux.

Nothing weird in the bedside table. Nothing dangerous in the medicine cabinet. Master bath was amazing. The shower was a walk-in with a built-in seat and shelves. Jon in the shower flicked through my mind. Then Jon with me in the shower flicked through.

There was a sound system in the living room with lots of CDs. The TV was a large flat-screen. The couch could accommodate two horizontal or six vertical. The food in the fridge was fresh, indicating Belle had just bought it. The kitchen was beautiful with lots of pots and pans, mostly unused.

A basement could represent a major philosophical statement or it could be a dumping ground. Jon's was a statement. It had more carpentry tools than the kitchen had cooking tools. These, however, looked well used. I headed back upstairs. He didn't have any sex toys, women's underwear or even condoms in his house, so I figured he wasn't involved with anyone. I tried to ignore the relief centered somewhere south of my stomach.

I decided to see if Jon's renter in the other half of the house was a hot babe who kept all the sex toys on her side. Or maybe a hot guy and I could forget all about Jon. I was sure Jon wasn't gay, but I was always up for meeting a hot person of any gender or sexual persuasion. They tended to be entertaining.

I looked out the front door to check for bad guys. The street was empty. Mailboxes were side by side on the porch. Stevens was painted in white on a plain black box. The other box was a cute birdhouse with Emmy Lucille Streeter painted on it. I rang the doorbell. I hadn't decided what I was going to say if a blond bombshell opened the door.

It was my ash-lady airport run. No surprise in this small town, but she must have scattered Granddad's ashes in record time. It didn't seem very long since I'd dropped her off. I pictured her dumping the cardboard box under a rock at a highway rest stop outside an airport in Anywhere, USA. The overwhelming smell of baking cookies wafted out the door.

"May I help you?" She smiled beatifically at me.

"Uh, I'm staying next door temporarily, and I, uh, thought it might be nice to meet the neighbors." And find out what she looked like and how much she knew about Jon. "My name is Honey."

"Oh, how nice. I'm Lucille. And, no, you can't call me Lucy. Are you providing sexual favors for Jon while you're staying there? He's such a nice young man."

I almost choked on my tongue.

"Those cookies smell wonderful. Are you baking them yourself?"

"Oh, yes. I use them to attract the cute men at the senior center. Would you care to try one? You could give me an opinion about how lucky I might get."

"Thanks. I can't stay long, though. I drive for Cool Rides Taxi and I have a pickup pretty soon." I glanced behind me as I stepped through the door, just to see if Jon's request for someone to keep an eye out had been taken seriously. The only car on the block was a black Lincoln that had just pulled up, and the suits inside were not police officers. I moved to a window and peered out to get a better look at the passenger who was leaning his arm out the car window. It had a cast on it. I couldn't see his face.

"Why, who would that be? What an impressive car." Lucille had moved up behind me.

"I think maybe they tried to mug me yesterday." The one leaning out the window moved his oversize arm. His head came into view. By this time, I'd nicknamed my attackers Bozo and Bongo. I recognized Bozo's black-and-blue face.

"Really? Well, don't you worry, dear. We women take care of ourselves. I have just the solution." She disappeared into the kitchen and came back with a huge gun in her hand.

"Um, I'm not sure that's the right solution."

"Oh, sweetie. Jon keeps telling me to call any time I have any problems, but, you know, I've always been independent. I really do like to take care of myself. And I do believe I'm a better shot than Jon anyway. Shall we find out? I think I can nail that tire from here." She opened the curtain and took aim. POP! I jumped back from the window.

"I'm so glad I got a silencer for this gun," said Lucille.

The arm jumped inside the car, the window rolled up and the car skidded down the street. They didn't return fire. In half a block, their tire started to deflate with a kerthump, kerthump. They made it around the corner and disappeared. Guess they didn't have run-flats. Run-flat tires only handle marginally better than a tire with a bullet hole in it, in my opinion. I didn't have much experience with the bullet hole side of that equation. I had tested out a few run-flats.

"I think it's cookie time," Lucille said and headed off toward the kitchen. I continued to watch for the car or any of the occupants for a second, shrugged, and followed her. "I was the best shot on the firing range, you know." She tucked the gun into the back of the kitchen junk drawer.

Firing range? Where did Jon get his tenants? Then I noticed the framed photos and certificates on the wall. One of the pictures was of a younger Lucille with a well-known politician. She was wearing a badge and a jacket with FBI in large, very clear, white letters. The certificate next to it was one for achievement on the firing range. Nice neighbor. Handy to have around if someone is trying to knock you off.

I was on my second cookie when the doorbell rang. We both jumped a little, but Lucille got up and peeked out the window.

"Oh my, aren't we having the best visitors today? It's Officer Rodriguez. We have cookies, dear," she said as she opened the door.

"Lieutenant sent me over to make sure you got to work okay. Looks like breakfast is over." He glanced at the cookies.

"Why, dear, Honey and I have just been enjoying these freshly made chocolate chip cookies." Lucille pushed the cookie plate closer.

"Oh gosh, look at the time. I have an airport pick up in ten minutes." I headed for the door. Rodriguez was right behind me. I knew if I tried to explain the flat tire and the idiots changing it to Rodriguez I would be delayed for hours, miss my airport run and any other business I might do for the rest of the morning. I wasn't positive beyond a reasonable doubt it was the guys who tried to mug me anyway.

"I'll just make sure it's all locked up." He smiled. "Lieutenant's orders."

I glanced down the street, zipped in, got my bag, locked up and was backing the cab out of the driveway when Rodriguez and the patrol car pulled up behind me.

I drove slowly to the end of the block, taking care to do a cute finger wave at the guy changing the tire. He looked up as I drove by. His face was a mask of bruises with a bandage across the nose. He held up a finger as I drove by and dropped it quickly as the patrol car followed.

Chapter Ten

When I pulled into Cool Rides, the patrol car continued by, leaving me in the very public hands of a busy transportation service. Belle was waiting for me.

"How was choir practice?"

"I might have to start believing in God." She had added some makeup to her face and changed into sparkle and spandex. Black leather heels now added 3 inches to her formidable height. "Mona says I'm riding with you to the airport and then to meet Iggi Paluska."

The airport is an hour and a half round trip so we were calling it a little close, but with two people, one could lug bags and open doors while the other did car control and collected money.

I drove to the North Prince Motel on the outskirts of town. We usually pick up airport runs from in-town hotels. North Prince catered to a lower-income clientele who didn't usually travel far enough to need an airplane.

I saw the flashing lights from a long way away. As we got closer to the motel, I realized the cop cars were in the motel parking lot. And there were lots of them. Including Jon's nondescript police-issued clunker, a clunker that a friend of mine had told me could do zero to sixty in an obscenely short time and corner, stop, and provide cover for any officer who might drive it.

Belle looked at me. "Honey, I think we could turn around here. I just got an allergic reaction to this taxi-driving stuff."

"You're not allergic to taxi driving. It's the cop cars. We'll just pick up our fare and leave."

I pulled out my fare slip. The name written on it was Mr. Smith. Well, there are a lot of real Mr. Smiths in the world. I looked at the unit number Mona had jotted down. Number 5. Unfortunately, number 5 was occupied by a lot of police officers, probably none of them named Mr. Smith. As I thought about how to find out if I still had an airport run, Jon turned and spotted the cab. Then he saw me. He jammed his fists in his pockets and walked slowly to the taxi.

"Don't tell me." He leaned against the passenger door. Belle tried to sink lower. "What's the name of your fare?"

I stared at my feet and mumbled the name. "I don't have a fare, do I?" I asked.

Belle sank as low as she could in the seat. Jon alone, she could tolerate. A parking lot full of cops was too much. Six feet of female with another few inches of Afro is hard to hide in a Scion XB or, for that matter, in a tractor-trailer.

"We'll talk later." Jon ran a hand down his face, shook his head, and strode back to the crime scene. On the upside, we wouldn't be late for Iggi Paluska. I turned the cab around and headed back toward town. We even had time for a quick coffee before we picked him up.

Iggi was a regular user of our car service. Today's trip was to the hospital for blood tests and then back to his house to get his cat and truck it to the vet. I drove, with Belle riding shotgun. Once she knew his errand pattern, she could pick him up by herself.

At 88, Iggi had given up his car. This was good because he had a lot of memory lapses. Like where he lived and what he'd done yesterday. That had occasionally led to lost car syndrome. We were his only reliable form of transport.

I parked in the driveway. The garage door slid up. Iggi stood at the top of a long wooden ramp, back lighted by the windows in the house. His dogs set up a howl as the door closed and he descended the ramp, pushing his walker and oxygen ahead.

"He knows how to make an entrance," Belle said. She unfolded herself out of the car and opened the door for him.

"Hey, chicky, you the new driver?" Iggi looked Belle over as she loaded his walker behind the seat and set his oxygen tank on the floor between his feet.

"You bet. I'm gonna show this crew what real driving is about. I could do driving stunts for Hollywood." Belle smiled.

We got to the hospital, delivered Iggi to the entrance where a nurse met him and we went off to run his errands. We delivered his cleaning, picked up kitty litter, milk, Ritz crackers and Cheese Whiz. When we returned, the nurse said Iggi had finished and left. We circled the hospital until we found him at an unused side entrance, carefully studying a blank wall. No one was around to notice an old man standing alone. I wondered how long it might have been before someone noticed he was missing if we hadn't been the transportation company of choice.

As Belle got out to help Iggi, a black Lincoln town car slid up behind the cab. Bozo, surprisingly nimble for a man with his arm in a cast, jumped out, wrapped his fist in Belle's hair and yanked her toward the Lincoln. Iggi, sensing this was not on the agenda, raised his walker and charged after Belle. Except he forgot about the oxygen tank. It spilled off his walker, tubes trailing, and rolled toward Bozo and Belle. Bozo caught movement out of the corner of his eye, pulled his gun and fired off a shot. He missed the target but hit the tire of his car. Belle planted her feet and yanked back. Bozo stumbled and dropped his gun. It fired off another bullet which blew off the release valve on Iggi's oxygen tank. The tank took off like a rocket, blasting around the parking lot like the ball in a pinball machine. Belle jumped sideways as it whistled by her legs. It hit Bozo's foot and flipped him onto his back. His head hit the pavement with a kerthunk. The oxygen tank zinged off the rear bumper of the Lincoln, bounced off the fender of the cab and sailed straight up in the air. It turned a graceful arc, shot back down like an armor-piercing bullet, and stopped, stuck, top down, in the roof of the Lincoln. It fizzed out the last of the oxygen and stayed put.

Belle stuffed Iggi into the backseat of the cab, barreled into the front, and yelled, "Drive!"

I nailed it up the hill and out of the parking lot, looking back long enough to see Bozo lying on the ground with his leg sticking out at an ugly angle. My last visual in the rear-view mirror was Bongo trying to get Bozo into the Lincoln. I hoped they forgot to replace the spare tire.

117

"Hey, you guys are a lot more fun than Willie, but I think I have to add a new oxygen tank to my shopping list. You know those guys?" Iggi looked at Belle. His breathing was a little heavy.

"Unh, not really. Maybe friends of Honey's?"

"Nope!" I replied to Iggi's questioning look.

I glanced at him in the rearview mirror. He was grinning from ear to ear, but his breath had started a wheezy, sucky sound. The oxygen tank definitely needed to be our next stop. I headed out North Prince Street to the medical-supply store.

Now I needed to assess the danger level and decide how much, if any, of this stuff I should tell Jon, who, being a cop, would act like a cop. Belle wouldn't talk and Iggi Paluska would forget it before we got his new oxygen tank.

If I told the police about Bozo and Bongo stalking me or Belle, Jon would have a patrol car on my tail. That would seriously cramp my style and cut into my tips. And I didn't want to squeal on Lucille. I didn't know whether Jon even knew she had a gun. I was sure Officer Rodriguez had told him about the guys changing a tire near the house. But I didn't think Rodriguez knew why the tire was flat.

This time they had gone straight for Belle, so I figured I wasn't as important to them. They had made their move when a quiet opportunity presented itself, which meant they were watching us. I didn't think anyone had witnessed the hospital attack because no one came to the rescue and no police arrived. If I reported this to Jon, he might slap Belle into protective custody or something equally self-defeating. I was getting to know Belle and I was sure she wouldn't react well. On the other hand, there might be some real danger. And I didn't want to make Jon angry enough to damage our budding relationship. I decided to think about it for a while before I over-reacted.

We arrived at the medical-supply store and I hopped out with my charge card. I really didn't think Iggi should pay for this.

Belle beat me to the door. She had her credit card in hand as well.

"I'll get this one. Those assholes weren't after Iggi…or you." She opened the door.

"Belle, you haven't made any fares yet. Ever hear of cash flow?"

"Sweetie, don't you worry about Belle. I made plenty of money as a ho. I stashed some and invested most of it. Cash flow is not my current problem."

We got Iggi's canned breath and took him home. He said he was feeling lightheaded, so I told him the cat could wait until tomorrow. I helped him make an appointment with the vet for the next morning, promising to pick up, transport, and return the cat, whose name was Ferocious. It was one of those laid-back-rag-doll kinds of cats and Ferocious was as far from a fitting name as possible. It took a lot to get Ferocious excited but Iggi said it occasionally happened and then the feline definitely lived up to his name.

I went back to work, taking an elderly lady to the grocery store where she examined every can of cat food with a flashlight and a magnifying glass. Belle was in a cooking mood so she went back to Jon's house. Acting normal is how I deal with not normal. Belle seemed to share my approach.

The elderly gentlemen had visited the porn store again and needed a ride to the retirement home. They argued over who would wear the black thong that had Northampton, eat here embroidered in candy apple red on the crotch.

My next fare was a fifty or older woman suffering through the change of life. She turned the air conditioning on full and fanned her face.

"Raging hormones, sweetie. That's what this is about. If I had a sex life, I bet this wouldn't happen. My hormones would get all used up. What I need is a young stud. And maybe a good dildo. Can't you turn the air conditioning up any higher? It's hotter than a whore's tit in here."

My teeth were chattering.

"How much you figure a good gigolo is gonna cost me? Would that be a problem in a divorce case?" She dropped the fan. "Jesus, it's cold in here. Maybe you should turn on the heat. What, is your air conditioning busted?"

Her flushed face had turned pasty white. I flipped the air off, thinking fifty is only twenty years away from thirty and that milestone wasn't that far away from me.

When I got back to the garage, I decided to wash the car. I was rinsing it off when Jon sauntered out of the office. He was in blue jeans and a black T-shirt, with no indication he was a cop. Belle would approve.

"Need some help?" He took the hose from my hand. I was hot and sweaty from working on the car, and my excessively curly hair was in an uproar.

Jon smiled. "I see wet T-shirts in your future."

And he held the hose over my head. I squeaked and grabbed for his hand which he held out of reach, grinning broadly as he checked out my wet T-shirt. We looked like a couple of teenagers, wrestling for the hose until we were both soaked. Suddenly we were close up and personal and his hand was on my butt. The hose cascaded water over the car and the office window. Mona came barreling out the door just as Jon's other hand lowered itself to cup my head, changing the direction of the hose. Mona got drenched. Jon kissed me anyway. Did my toes curl? You betcha!

"Aaack," Mona spluttered. "It's clean enough already. Go home! Find a bedroom." She turned off the water at the faucet and stomped back into the office.

I backed away from Jon. His eyes followed me. "I'll give you a ride to my house."

We made it to Jon's doorstep before his cell phone rang.

"Shit," he mumbled and turned away. "Yeah, okay." He pushed a stray hair out of my eyes, brushed his lips over mine and sighed. "I've been summoned," he said and turned back to his car, walking a little stiffly.

I couldn't decide if I was relieved or disappointed. I hoped he had a change of clothes at the station.

"Oohwee, what was that about? And what happened to your clothes?" Belle came out of the kitchen and looked at me.

"Give me dessert. I'll skip dinner." I went inside and locked the door. Jon didn't get home until sometime in the wee hours.

Belle and I left early and didn't disturb him. There was no sign of any bad guys.

We had to pick up Iggi Paluska's cat for a few minutes of pain and then we could bundle it back home.

When we arrived at the Vet's office, the parking lot was empty. After twenty minutes, Belle came out with the cat slung over her shoulder like the rag doll that it imitated. She had the carrying box under her arm. I was moving her oversize bag off the seat when I heard the screech of brakes. The Lincoln Town Car rocked to a stop behind the cab.

They had increased their ranks to three. The new guy was bigger but lost the intimidation factor by wearing a lopsided toupee. Bozo was at the wheel. The other two jumped out and flanked Belle. One pulled, the other pushed. Belle balked. Ferocious the cat saw an escape route. He bounced off Belle, onto the toupee and dug in. The rag slid down over new guy's face. Feline claws sank into bare flesh, launched off, and the cat slithered under the cab. Lines of blood oozed down the bald head. It was like a target. I swung Belle's purse as hard as I could and scored a direct hit. He went down like a tree in the forest, but definitely with noise. The Lincoln screeched out of the parking lot with me screaming obscenities as it flew off down the street. Belle's foot hung out the window. Her gold shoe sparkled in the sunlight. It flipped off and flew a graceful arc onto the pavement as the car door slammed shut. The string of profanities that came out of my mouth shocked even me. I bent and picked up the shoe.

I couldn't catch up with the retreating car, so I turned back to corral the cat. The third guy was still spread-eagled in the parking lot next to the cab. I wondered what was in Belle's bag. I bound his wrists and ankles with my roll of duct tape and accidentally kicked him in the ribs. I managed to coax Ferocious, who had regained his composure and was relaxing in the shade of the cab, back into his mini-house and tripped over the bald guy's head. I stepped on his leg on my way to get the cell phone to call Jon.

"Stevens."

"They got Belle. They snatched her in broad daylight at the vet's office. But I got one of them. I hit him with Belle's bag." I was past the adrenaline rush and my speech was getting slightly chaotic.

I leaned on the car and looked at the shoe in my hand. All I'd wanted was to make the rent. Belle had become a friend and I wanted to keep her. Someone was derailing my plan. Anger replaced adrenaline.

"I'm on my way. Give me a description of the car. Did you get a license?" Jon sounded unusually frantic. He screeched into the parking lot in two minutes, jumped out almost before his car stopped and grabbed me, pulling me up against his nice, safe, masculine chest.

"I'm fine," I said into his shirt.

By the time the first patrol car arrived, I had added more tape and the guy had gone from looking like a roped steer to a movie prop out of Cocoon. With great restraint, I left breathing space around his nose.

An hour later, I had finished giving my statement to Jon, who was reluctant to let go of me but looked at the cat and mumbled about being careful, please.

I delivered the cat back to Iggi and we all headed home. Without Belle.

By this time, I knew Bozo well enough to identify him if the police could drag his ass into the station. Jon had seen him when we were leaving Holyoke and knew him as one of Scarpelli's goons. It was only a matter of time before they found him—if he stayed in the area, and if he stayed alive. No one knew what made Belle valuable to the Scarpellis. They seemed to want her alive, so my guess was information.

Money, drugs, and guns came to mind. The guy I had nailed at the vet's office was in police custody. I hoped he would talk his toupee off.

My apartment had been processed for evidence and cleaned in record time, but I didn't feel like facing it right now. And Jon didn't want me wandering around by myself. I slumped on the sofa in Jon's living room while he paced around me.

"Jesus, this is Northampton. How can we be getting this kind of violence? Springfield is giving me a hard time about trying to find Belle. Either they aren't interested, or they don't want her to be found. They told my superiors it's a turf war and implied she went off with a new pimp. Tell me she hasn't gone back to turning tricks."

"When would she have time? She hasn't even started driving by herself yet." The implication I didn't know the difference between Belle going willingly or being taken bugged me. "She's spending her nights here, days at the cab company. I refuse to believe she could be doing that kind of business out of the taxi between fares, which she hasn't had yet. We would notice if that ever happened with anyone." I was pissy already, and Jon's question, justified though it was, sent me over the edge. I stomped off to my assigned bedroom.

Chapter Eleven

In the morning, Jon was gone. I stuck my head in the fridge. Nothing screamed breakfast to me. God, I missed Belle. I decided to go to the mini-mart for some orange juice. And some donuts. And some coffee.

The store clerk was restocking shelves and dancing to the iPod noise streaming directly into his skull. I walked to the big cooling unit in the back. Another customer was head in, rear out of the fridge. I had seen that butt before. The door was opened wide to accommodate his shoulders and the glass reflected his face. Shit! Bozo! I should have called the cops, but rage short-circuited my brain. I went straight for revenge. I snuck up as quietly as sneaker-sucking floors allowed. The reflection of his face didn't look good. His eyes were turning yellow and he had the same band-aid on his nose. As he began to back out, I slammed the door on his head. He went to his knees. I grabbed a half-gallon of frozen ice cream and hit him in the face. Then I grabbed a gallon of milk. Then I grabbed a bottle of soda. I was out of control. His eyes were wide and glazed. A can of Cheez Whiz somehow ended up in my hand. I sprayed his face. I wondered what was in Cheez Whiz. He screamed and flipped over backward into a shelf of ancient Twinkies. His feet slid on the Twinkies and he landed headfirst on the floor. My rage began to fade as I fished out my duct tape.

By the time Jon got there, I had calmed myself down. I had calmed the clerk down and helped him restock the Twinkie shelf. I bought the OJ and the extra-hard ice cream and a package of doughnuts. I recapped the Cheez Whiz and put it back on the shelf.

"Honey." Jon nodded to me. He looked around the 7-Eleven. "You're depleting Scarpelli's ranks."

I looked down. "I got some orange juice and doughnuts. In case you forgot breakfast." I paused. "And ice cream. It's too hard to eat right now."

I looked at the carton in my hand. There was a head-shaped dent in it. Maybe I didn't want it for breakfast.

"You need a ride? We need to talk," Jon said. The officers loaded Bozo into the patrol car.

"No, I have the cab. I need to go make a living. You will call me with any new developments, right?" I tried to look deeply into Jon's eyes. He was wearing sunglasses and was in his cop head again. All I saw was my face reflected back at me.

"I need to see that house where they tried to take you. I don't think Scarpelli is dumb enough to use one of his own, but so far smart hasn't been his M.O. All this shit has to be related to getting the damn drugs up the interstate," Jon said.

"I guess I could call Willie. See what's happening right now."

"Good," Jon said. He walked over and talked to the uniforms. One of them got in Jon's car and drove off. I called Mona.

Jon looked at me. "We have a person-of-interest warrant out on Bozo, so we can hold onto him. I don't think he's going to talk, but it's gotta piss Scarpelli off. Maybe he'll be even more stupid."

Yeah, like shoot me. I didn't say this out loud since Jon might move me to a more secure place…like jail.

"Mona wants me back at the office by 10. Have a doughnut." I tossed the ice cream into the trash.

We found the house on Route 5. Jon circled around it and pounded on the door. No one home, no nearby neighbors. We drove back to Northampton. Jon would do more research on the address. He might be able to get a search warrant from a judge, but he had his hands full right now and search warrants were not easy to come by. Since he had two of the goons who had grabbed Belle, the uniforms would start doing a door-to-door with their photos near the two murder scenes. Murder was, I remembered, the crime he was trying to solve. Springfield and Holyoke were pretending to cooperate with the effort to find Belle, but it was common knowledge they had mixed feelings about Scarpelli. Some of them liked him. Some wanted to bust him. Some considered him a pillar of the community. One way or another, a lot of them made a living because of him. And how Belle had made a living was also common knowledge. I didn't think prostitutes were very high up on the police list of people to be grateful to or interested in tracking down.

"I'll see you tonight. Try to stay out of trouble," Jon said when I dropped him off at the station.

Humph. He was assuming I would be at his house that night. I still had mixed feelings about Jon's in-charge attitude. It was fine as long as it wasn't me he was trying to be in charge of. I took my bag of breakfast and headed for Cool Rides.

Mona met me at the door. I held the doughnuts in front of me defensively.

She scowled. "I hate it when it's slow." She plopped herself into a chair. "Give me those damn doughnuts."

We ate doughnuts and looked bored. After 15 minutes I was pacing. After 20 I had eaten five doughnuts and was as bloated and grouchy as a pregnant cat.

"I'm going uptown. See what I can scare up." Susan, the crazy lady lawyer with the red shoes, inexplicably popped into my mind. She hadn't been heard from since Belle moved in with me. I had questions like, why did she shoot her husband's butt? The husband who now had a hole in his head. And how did that tie in with Horace? Or with Scarpelli? Was she still a friend of Belle's? Did she know about Belle's disappearance? Could she help me find her? And, of course, where did she get those shoes?

"Whatever," said Mona. She probably assumed I'd try to scare up some fares. I might do that, too.

I pulled up in front of the office of Susan Young, attorney at law. A bunch of miserable-looking people were sitting in front of the dentist's office, but the attorney's side was locked up tight. I drove back to Cool Rides and looked up Susan Young in the phone book. The only listing was her office. I went to the driver's log, checked to see if any other drivers had picked her up before, and there she was. Andrew had taken her from a condo to her office three weeks ago. If that was her home base, she lived in the old jail condos on Union Street. When the state finally shelled out the money for a new jail on the outskirts of town, some enterprising developer had bought the aging county jail and converted it to very expensive condos. Sometimes the law pays well. I wondered when the city of San Francisco would see Alcatraz for its real potential. What kind of cool condos could that rock be?

Susan Young had a three-bedroom on the first floor, partially below ground. I parked the cab around the corner on the street.

I rang Susan's bell and waited. Ten seconds passed. I could hear someone on the other side of the door, but it was muffled. Good soundproofing. I waited another 10 seconds and rang again. Susan opened the door.

"Honey, what are you doing here?" Her mouth formed an O of surprise and her forehead wrinkled.

"I just stopped by to see if you had any thoughts on Belle. You know she's been kidnapped." I leaned against the door to force her to ask me in. It didn't work.

"Now is not a good time." She didn't back up. I changed tactics.

"I could come by later." I stared at her.

She shrugged. "Call the office. Make an appointment. I really don't have time right now." She sounded angry.

"I'll do that." I turned and walked away. When I looked back, she had closed the door.

I trotted around the block until I was behind the jail. There were ground-level windows on the side of the condo, hidden behind foundation plantings. I wiggled between the bushes. Bars covered the window on the inside. I looked in and saw Belle sitting against the wall with her butt on the bare floor. There was no furniture. I tapped on the window. No reaction. I banged harder. Belle finally noticed me.

She pushed herself to her feet, gesturing wildly. I couldn't hear her voice. Soundproof glass? Finally, I read her lips.

"Get help, stupid!"

I wiggled back out of the bushes, stood up and found myself face-to-chest with a very large man in a black suit.

"Inside." He gestured with the gun in his hand. We paraded around the corner and up the front steps to Susan's condo. He knocked and the door jerked open.

"What now?" Susan Young stood there, holding the door and looking really pissed.

"Uh, I found her at the window. The special-room window." His speech was slow and he sounded uncertain about what he was doing and why he was doing it.

"Jesus Christ, you just never give up, do you?" Susan stepped back. The big guy shoved me inside. "Search her and put her in with the other stupid."

I was escorted down the hall to the bare room where Belle was sitting, again on the floor.

"Man, oh man. I can't believe they caught you. All you had to do was get out of here." Belle rested her head against the wall.

"Belle, what the hell is going on? What's wrong with Susan? Is Scarpelli holding her hostage?"

"You dummy." Belle sighed. "Susan is Scarpelli's kid. Like father, like daughter. Only, I'd guess, she's tryin' to run the whole show. I'm thinkin' Daddy isn't too happy."

"Susan Scarpelli? How come the cops didn't know about this?" I couldn't believe she could float right under their radar.

"Nobody knows. I only found out because one of the goons slipped and called her Miss Scarpelli. I'd heard through the grapevine the old man had a daughter out on the West Coast. I guess she decided to come back and join his 'family'." She made the word sound obscene.

I was on information overload. "So, what's with her husband getting whacked?"

"Turf wars?" Belle stood and went to the window. "Horace must have got mixed up in it. He wasn't too bright sometimes."

I joined her at the window. We could see the infamous Lincoln Town Car through the bushes.

"Like between her and her dad? Why shoot Horace?"

"He had something. I don't know what. Damn. They think I know where he stashed whatever it is. The bastard must've told them I knew. Which I don't." She kicked the wall and grabbed her toe.

"Fuckin' solid walls. Shit."

I kept looking out the window. "Hey." I pointed at Susan and two of the men getting into the town car.

"That means they left the idiot guy here with us." Belle paced.

"He must have the keys to open this door. We need a plan." I pretended I had just eaten a handful of Lucille's cookies. Sugar always makes me think more clearly.

"Yeah, and he's also got a gun. A big stupid gun with a big stupid body and a tiny stupid brain. He opens that door, most likely he's gonna shoot you. Be sure you put that in your plan."

"Can he hear us through this stuff?" I pushed on the door. Solid.

"It's soundproof, so only if you scream. I found out when I needed to go pee. Jesus, did I scream. That's the only reason he'll open the door."

Soundproof doors and barred windows required some paranoia. Susan's grasp of reality was beginning to seem less and less solid.

"He won't shoot me." I stripped off my T-shirt and handed it to Belle.

Then I dropped my jeans and lay down on the cold, hard, bare floor.

"Strangle him with the T-shirt." I spread my arms and legs. "Start screaming."

Bell stared at me for about two seconds. Then she pounded on the door and screeched, "She's trying to kill me. Heeelllppp, get her off me."

The guy who had found me at the window opened the door. He held a big gun with an even bigger silencer on it. He stared at my mostly bare body. He looked like he might have a regular relationship with a bottle of steroid pills. Great for bulking up the body, but they don't do much for brain function.

"Wow!" He grinned and took a step forward. Belle was behind the door. She threw the T-shirt over his head, executioner-style, jumped on his back, and wrapped her legs around his middle. He careened around the room, arms cartwheeling the air. I jumped up, shoved my hands between his legs, grabbed the big squishy and twisted as hard as I could.

"Aurrrgh!" he screeched. I guess the gun went off because his foot exploded. Bellowing like a bull, he launched himself, headfirst, into the wall. And sank to the floor like a wet mop. Belle dismounted.

"Hot damn. We're outta here." She pried the gun out of his hand and snatched the key from his pocket. I grabbed my T-shirt off his head. Ugh.

"Wait." I shimmied into my jeans, rammed feet into sneakers and staggered out the door. My oversize bag was sitting on the kitchen counter. I pulled out the duct tape and finished the job. I promised myself I would call Jon as soon as we were safe. Right now, I was on adrenaline overload and I was sure I was Wonder Woman even with the wrong fashion statement. Belle locked the door to the special room.

We went out the front door and raced down the steps and around the corner to the cab. Amazingly, it was still there. The keys were in my bag. No one ever said the bad guys were smart.

"Honey, you got steel nerves. I can't believe you dropped your drawers like that. I can't believe you even thought of it. Yeah, lady, nerves of steel." Belle laughed and crammed herself into the passenger seat.

I giggled, "You want rock solid nerves, try driving down the interstate at 80 miles an hour in one of these units with 18-wheelers on all four sides of you." In a Scion XB, the peripheral vision is so good you can see the fine print on the truck next to you. I'd done early-morning runs where the night crawlers were just coming off shift and the day hoppers were joining the crowd at the same time. The road was coated with trucks of every size, shape and color. I'd gotten boxed in more than once and it was really scary, almost up there with big guys with guns.

I jumped in and took off. I was giddy with adrenaline and put a little more foot into it than I needed. My mind was racing around thinking about weird stuff, like trucks and the interstate. And Jon and sex, oops!

"Where do you think Susan went?" I asked Belle. I had no idea what to do. I thought for two seconds about the police. Other than our firsthand experience, we had no hard evidence Susan was involved in any illegal enterprises. By the time Jon got a search warrant, if he got one, Susan would have come back and the guy we left in her condo would be gone. Belle's credibility was shaky, given her previous profession. Susan was a lawyer and very slippery. I bet she had plenty of good explanations for what had happened. We decided to hole up in Jon's house while we came up with a plan.

I pulled the cab into Jon's garage and let the door down. No reason to advertise our presence. We struggled inside, our bruised bodies suffering from an emotional high that was dropping like bird shit. I sagged against the door.

"Lock up," I said to Belle. "We can go next door and see if Lucille is home. At least she's got a gun."

"A gun? I had a gun. In my bag when I was snatched."

"Your bag! I've still got it." I went into the guest bedroom and came back with the oversize bag. I upended it on the kitchen counter. Shit. She had a gun, all right. And a couple of pounds of ammo to go with it. No wonder the guy at the vet's office had gone down fast.

"Oh my, where did all that come from? Someone must have left it in my purse. What's a woman to do?" Belle blinked in wide-eyed wonder.

"Right. We need to get a plan together. Susan won't be happy when she gets home." I hoped she'd gone out for a long time. I thought about Jon and his reaction to what had just happened. I'd have to tell him and we needed to make the decision about how much to tell, soon.

I unlatched the locks and peeked out the door. No action outside. I reached my hand around and knocked on Lucille's door.

"Coming." I heard her sing out. These walls were not as soundproof as Susan's.

"Why, hello, dearie." Lucille's head popped out. We could have held our conversation door to door, but I liked her for backup. I had seen her in action. Big gun, good aim. "I have cookies," she said.

From mayhem and murder to cookies and tea. Belle and I slipped out Jon's door and through Lucille's.

"Hi. We didn't really have time to meet properly before. This is Belle, and my name is Honey. How's the cookie baking? Getting lucky?"

The old lady extended a hand with a smear of cookie dough across the back. "I'm Lucille. And, no, you can't call me Lucy," she said to Belle. "I'm trying

136

a new recipe. I got lucky with the last one, but there's always room for improvement, I say. The better the cookies, the better the sex. Men will extend themselves a bit more if the rewards are great enough." She nodded her head. "Although I don't believe Jonny needs cookies to perform well."

And how would you know? I wondered.

I edged closer to the source of bliss.

"Go ahead now, take as many as you need. They may enhance your performance as well. I'll ask Jonny next time I see him. Where is he anyway? I don't see him much anymore. I hope that means you're keeping him busy."

Oh, yeah, we were doing that.

"Cookie-enhanced sex performance?" Belle asked and snatched the platter off the table.

"Um, maybe we should give Jon a call. Let him know we're all sitting around eating cookies. That is, you and me and Belle." I was hoping Lucille would volunteer to call him and mention Belle. Then I wouldn't have to.

I was on my third cookie when we heard a car in the drive. I jumped.

"Nervous, dearie?" Lucille went to the window. "I know an affair with Jonny might fill me with anticipation. Oh good, it's him," she said, looking out the window. "I'll just put some cookies on a plate for you to take over to him. And let me add these. I got the extra-large size. I've only seen him naked once, but Jon is well hung. He worked undercover on a male-strip-club bust. They were running a hijacking ring specialized in stealing shipments of sex toys and selling them out of the back of the strip joint. I just happened to be in the audience one night." She handed me a package of extra-large condoms. I tried to imagine Lucille stuffing dollar bills into Jon's G-string. I was envisioning Jon as a male stripper when his front door slammed. Lucille stared off into space, maybe rerunning the picture of Jon in his stripper outfit. "Of course, sometimes they stuff socks in those stringy men's panties. You know, to make it look more enticing." She smiled absently and patted the condoms in my hand. "But I'm sure Jonny is for real." I suspected she was right, but I decided not to add to the image.

Cookies and condoms. The complete guide to my life. I opened Lucille's front door, stuffed the condoms into my pocket and led with the cookie plate. We hadn't called Jon and neither had Lucille. I wondered what he was doing home at this time of day.

"Stop dragging your feet. And hold your chin up. You're in charge here. Besides, surprise is on our side," Belle said, slapping open Jon's front door. She strode across the doorstep.

And there stood Lieutenant Jon Stevens in his underwear.

His clothes lay in a heap beside him.

Belle was ahead of me when Jon looked up.

"Jesus. Don't you knock?" Then he realized who was watching him so intently. "Where the hell did you come from?" He stared at Belle. "Honey?" His voice was low and controlled as his eyes met mine. I was hiding behind Belle.

"Wow, what's that smell?" Belle inched closer to Jon's really nice, mostly naked body. He had just the right amount of everything. Muscle, hair (not much) and other yummies. They were boxers, so determining his amount of hungness was difficult. Which is not to say I didn't try in the few seconds we got to take a look.

"Huh? Oh, domestic dispute gone bad. Vomit from the husband, disputed dinner from the wife. Dinner was worse. That's why I'm standing here. Shit!" He turned and stomped into the bathroom. I heard the shower running. Five minutes later I heard drawers opening and slamming shut. His problem made me consider, however briefly, my own lack of culinary skills.

"Maybe we should put those clothes in the laundry," I said.

"Maybe we should put them in the garbage." Belle wrinkled her nose.

"Maybe I'll make that decision." Jon was dressed in clean clothes and was rubbing a towel over his damp hair. "Care to tell me about how the two of you got here? And where you've been? Last I knew there was some doubt about where you were and whether you were there voluntarily." He looked pointedly at Belle.

"We drove in a taxi," I said.

"There's a care package for you at Susan Young's condo on Union Street. And by the way, it's Susan Scarpelli." Belle drew out the name and said it as if she were handing Jon first prize. She retreated to the kitchen, out of the line of fire.

"Let me guess. The package is wrapped in duct tape. And I know it's Susan Scarpelli. We finally got the connection from Springfield. And speaking of Springfield, what would you like me to tell them?" Jon looked at Belle.

"Forget Springfield. And that package? It's big and ugly and if you don't get it soon, it'll be gone." Belle smiled broadly.

Jon turned back to me.

"You are a constant source of entertainment." He picked up his cell phone. "Yeah, Stevens. Get someone out to attorney Susan Young's condo in the old jail on Union Street. Fast. No, there may be a hostage inside." Jon looked at me again, raising his eyebrows. "I'll meet them over there." I guess the hostage possibility bypassed the need for a search warrant.

He pocketed his cell phone, grabbed his gun off the counter, stuffed his shield onto his belt. He was at the door when he turned back. "Stay here. Do not move from this house." And he left. His attitude was beginning to piss me off. Like I couldn't take care of myself. Who had rescued Belle, anyhow?

We lasted 20 minutes. Belle and I fed each other's bravado. She thought I had nerves of steel and I thought she had the chutzpah of a chocolate chip, macadamia nut, raisin, oatmeal cookie walking down Sesame Street and making rude gestures to Cookie Monster. Together we became Super Girl or, more accurately, Super Women. The only question was where we most wanted to go. Belle wanted to go to Susan's condo to see if the cops got the mess we had left. If the goon was still there, she might be able to accidentally stomp on him a few times. Belle had a great deal of confidence in her ability to penetrate police barriers, with some justification. Her anger had overcome her cop phobia. I wanted to go back to Lucille's for more cookies.

We compromised and ate all the cookies we had brought for Jon. Then we got in the taxi and headed toward Susan's condo.

We arrived just as they were bringing the "hostage" out. He looked a little battered, like he'd been rolling around on the floor. His feet had been cut free, but his hands were still taped. He was limping.

Jon came out of the condo after them. When he saw us, the word scowl took on new meaning. He walked over to us.

"What part of stay don't you understand? I feel like I'm training a fucking puppy." He jammed his hands in his pockets. "Ah shit, Susan Scarpelli is probably more interested in saving herself than murdering you. Although if it were up to me, it might be a close call." He looked like he wanted to kick the puppy, but he turned and stomped toward his car instead.

Halfway to the car, he turned around and stomped back to me. He grabbed my face in both hands and kissed me hard on the mouth. Then he walked back to the car, got in and drove away.

"I'll check in tonight, sweetie. Maybe." I smiled goofily, and did a little finger wave at the retreating car. Even if I wasn't sure about my relationship with Jon, Jon seemed to know what direction we were headed.

Belle stared at the man who was being loaded into a cruiser. I could see visions of trampled flesh running through her brain.

We got in the taxi. The car must have felt the need to be among friends, because five minutes later we found ourselves at the Cool Rides office.

It was late afternoon and all we had eaten was a few dozen cookies, so Mona ordered pizza. Comfort food would help us all talk more freely.

"So," I said, turning to Belle, "what did Susan say to you when they snatched you? What did she want?"

"Mostly she just slapped me around. I think she's into it. Like fun with S & M. Only she was S'n and I wasn't M'n. She'd be real good at the dominatrix trade. She kept babbling about a disc. Said Horace told her I knew about it. Bastard. He was always shoving stuff off on me. She ranted about increasing some corridor. I think her daddy has her climbing walls. There's a big weird goin' on there. Those Freudian freaks would have a heyday."

"And sometimes a cigar is just a cigar. Maybe she has her own agenda. Have you run this by Jon? I know both of you have a problem with authority, but..." Mona trailed off.

I spoke around a mouthful of cheese and ignored her question. Mona was right about the authority though. "So, Horace never kept any books, like about the business? Did he have a computer?"

"Not that I knew of."

"Maybe it was his contacts book, on a disc." Mona said.

"What's a contacts book?" I was new to the language of illicit businesses.

Belle swallowed a bite of cheese, pepperoni, peppers, onions, and something else I hadn't figured out yet. "Could be a list of my customers or which police could be bribed. But why would Susan want it? Why wouldn't it be old man Scarpelli who was after it?"

142

"Or maybe it didn't belong to Horace," I said. "If he got his hands on it, where would he stash it? Susan must have searched the apartment before they shot Horace. When you moved in with me, they ransacked my place. Then they staked out Jon's house. Belle, they think you know where this disc is."

"I knew Horace inside out. I don't think he had the balls to steal from Scarpelli. Possibly from Susan, though. He was a sexist pig. He might think a woman wouldn't have the balls to shoot him. Based on my most recent interaction with her, I think she'd enjoy drilling someone between the eyes. She'd like to see brains splatter all over the wall. She'd want to watch someone get hacked up like a pig into pork chops with blood dripping down and pooling on the floor. She'd..." Belle stopped.

Mona was staring at her half-eaten piece of pizza. My hand had paused halfway to my mouth. Belle was in her British upper-class mode of speaking, but the words coming out were too coarse for the accent. It was lousy dinner conversation too. I wondered if she was aware of how odd it was.

"Okay, we're trying to eat here. Sorry." Belle took another bite.

"Maybe Susan was getting ready to off the old man," Mona said and resumed eating.

This was beginning to read like an episode of The Sopranos Godfather Ten. While I was trying to sort out characters, the dispatch phone rang.

"Cool Rides, the best ride ever," Mona purred into the receiver. "Where are you and where do you need to be?" She jotted info on paper. "Short haul. Wal-Mart to Hampshire Heights."

I groaned and looked at Belle. No tip, would probably want us to wait for "just a minute," which would turn into 10 minutes while they dug up the fare and no wait fee.

"We'll take it," Belle said. She grabbed her bag and headed out the door. I lifted the fare slip from Mona's fingers, shrugged and followed.

When I got into the car, Belle was fastening her seat belt.

"What's with the hurry-up?"

"Hey, we're going to Hamp Heights. I might want to stop at my old digs and pick up a few things. I'm running low on spandex."

The fare turned out to be a friend of Belle's from her previous profession.

"Honey, this is Miss Pussy Galore named after the James Bond character with no moral principles whatsoever." Belle waved toward the slightly less spangled but equally voluptuous Pussy. I drove while they reminisced about the good old days of ho.

"I was sorry to hear about Horace. I know how he was, but he did have his good times." Pussy touched Belle's shoulder. "That last day, I remember seeing him skateboarding with the kids. Of course, he stole the skateboard. Maybe that's what got him killed."

"Huh? I don't think those punks would shoot him for swiping their board," Belle said.

Pussy shook her head and gestured with perfectly manicured fingers.

"Oh no, I didn't mean that. He was riding one of the boards. He started getting cocky about how good he was and miscalculated. Rode it straight into the bushes, and that board launched Horace right through the front window of his own apartment. It was open 'cause it was hot and the air conditioner wasn't working. It woulda been funny except, well, you know—what happened and all. Then I hear a pop. It sure sounded like a gunshot. Musta hit Horace."

"Did you see who did it?" My heartbeat picked up a notch.

She looked at me like I was the dumb duck in the water watching the sharks circle.

"Are you kidding? You hear gunfire around here, you get down. I don't think he knew they were in there. Probably scared the shit outta them when he sailed through the window."

I hadn't asked Jon about the autopsy report. Not that he would have told me. I had assumed it was an execution-style shooting. I might pass this information along. If Jon was really nice to me. Or even if he wasn't.

Belle's friend was true to form and emptied the loose change out of her bag to pay the fare. Belle dug a key out and slipped under the police tape which still hung limply around the crime scene. I collected my money and joined her.

I was on the top step when a wizened old geezer staggered up the sidewalk. His arms were thrown wide, his pants drooped and his fly was open. A little pink penis hung out.

"Belle," he moaned loudly.

Belle stuck her head out the door. "Why, hello, Mr. Ding. What's up?"

Certainly not him, I thought. Mr. Ding stumbled forward.

145

"For old time's sake?" He wiggled his hips. His penis flopped around like a rubber hot dog or a short, fat, worm. He took another step and fell, face first, into the bushes.

"What do you want me to do with him?" I asked.

"Is he breathing?"

I leaned a little closer. "Yeah." The air around him smelled horrible.

"Leave him be. He'll sleep it off."

I went inside. "Did you use to…uh…service him?"

"Mr. Ding? God no. I used to cook for him. But he knew what I did. He was forever trying." She smiled.

I thought about Belle's previous employment and wondered what it would be like to choose your sexual partners based on their wallets. A lot of women do that. Prostitution was just more upfront about it.

Belle came out of the bedroom stuffing a few spandex tops in her bag. She seemed to have a never-ending supply.

"I've been thinking about where Horace might hide something. I say we search the joint," said Belle. There was fingerprint powder on a lot of surfaces. The carpet had an ominous dark brown stain on it.

We found mostly dust. All the illegal substances had apparently been confiscated by either the police or, more likely, the murderers.

After 10 minutes, Belle flopped onto the sofa. The apartment was hot and stuffy. I wandered over to the air conditioner.

"Don't bother," Belle said. "It stopped working months ago. Horace was supposed to get it fixed. He didn't get to it before..."

I punched the power button anyway. The fan came on. It made such a racket I turned it off. "Something's caught in the filter." I gave it a little shake and turned it on again. The rattle got louder. I pulled the filter out. A CD clattered to the floor. Well, duh!

I picked it up.

Belle stood. "Well, what the hell! That's gotta be it."

"Time to go." I was reaching for the door when it flew open. I jumped behind it.

"What the fuck are you doing here?" Susan stepped in and glared at Belle. I kept quiet.

"I fuckin' live here. What are you doing anywhere, bitch?" Belle charged Susan with head down in true dirty wrestling fashion. They toppled down the steps. Belle was on top, so I stayed where I was. Suddenly there was a gun in Susan's hand.

"Back off, bitch!" she screamed. Belle rolled off Susan and stood up. I retreated unnoticed behind the counter that separated kitchen from living room.

"Inside." Susan waved the gun at Belle. "I'm going to search this fucking pit until I find that damn disc. Horace said you hid it in this hellhole and I came here to find it. If I have to whack you around, so much the better."

I grabbed a frying pan off the stove and ducked out of sight.

When I looked out from under the bottom of the counter, I saw three pairs of feet. One of them was large and masculine. Susan had brought backup. And

147

another pair of nice shoes. Those would be Susan's. No matter what else we felt about Susan, she had great taste in shoes. The masculine shoes were big and flat and plain and stood next to the counter. The addition of the bad shoe guy meant not good odds for us. On the upside, neither of them had noticed me.

Chapter Twelve

"Sit," said Susan, motioning Belle to the nearest chair. Belle sat. Susan stepped forward and slapped her hard across the face.

Belle's arm jerked up defensively and punched Susan solidly in the head. Who doesn't know to tie up their victim before the torture begins? Susan staggered backward, dropping the gun. Belle dove off the chair after it, the bad shoe guy charged after Belle. I jumped up and put all my muscles and a lot of adrenaline into connecting the frying pan with his face. He toppled like a giant sequoia. Belle snatched the gun off the floor. Susan had the sense to retreat in the face of superior force. She tripped over Mr. Ding on her way out, made it to the car and smoked her tires as she left.

"Bagged another one," said Belle, looking down at the comatose body.

I pulled the duct tape out of my purse.

Belle nudged the body with her foot. He didn't move. He was breathing, so we decided to leave him for the police. I added more duct tape. Belle placed a kitchen chair over him and I taped him to that as well. It would make escape a little trickier.

"I need comfort food," I said.

"I want to know what the fuck is on that stupid disc," Belle said.

"And we should call Jon," I added, feeling almost guilty about having found the disc before the cops.

"Lucille will have cookies, and I saw a computer on her desk," said Belle.

Police Dispatch put me through to Jon. "Stevens." He sounded distracted.

"Hi, Jon." I tried to sound cheery.

"Where are you?" he asked.

"Just leaving Hamp Heights. We had a fare. But you might want to send a squad car over to Belle's old apartment. Where Horace was shot." Where there was crime-scene tape all over the place.

"Why?" Jon's voice was beginning to sound wary, maybe even hostile.

"We left you a present."

"Does this involve duct tape?"

"Ahhh...yeah."

"Jesus, Honey. Scarpelli might take out a contract on you if this keeps happening." He sounded a bit peevish. "Where are you going now?"

"Belle and I are thinking we might head to your place and stay in tonight."

"How sensible of you. I'll be there as soon as I get the paper done on your latest trophy. And you better be there. I have a lot of questions." He disconnected.

"How's Jon?" Belle smiled one of her you should do it soon smiles.

"He's such a cop. I think he's feeling left out."

"He's just moving in the wrong circles. He hangs with us, he's gonna enjoy life more. Maybe he could enjoy you more, too."

"He's just too controlling. That stuff scares me. He did bust me for no good reason. I was just a kid."

150

"He busted you? Now that's a story I might need to hear, but yeah, cops do that. Doesn't mean he can't be good where it counts."

I sighed. It had been a long time since that counted.

"I say let's hit up Lucille and see what she's got cookin'," Belle said.

We rolled Mr. Ding off the sidewalk and hauled him back to his doorway before we left. Belle pushed his hot dog back inside his pants and carefully zipped him up.

Of course, Lucille had a batch of cookies in the oven and another on the table.

"Is your computer new?" I asked. My computer skills were nonexistent.

"Oh, my, yes. That's my new baby. I just love the Internet. And all those wonderful ads about penis enlargement. Why, it starts my day off just right. I can show you some of them. I save the best. There's one with a wonderful illustration. It looks a lot like my dearly departed husband. What a shame to cremate that part of him. But they wouldn't remove it for me before they burned him up. I thought about having it preserved." She took a dainty bite of cookie. "So, what do you think about this recipe?"

I was having trouble getting past the image of preserved parts. She didn't specify the method of preservation they had refused. My imagination couldn't stop coming up with possibilities—pickled, embalmed, stuffed like a hunting trophy. Wall mounted?

"Could you read a disc for us?" I asked, trying to control my overactive brain.

"Well, of course, dear. I get CDs all the time. They have most of the good classic movies, like Deep Throat, on CD now. I have a very complete collection."

I bet she did. Maybe I could introduce her to Tweedledum and Tweedledee.

"Can we, uh, turn this on?" asked Belle, gesturing to the computer.

"Boot up Baby? Well of course." Lucille joined her at the computer. She patted it and pushed a button. Baby came to life. "Did you want to surf the Net?"

"No, we have a special CD we wanted to take a look at."

Lucille pushed another button. The CD holder slid silently open. I handed her the disc. She set it in the round indentation in the tray. The holder slid closed. I can identify with computers. You have to push a lot of buttons to get a response.

A list of names flickered onto the screen. Belle crowded in behind me.

"Jesus, I know those names," Belle said. "Some of them work for Scarpelli. And look." She pointed an enameled, iridescent, silver glitter fingernail at a name on the list. "That's a cop." Her perfect fingernail traced down the list. "Another cop."

It pays to have someone in the business on your side. Belle knew all sorts of people I'd never heard of.

"So, what do you think this is? And why did Susan want it so bad? If it's just Scarpelli's goon squad and some bad cops, that must be common knowledge."

"Susan is relatively new in town. Maybe she wasn't privy to common knowledge," said Belle.

152

We were contemplating this when there was a knock on the door.

"Should I get my firearm?" Lucille asked.

"Let me see who it is before we blast them to kingdom come." I stepped to the door and cracked it open.

"Hi, Jon." I opened the door farther.

"Honey." He said it with some wariness in his voice. "You going to let me in?"

"Oh, Jonny, dear. Honey and Belle and I are just having cookies and talking about lists of police officers. Do come in. We have plenty of cookies. And maybe you know some of the officers." Lucille's voice had the maternal ring I had learned she used around Jon.

Jon walked over to the plate of cookies. He took one and continued to the computer. "Playing with Baby again?"

"Did you get my package at Belle's apartment?" I asked.

"Do you know how much paperwork this is taking? Do you know how hard it is to hold someone who doesn't want to be detained? We let him go because we didn't have any witnesses who would press charges. You both left and he sure as hell wasn't talking. Sooner or later we'll have to come up with charges against somebody or Scarpelli will charge us with harassment. My fellow officers were taking bets on how you two got him on his back." He eyed me speculatively then looked at Belle.

I turned to the computer.

We stood around Baby with Lucille at the controls. I was having trouble thinking of a piece of plastic and metal as having a nick name. But then I thought about the variety of things we name. Lots of parts of the human anatomy, for instance. And cars. Willie had names for all the Cool Rides cars.

"Where did you get this?" Jon leaned over. "Shit, what is this? Half of these guys are known felons and the other half are cops. Mostly Springfield." Jon scrolled down the list. "Where the fuck did you get this?" He wasn't yelling, really. His level of frustration at being out of our particular loop was showing.

"Why, Jonny." Lucille patted his hand. "Is this police business?"

Before he had a chance to answer, I jumped in. "I think this is what Susan was after. Horace being killed might have been an accident. Belle's friend heard the shot."

"Wait, wait." Jon needed time to process and catch up. "We questioned everyone in the Heights. Just who was this witness?" He looked sharply at Belle.

"I ain't talking. She wouldn't be around if there were cops around. Her business ain't compatible with yours. Besides, she didn't see the incident. She just heard some shots."

"And she didn't bother to call the police?"

"We talkin' about the same Heights? You hear that sound, you don't hang around." Belle's voice dripped scorn. "Duh, reality check."

I could see a tic starting in Jon's jaw. He refocused on the computer screen. "I need to take this CD into evidence."

"How do you know it's evidence you'd be interested in?" Belle was getting belligerent.

154

"Duh, reality check," Jon replied. His hand moved to pop the CD out of the computer.

Belle slapped his hand away. "Wait a minute. Wait just a damn minute. I remember Horace talking about some of Scarpelli's men being ready to jump ship. That the old man was getting a little fuzzy."

"Yeah, I heard that from one of the Springfield cops. They said he was getting ready for the leg breaker in the sky to take him away. They're worried about the aftermath. No heir apparent," said Jon.

"So, maybe Susan was going to move in," I said.

"A woman? Scarpelli would never approve it. He has a real limited view about what a woman can do. Maybe he just didn't know the right woman." Jon glared at me.

"Yeah, but Susan might not have cared. It isn't your average father-daughter relationship." Belle was back at the cookie plate.

Lucille was staring at the screen. "I think this is a coup list," Lucille murmured.

"A what?" Jon leaned in closer.

"It's a list of people she could trust. Or people her father couldn't trust. The cops are dirty. I'm sorry, Jonny, but I think they are. So blackmail may be involved." Lucille's face had developed an expression I hadn't seen before.

"If that's what this is, maybe she didn't want Daddy to know about it. He'd recognize it in a heartbeat. If he can recognize anything anymore," I added.

"She'd sure as tootin' kill Horace for it. I wonder which side her husband was taking," Belle said.

155

"From his status in the morgue, I'd say it was in question, by both sides," said Jon. He reached for the disc.

"Just a damn minute." Belle tried to slap his hand away again.

He gave her his cop stare and slowly moved his hand to the disc. "This is not only evidence. It's dangerous evidence." He removed the disc. "You still don't get it. Two people are dead, possibly because of this list."

Jon turned to me. "And you should have brought this into headquarters when you found it. You can't just keep evidence until you feel like telling me about it."

"Yeah? And I found out Susan is a Scarpelli from Belle. When did you plan to tell me about that?" My voice was rising. "If I'd known, I might have been more careful when I went to her condo." Knowing that probably wouldn't have stopped me, but I could have slowed down to think about a more devious plan. Jon's attitude was pushing my buttons. I should have been directing my anger toward Susan and her agenda. But Jon was an easy target. I stared at him for a few seconds and turned and stomped out of Lucille's side of the house, next door and into my bedroom. Which was really Jon's bedroom because it was Jon's house. And that pissed me off even more.

Chapter Thirteen

The next morning the kitchen was empty with a note from Belle on the counter telling me she would be at the Cool Rides office. I fiddled with the coffee maker and actually found the coffee, but I wasn't sure enough of my culinary skills to go as far as making it. I opened a few cupboards and didn't find anything appealing to my morning need for sugar and carbs. I decided to see if Lucille would provide the kind of breakfast I was craving. I slung my bag over my shoulder and knocked on her door.

She opened it and I followed my nose to the breakfast platter.

"Why, hello, dear. Won't you join me?" Lucille said to my back.

I had one cookie in my mouth, another in my hand and was stuffing one in my bag. Lucille was pouring coffee when we heard a car out in front of the house. We looked out the window together.

A long black limo sat ominously at the curb.

"Should I get my gun?" Lucille asked, holding the curtain aside.

As we considered this, a very large man I didn't recognize got out of the driver's side. He raised a limp white, lacy square over his head and waved it in the direction of Jon's front door, a slight smile sort of pushing the sides of his mouth up. The impression was of someone who felt he shouldn't be smiling but couldn't stop it. Sort of like laughing at a funeral when you didn't like the deceased and found out he was wearing a peanut outfit and got trampled by a rogue elephant. Inappropriate, but justifiable—and right out of a Mary Tyler Moore show.

"What is he doing?" Lucille moved to the door and opened it a crack.

"Miss Walker?" The driver's attention changed to Lucille's door and he moved forward cautiously. "Don't shoot. I got Mr. Scarpelli here. He wants to talk. If you could come out to the car."

"Don't let him fool you for a minute," Lucille said. She yelled at the driver, "You tell your boss if he wants to talk, get his ass in here. We women don't get in cars with strangers. Besides, we have cookies."

Whatever her background, Lucille hadn't sprung into life baking cookies. I realized she had a lot of characters in her FBI-jacket-wearing repertoire.

The dark window of the limo glided down silently. A head full of white hair popped out. "Cookies? Who has cookies?"

"Hey, he's a hot one." Lucille smiled.

"Ah, I think that's Mr. Scarpelli. Should we really let him in?"

"You don't think he would shoot us for chocolate chip cookies, do you? He doesn't look like that kind of man."

"Probably not for the cookies," I admitted. Lots of other possibilities, though.

The driver opened the door and a cane emerged. Mr. Scarpelli leaned on it and hobbled up the walk. Lucille was right. He was stooped and moved slowly but he had piercing dark eyes and Mediterranean good looks. His eyes softened as he approached Lucille.

"Why, what a lovely lady." He took her hand gently in his and raised it to his lips. "And such a heavenly aroma."

"Oh, get over it. You can have a cookie. But don't try to charm me into thinking you're just some nice guy. I know who you are. Come on in and we'll negotiate." Lucille turned on her heel and headed for the kitchen. I shrugged and followed. I didn't know enough about the Scarpelli family to face him alone, so any help Lucille chose to give was welcome.

Mr. Scarpelli had a slight smile on his face. The driver was now grinning openly.

Lucille and Scarpelli sat down at the table. The driver/bodyguard stood behind his boss. I pulled the duct tape out of my bag, set it on the table and took a seat. Mr. Scarpelli kept smiling.

"So, I hear you've met my daughter," he said to me.

"Numerous times," I said. With varying results, I thought.

Scarpelli devoured a cookie. His bodyguard watched the cookie disappear.

"I got a problem," Scarpelli said. I swallowed hard and had second thoughts about Lucille's gun.

"It isn't you. It's the daughter." He snorted. "Kids. What can you do?" He shook his head in mocking self-defeat.

Shoot her, I thought. Susan Scarpelli Young was a parent's nightmare. Daddy wasn't going to survive his daughter's planned business merger. She was reversing the empty-nest syndrome, watching his nest like a vulture. If it didn't empty, she would empty it. But I didn't really know how he felt about her. Family can be dysfunctional and still have an amazing degree of loyalty.

"Horace—God rest his soul—got some property back from her, for me. She should take more care with her possessions. I would like to know where this property of mine is and what's on it. My daughter is quite determined in her pursuit of it. It might help settle some, ah, family differences if I could get hold of it." Scarpelli stared at me with a tired expression. I reminded myself, again, he was the ruthless head of a small crime family. If he needed a report to tell him his daughter was a backstabbing bitch, maybe his level of awareness really was fading.

"My estranged wife may have expressed different opinions about the nature of my business than I would have to my daughter. In any event, the daughter seems to have a view about her place in my life that is not very realistic." He stared off into space and seemed to have lost his train of thought. After a few seconds, his focus drifted back.

"She seems to have a somewhat unrealistic view about the whole world, come to think of it. She may be a bit unstable, actually. She doesn't take 'no' for an answer very well." He said this to himself more than to me or Lucille. The bodyguard stared at the floor. "Maybe I shoulda let her run a job. But she don't got the control, and I don't see her learning it. I don't disapprove of her goals, but her method just ain't gonna work. She's not a real good judge of character." He paused again. "Whatever. I would still appreciate getting back what Horace had."

"Whatever it was, we don't have it." I stared back at him with less effect.

"But you know where it is." Scarpelli's bodyguard moved closer. His looming presence was uncomfortable. The old man made a gesture and the ape backed up a step. "This thing may reveal other things that are interesting to the wrong people."

Lucille passed the cookie platter to the bodyguard. He took a handful and kept some distance between him and his boss.

I was good at lying, sometimes—sometimes, not so much. Luckily, I knew this. Otherwise some people might have gotten testy. "It's nowhere you can get it."

"Ah, you gave it to your friend from the police. Well, that won't be a problem for me. A bit inconvenient, perhaps. There was some information on it that might help me sort out who considers me more important than my daughter to my humble organization. My daughter will have to get her own ass out of the fire." He turned to Lucille. "Please forgive my language."

Lucille raised an eyebrow and nodded graciously.

Scarpelli rose and was heading for the door when we heard a screech of tires outside. A car door slammed. Then Jon's door opened.

Mr. Scarpelli turned when he reached the door. "If you see my daughter, tell her bon voyage for me."

I heard him mumble as he stood at the door. It sounded like "complete nut-case."

He opened the door and stared straight into Lieutenant Jon Stevens' gun. His bodyguard had one hand full of cookies, and the other one was groping for his own weapon.

161

"Where is she?" Jon's voice was barely a whisper. He grabbed the old man by the lapels and pressed the gun under his chin. Both Scarpelli and his bodyguard froze. I had never seen that look in Jon's eyes. Hard, cold, scary. Beyond cop face.

"I'm okay. And so is Lucille." I moved to where Jon could see me.

He looked at Scarpelli. "Don't ever come near my house again. Ever." He pulled the old man out the door and released his fist slowly. The bodyguard had seen some secret signal only those guys know and stopped trying to find his gun. Jon lowered his weapon. I blew out a deep breath I didn't realize I'd been holding.

"Cookies?" Lucille beamed and pushed the plate across the table. She had turned into everyone's ditzy grandmother. I felt like I was back from Oz as she quietly returned the gun to the kitchen drawer. I hadn't seen it come out.

Scarpelli hobbled slowly to his car, his goon supporting his elbow. Jon stepped into the house, closed the door and sank into the chair recently vacated by Scarpelli.

"What in God's name were you thinking? I can't believe you let him in."

"He wanted me to come out and get in his car. Lucille wouldn't let me go. She lured him in with cookies."

"I'm glad you had the brains not to get in a car with him. I think."

"Jonny, he was very sweet," Lucille said.

"Sweet, my ass." Jon frowned. "Are you going to tell me what he wanted?"

"He wanted to know where the disc was. I didn't exactly tell him. He guessed."

"Does he know what's on it?"

"I think so. He knew his daughter wanted it for something, probably illegal. Or maybe just illegal in his system of laws. He thinks his daughter is a bit unstable."

"Or maybe against his better interests. She might want to watch her back. Probably he should too." Jon stood up. "I'm gotta get to work. We haven't finished processing that disc."

"Jon?"

"What?"

"How did you know he was here?"

"I'm a cop," he said. And closed the door behind him.

I considered my morning. I could move back to my now-clean apartment any time. Being there alone with Susan Scarpelli Young still on the loose might not be too smart. But that was only a temporary setback. I loved my apartment, no matter what either Scarpelli decided to do. Or what Jon decided to do. I needed my space.

Lots of people lived with danger. Some people swam in rivers filled with crocodiles. Hell, we all shared the universe with millions of asteroids, comets, space dust. You needed to be careful. I wasn't sure if Susan Scarpelli and her father were more or less as inevitable as an asteroid but I resented sharing my space with the danger created by their disagreement.

Unfortunately, no matter what anyone else was doing, I still had to make the rent money. I had another breakfast cookie, thanked Lucille for her support, and went to work. I needed some normal fares and, hopefully, some good tips.

Mona had sent Belle out in one of the other cars and was pacing the office, waiting for it to come home.

"She should have been back at least five minutes ago. She's only doing a local."

"If you're worried someone might try to grab her again, I don't think anyone has her on their agenda right now. They have too many family problems."

"Grab who?" Mona looked at me blankly.

"Belle."

"Who cares about her? If that car comes back with so much as a scratch, I'll have her hide. Or better, I'll have the shoes she was wearing."

"Oh." I fidgeted for a few seconds. "What were they?"

Mona sighed. "Rhinestone high-heeled flip-flops. They would make me at least 4 inches taller." Mona carried a fair amount of weight on a short frame but she carried it well and knew how to use it to intimidate as well as how to make it very sexy. The right shoes could do wonders for anyone of any size, shape, or gender.

"Where did she get them? Did you get a source?" Unfortunately, to get the shoes, I had to drive some fares so knowing the source was only for future dreaming. I looked at the slip of paper in Mona's hand. "What you got for me?"

Mona smiled and I remembered that normal fare was a relative term in this business.

"Wonder Bread man wants a ride home from the grocery store." She grinned.

I groaned.

Wonder Bread was introduced in 1921 by the company that makes Twinkies, and you haven't lived until you've had a deep-fried Twinkie. My fare knew his bread history, and anyone who picked him up knew it, too. I had heard that, before the heat of corporate stress baked his mind, he had been high up in the Wonder Bread company chain. Now he's in subsidized housing, but he paid for a cab and if you listened to him, he tipped well. His real name was Tommy.

Tommy stood in front of the mega-grocery with a shopping cart overflowing with the signature blue, yellow and red packages of Wonder Bread. There were a few Twinkies tucked in, filling the spaces between the loaves of bread. The load swayed and jiggled precariously, but he made it to the taxi without losing it and we off-loaded into the backseat. The bottom ones looked squashed, but isn't that part of the appeal?

He wore a black armband. His face sagged into a pile of unhappy wrinkles. He looked like a bloodhound that had lost the scent.

"They're gone!" he wailed. "Gone, gone, all gone."

If he was talking about Wonder Bread, it was because he had just bought the entire supply. I envisioned green bread mold erupting from his apartment and engulfing Northampton.

"They stopped production. In 10 years, all this bread is going to be worth a fortune to the collectors." Satisfaction mixed with some greed spread across his face like fluffernutter on cheap margarine.

He asked me to help move his stash into the elevator and up to his room in the dismal gray cement smudge that is the city's public housing. We loaded up an abandoned shopping cart that sat by the door and headed past senior citizens sitting outside sucking in nicotine. A few followed us in, trailing smoke.

"Hey, is that Wonder Bread? I heard they was closing the plant. Ain't gonna make it no more."

"You're kidding. I was raised on that stuff."

"How come you got so much of it?"

Two more residents hobbled into the group. A few more came out of the restrooms. There were at least 10 wheezing geezers standing around observing the cart overflowing with plastic sacks of bread.

"You ain't hoarding it, is you?"

The elevator doors opened and I shoved the cart and Tommy inside. As the doors started to close, a wrinkled hand reached between them and they slid back open. The whole crowd trooped in and the doors shushed together. I was crushed to the back wall.

"I could use a loaf for peanut butter and pickle sandwiches. It's the only kind of bread that works." A gnarled hand reached out and snatched a sack.

"Yeah, I use it for liverwurst with pickles. Them pickles go with everything. And you can get 'em by the gallon at Wal-Mart." Another package disappeared. Two loaves toppled to the floor and were gone.

Tommy slapped wildly at grabbing hands.

"Hey, gimme that!" a cracked voice squeaked.

"That one's mine."

"Back off, asshole."

The cart was almost empty when the elevator labored to a stop. The doors creaked open and everyone spilled out into the grungy hallway. I stayed plastered to the back of the elevator. Tommy stood next to me, shoulders slumped in a defeated posture.

I left the cart blocking the door open and peeked into the hall. There were two people still visible. Unless you counted the body laid out on the floor. One of the upright bodies nudged the horizontal one with his toe. The elevator door tried to close, banged the cart and slid back open.

"Don't know where he came from. I heard his head hit the wall. He shoulda known better than to stand in the way like that. Old Ethel there was in a hurry to get home. Talking about her Depends." He nudged the body again. "I wonder if he's dead."

"I remember when Harry came out into the hall to die."

"Yeah, what a mess he made. Sometimes when you die, you shit in your pants."

"I heard that."

I slipped around the cart and stepped out of the elevator. The door tried to close again, bounced off the cart and opened again.

"So, he's still breathing." One of the old men turned to me.

"I think we should roll him over."

We each pushed with a foot, and the skinny body flopped over onto its back. He looked about 25 years old. He had a number tattoo on his upper arm. It said 18th. I wondered what he was 18th in and why he would be proud enough of coming in 18th to tattoo it on his arm.

"Hey, I recognize him. He was just on the news. You know, one of them bulletins. Wanted for some kind of drug deal. He had what's-her-face, down the hall, handing out free samples."

"'Member that horsey-looking lady, came with him one day? She wanted to swap some funny-looking pills for Anwar's oxy. I heard her tell him she was trying out new territory."

"Yep, this guy's the one did a high-speed chase, driving a truck full of Porta Potties. Dumped the shit-mobile on its side and run off into the woods. They never did nab him. Found a bunch of 'suspicious white powder' in the cab of the truck. Porta Potties were clean as a whistle, though. I betcha he's part of some big drug cartel. Think there's any reward?"

The other old guy whipped open his cell phone and dialed 911. He turned to me. "You know this ain't just any old subsidized housing. We're a regular stop on the interstate drug-running corridor. I read that in one a them national magazines," he bragged.

Any drug runners who stopped in here were putting their lives in danger. Unless they were supplying the senior citizens who lived here, their chances of survival were pretty poor. I wondered what kind of samples were being passed out. The apartment complex housed a population of elderly and disabled, so there were lots of medications floating around. I could see some enterprising business involving the heavier painkillers.

The body groaned.

"Maybe we should tie him up. Anybody got some string?"

I shrugged and pulled out my duct tape.

Tommy finally staggered out of the elevator and looked sadly at the last three loaves of bread in the shopping cart.

"It's nice to know they like the stuff so much," I said, trying to put a positive spin on it. He shuffled out and down the hallway, dragging the cart behind him. The elevator, having nothing to bump against, finally closed. I took the stairs down.

The police cars were pulling up when I got to the lobby. Jon's unmarked was first in line.

"How's your duct-tape supply?" he asked.

"Are they sending detectives to bust senior citizens now?" I snapped back.

"Dispatch said there was a possible drug dealer in the area."

"It was all about Wonder Bread," I said.

Jon shook his head. He looked at me and smiled. He leaned over and handed me a stray loaf that must have fallen out of the cab.

"I can't keep up with your crime-fighting spree." He looked toward the building. "So, where's the body?"

"Upstairs, third floor. And he's alive."

"Contained?"

"Very."

"Duct tape?"

"Yes, but I just loaned it out," I said defensively. "It was the senior-citizen brigade who used it and called emergency."

Jon motioned to the uniforms and they went inside. "Any idea who it is? Or why they called 911?"

"Those old people watch news television 24/7. They saw the guy on one of the local channels, a trucker who fled the scene after a high-speed on the interstate. They were talking about Porta Potties and suspicious powder and being a stop on the drug runners' route. He has a tat that says he's 18th."

"Shit, 18th Streeters and Porta Potties. That just makes my day," he said, looking a little overwhelmed. "I need to talk to that guy. And I'll talk to you later." He ran his hand down the side of my cheek, along my neck and onto my shoulder. He sighed and disappeared inside.

Jon knew things he wasn't telling me. In a small community, people share stuff with a taxi driver. Jon wasn't sharing.

I decided to live in the moment. Tommy had paid up and tipped well before the riot. I got a loaf of sort-of bread out of it. With thoughts about the guy at city housing and drug runners flipping around my brain, I headed back to scare up more rent money. Crime in Northampton is either personal and domestic or about drugs and money-laundering. The domestic problems are local. The drugs and money laundering are usually controlled from outside the city. The victim of the Wonder Bread riot was an outsider. It got me thinking about how important Northampton was to the drug trade. Lots of small towns, especially those with colleges, were feeling the pressure of increasing drug presence in the population. I was sure I had inadvertently transported drugs up the interstate. We avoided doing it, but the quantity was overwhelming and it was getting increasingly difficult to sort out the drug runners from the rest of society. A driver for another company told me about a woman who paid him to deliver her illegal drugs and to collect payment.

She used her American Express card for both the taxi fee and the drug payment.

Mona and Belle were sitting down to lunch when I got to Cool Rides. It was pizza loaded with, thank God, no Wonder Bread.

"So, how was he?" Mona asked around a mouthful of sausage.

"We had a little accident."

Mona rushed to the window to check out the car.

"Not the car. The car is fine. No scratches, no dents. Honest." I told them about the bread riot.

"Yeah," Belle said, "those old folks, they have real chutzpah. Gotta be careful around them. Look at Lucille. She's murder with those cookies."

A good shot with a large gun, too.

"The senior citizens called the cops but it wasn't about Tommy or Wonder Bread. They bagged a drug dealer." I turned to Mona. "You got fares?"

"Yeah, King Street porn store to Easthampton. Don't worry," she said at my look of dismay. "It's one of the clerks."

"Like he's gonna be normal." I turned back to Belle. "Want to come along? You still need some drive-time experience."

"Yeah, from super-pro driver here." Belle got up and headed for the door. "I can run bodyguard. Protect you from the big bad porno clerk."

I rolled my eyes and followed her out.

We picked him up and delivered him to an apartment building in Easthampton. Belle fidgeted the whole way, bouncing her leg, cracking her knuckles, shifting in her seat. He paid up and disappeared into the ancient, crumbling brick structure. He was big and mean looking. I tried to envision him selling accessories to horny senior citizens.

Excuse me, sir, but how many tubes of lube did you want with that elephant-sized dildo?

When he was out of sight, I turned to Belle. "Okay, what is wrong with you? You're acting like there's a bomb in your britches."

I backed into a side street to turn around.

"I know that guy. I saw his portrait in the police station. He's up for a mob hit."

"Are you sure? Some of those wanted pictures are awful fuzzy. And way out of date."

"I know who he is," Belle said with certainty.

I slowed to a crawl and studied the side-by-side brick buildings where we dropped him. There was an alley between them that dead-ended into a brick wall. Unless you like brick, the landlord wasn't charging for the view. The side door emptied into the alley.

Suddenly the door slammed open. A woman charged out with our fare in hot pursuit. He grabbed her hair with one hand. The other hand was holding a gun. The woman lost the battle to get away. He forced her to her knees, raised the gun and pressed it to her head.

I jammed the car into drive and mashed the accelerator to the floor. We squealed another few feet and careened into the alley. The guy's head jerked up. He dropped the woman. She did a fast crab walk back to the doorway. He turned toward the cab. Too late, asshole. He must have thought the same thing because he wheeled around, took two steps, smacked into the brick wall, bounced off and planted his butt on the hood of my car. I slammed on the brakes. When I

172

opened my eyes, he was spread across the front of the car. His hand twitched, and he slid to the ground.

Belle called 911. I got out of the car to find the gun. His victim had come out of the doorway and was looking for it too. I found it first, probably because she had stopped to kick him a few times. I was less inclined to shoot him than she might have been, so I might have saved his life. I couldn't decide if that gave me my good karma or my bad karma for the day.

By the time the cops arrived, the guy was starting to come around. They checked his pulse, cuffed him and loaded him into the back of the cruiser. His lady friend and one of the cops disappeared into the building. Jon had been visiting the Easthampton station, swapping paperwork, when the call came in. He stood with Belle and me while the Easthampton cops did their capture and cuff. One of them came over to Jon.

"You know who that guy is?" He glanced at me. "That's Ruzzi. He's wanted in five states for murder. They finally got enough evidence to nail his ass in New Jersey."

"Jesus, Ruzzi. Did you get all his weapons?" asked Jon.

"Two guns, a knife and a bottle of unknown substance." The other cop looked at me again.

"Strip-search him when you get to the station. Meantime, keep your gun handy. What the hell is he doing here? He's a freakin' mob hit man. Shit." Jon looked like he wanted to kick something. The name Scarpelli wandered around in the back of my head.

"You want to take him to Northampton?" the cop asked, pride of possession battling with the reality of a truly bad guy.

"Nope, he's your collar. Just be careful. I'll do interviews with the taxi driver for you and forward the paper." Jon turned back to me.

"Honey, you are truly frightening," he said. "I will see you later in my private interview room," he added, running his thumb over my lip, and he left.

Belle and I went back to Cool Rides. When you're high on adrenaline, it's best to keep moving. Belle went to a pickup at the movie theater. Mona handed me a slip.

"This one is an accident. No fatalities. Just need a ride back to town."

"Who called it in?"

"Lieutenant Jon was on his way back from Easthampton when a car crashed coming the other direction. He called the ambulance, the tow truck and us. Said you are one scary woman. What's that about?"

"I don't know. I just do my job," I said and snatched the fare slip.

Jon was still at the scene when I pulled up. The driver and passenger had declined medical treatment, so the EMTs declared everyone lucky and left. The tow truck was leaving with a bent-in-half car. A tree on the side of the road had lost some skin.

"Hey, hi again," I said to Jon.

"Hi, yourself. I wondered if Mona would send you."

"So, what happened? Talking on the phone?"

"Nope." Jon grinned. "The driver's airbag deployed."

"Before or after the crash?"

"After. His fly was unzipped. And her face had airbag burn."

"Gak," I replied.

I dropped the couple from hell downtown. He said she was a controlling, brain frozen bitch. She said he was a manipulating cocksucker and from now on he could suck his own cock, 'cause she sure as shit wasn't going to. They split the fare and argued over that. They didn't split the tip because there wasn't one.

I headed back to the office. The phone rang as I walked through the door. Belle had returned and volunteered to ride along to whatever Mona had.

"Yeah, we could do that." Mona flipped the phone closed. "Woman wants a ride out to the bridge as soon as possible. Pick up in front of the Deep Hole bar."

The Coolidge Bridge is named after President "Silent Cal" Coolidge. It's the only way to cross the Connecticut River from Northampton unless you go twenty miles north to the next bridge or find out if your car floats. Traffic is always backed up inducing occasional bridge rage.

We pulled up in front of the Deep Hole Bar. There was a girl of about sixteen with a huge shoulder bag listing to the side as if the bag carried some excessive weight. She stepped forward tentatively.

"Are you my taxi? Can you take me to the bridge?" she asked as Belle opened the back door for her.

"So, you going out to the bridge for a swim?" Belle asked, sliding into the front.

"I'm going to jump off and kill myself." The girl opened her bag and took out a medium-sized brick.

"You have got to be shittin' me." Belle turned in her seat to get a better look at the girl and the brick. "Lady, no one takes a cab to commit suicide. You better pay me right now. And a big tip would be nice so we don't take a detour to the police station. And that brick—that ain't gonna help drag you to the watery depths. You want us to stop at the hardware store first and get you a cement block? I mean, how serious are you about this? 'Cause if you change your mind, we charge a wait fee."

A cabbie's first concern is collecting payment, but I thought Belle was being a bit insensitive. I turned around. "Fasten your seat belt, please. You can kill yourself, but if I kill you, it's going to raise my insurance rates."

Belle and I stared at her. She fastened the belt.

"Okay? Happy?" She did the pout and slouch that only a teenager can do well.

Oh, yeah.

"So, what you want us to do? About that silly little brick. I mean, you need to get realistic about this. The fall will probably kill you, but just in case, we should get a cement block, and some rope would be good, too. And, hey, are you old enough to commit suicide without your parents' permission?" Belle gave the girl the raised-eyebrows look.

"I'm 17 years old. And Mom, like, doesn't care what I do." More pouting. "You really think the fall will, like, kill me?"

"Sweetie, it's over a hundred feet before you hit the water. That's like hitting a sidewalk from a 10-story building. You're gonna be a mess. But most likely you'll be too dead to worry about how you look.

176

Of course, you could have dressed better." Belle gave the girl's outfit the once-over. It was blah and baggy.

"You got clean underwear on?" I asked. "'Cause in my limited experience with suicide, clean underwear would be high on my list of stuff to do before." I didn't think it was close to a hundred feet from the water, even at the bridge's highest point but it wasn't an argument I was going to start since even a forty-foot drop could kill her.

The young woman's bottom lip quivered a little. We reached the parking lot next to the bridge. "I don't need a bigger brick. I got, like, three of them in here. I'm going to, like, hang the pocketbook, like, around my neck."

"Oh, that'll look real nice. It'll probably fly up and smack you in the nose on the way down. I hope you didn't ask for an open casket, 'cause your nose will be flat, flat, flat. You did make some arrangements for after?" Belle opened her door and got out.

"I didn't really, like, think about all that. Suicide seemed like the simple way out. I guess it's more complicated than I thought." Our passenger had begun to look more morose and less certain. Belle held the passenger's door open.

"Well, come on then. Honey and I will walk up with you. We can throw one of the bricks off. That way, you can test the distance. See how long it's going to take you to hit."

"Why do I need to know that?" She was starting to whine.

"You want your last minutes on earth to be quality time, don't you? It's good to know how many you got. That way you can think worthwhile thoughts during

177

the last few breaths you suck in." Belle started to walk up the sidewalk that edges the bridge. She turned back to our young passenger. "That's ten dollars, by the way."

The girl looked at her blankly.

"The fare, sweetie. It's ten bucks."

"Oh, yeah." She started digging in her bag. She came up with a few dollar bills and a lot of quarters.

I sighed. "Keep the change. It'll help weigh you down." I got out of the car wondering if there was a "like" free zone somewhere close by that I could retreat to or, if I was serious about the Queen's English, to which I could retreat. Before I could retreat to anywhere else, we all went about a third of the way up the bridge. Belle and I were walking faster than the girl who was slowed down by her load of bricks. We stopped to let her catch up.

Belle leaned over the railing. "This is probably far enough. Should do the trick."

We were over the water now. I knew no one had ever died jumping off this bridge and it was not close to ten stories high. Our young passenger must not have had that piece of information.

She caught up with us and stared over the railing.

"What's your name anyway? You know, for when the cops ask us if we knew you. That's if they find your lily-white, crushed and broken, bloody, chewed-on-by-fishes, body. Be good to have a name. And any special reason for taking this swan dive, just in case the press wants a caption for that photo of your flat, crumpled, compressed body on the front page." Belle put a friendly hand on the kid's shoulder.

"Umm, my name's Galaxy."

"Galaxy?"

"What?"

"No, I mean, that's your name?"

"Yeah, why?"

"It's a real interesting name."

"My mom's, like, an astrologer or maybe it's an astronomer. I'm not sure what she does."

"Your mom, huh. So, give me one of those bricks." Belle held out her hand.

"I guess two will be enough." Galaxy reluctantly slipped a brick into Belle's hand. "My mom told me I couldn't go to the hospital to, like, visit my friend. She overdosed on heroin. She's only, like, fifteen. She has some problems with drugs and all that shit, but she's, like, really a good person."

"Your mom?"

"My friend!" Galaxy rolled her eyes. "Mom said she was a bad influence and she didn't want me around friends like that."

"Oh." Belle hefted the brick in her hand. "So, let's see how this goes down. Honey, you got a watch with a second hand?"

I raised my hand. "One, two, three."

Belle dropped the brick. "Bombs away."

We all watched it careen toward the water. It dropped like a, well, a brick. Splat.

Galaxy stood back from the railing.

"How long?" Belle asked.

"Less than 30 seconds." A lot less, but I didn't want her to think it would be over quickly so I didn't say it only took about five seconds for the brick to go from being a weight in Belle's hand to being a ripple in the water. Galaxy's eyes had followed the brick from hand to water and were now glued to the ripple.

"Wow, I could have an orgasm in 30 seconds." Belle smiled.

I looked at her.

"Well, if I really concentrate," she said.

Galaxy shifted her gaze to her feet. "So how much will it cost to take me back to town?" she murmured.

"Sweetie, why don't we take you home?" I put my hand on her arm. "No charge." Sucker, I thought to myself.

We all trooped back off the bridge, loaded up and took her home. We watched the hugs and tears for a few seconds when her mom came to the door.

"I'm so sorry I was harsh about your friends. Friends are important."

"I'm sorry I said you would never see me again."

Then Mom noticed us. "Who are you? And where did you find her?"

"Cool Rides Taxi, ma'am." I handed her a card.

"Mom, I think I owe them some money."

"Oh, let me get my purse." Mom dug around and handed me a 50-dollar bill. "Keep it. I can't tell you how grateful I am."

We left them at the kitchen table with soda and chips. I thought about mob hit men, drug runners, and all the horrible stuff Jon had to face in his job. Even if her friend had somehow landed in the hospital, this young girl lived in a nice house in a nice neighborhood in a nice town. I thought about the kids from Holyoke and Springfield growing up with drive-by shootings, surrounded by drugs. Suicide seemed like an overreaction. But she was a teenager and that job description comes with a lot of drama.

"Wow, that wiped me out. I need fuel." Belle settled into the cab.

I called Mona.

"Cool Rides Cab, where are you and where do you need to be?" she sang into the phone. "Oh yeah, you guys. You can head home. Night shift is here."

We headed to Jon's house. He greeted us at the door.

"Been a full day on the crime-fighting front?" I asked.

"For both of us, as I recall."

"Yeah, we've been busy saving lives," Belle said. "And busting heads. I'm calling takeout." Belle thumbed through a stack of menus by the phone.

"Let's see...we got Chinese, we got more Chinese. Ah, here we got Italian, and Indian, and Mexican, and pizza...and Chinese.

"Lucille brought us cake. Should go well with Chinese." Jon pointed at the counter. "And she left a package for you." He handed me a manila envelope.

I pulled scissors out of some deep recess in my shoulder bag and sliced the envelope open. Jon was standing close behind me, almost leaning against my back, looking over my shoulder as I stared at the multicolored, Day-Glo, extra-sensitive, extra-large condoms. The note said, "Hope you get to try these out. I'm still waiting to get lucky. Let me know if I should invest in a box for myself. Enjoy, Lucille."

I blushed and slapped the envelope closed.

Jon's fingers rested on my neck. They started a slow, sensual movement down my arms.

I whipped around and took a step backward.

He grinned. "Love Lucille, she's always looking out for my best interests."

"Are you laughing at me?"

"Absolutely." Jon looked at the envelope. "And with you."

"You aren't laughing with me. I'm not laughing. I'm not even smiling."

"I could change that. I could make you smile all night and half of tomorrow."

Self-confident bastard. But he was probably right. Of course, he would be smiling too.

I was edging forward when the doorbell rang. Belle came out of the bedroom.

"Give the man some money," she said, snatching the bags of takeout and heading for the kitchen.

An hour later we slowed to a nibble and the rest went into the fridge for breakfast. Cold Chinese for breaky, yumm!

Belle had another choir practice. That meant a severe dress-down. Her boob-announcing spandex top became a plain white shirt. Her butt-enhancing pants changed into a long black skirt.

Jon looked at her appraisingly. "Changing our wicked ways?"

"Mine were never wicked. But I bet yours haven't changed one bit. Don't wait up, sweeties." She sashayed out the door, closing it with an exaggerated softness.

Jon started clearing the dishes. I put my plate in the dishwasher and turned for the next plate, brushing against Jon's chest which was two inches from my own. I stood there, staring at his shirt and put a

182

tentative hand on the first button. I slid my finger past the button and felt warm skin. He put the plate on the counter and I felt his hand come back to my waist.

"Honey," he said.

"Mmm?"

His hand spread across my back and his other hand moved behind my neck. I let my eyes wander up to his mouth and, finally, up until I was looking into those blue eyes. His thumb ran over my lower lip and I opened my mouth slightly. Feeling like a sixteen-year old on a first date, my expression frozen, I ran an experimental finger further up his open shirt.

Suddenly we were kissing and stumbling toward his bedroom. We were through the door and on the bed. His hand was under my shirt and heading upward when I heard a distant ringing.

Jon yanked the offending phone off his belt and tossed it over his shoulder. It hit the wall with a thud, dropped to the floor and stopped ringing. His lips were working their way down my neck and his hand was working its way up my body when the landline started ringing. His hand slowed and his mouth stopped.

"Shit." He rolled away. "I have to get that. Probably work."

Telephonus interruptus.

He seized the phone. "What?" he snapped. "And this better be good." He listened for a few seconds. "You have got to be kidding. And you need me because?" He listened for a few more seconds. "Rank?" he yelled into the phone. "Bust me to foot patrol for the night, for Christ's sake. Yeah, okay."

183

Jon flopped back onto the bed. "I have to go in. They're about to do a takedown and they need my Lieutenant-hood."

"What happened?"

"Two idiots tried to pull the front off an ATM."

"And they didn't catch them?"

"They took off after the ATM pulled the bumper off the truck. They left the bumper attached to the ATM."

I grinned. "With the license plate."

"Yep. DMV says they live off King Street. I'll be back. Don't move."

My body was pulsing like a bass drum and he thought I would stay there for the hours it took them to grab the bad guys, fill out the paperwork and finish the questioning? I needed a cold shower or a long walk. I thought about walking to Belle's choir practice. But that was probably a no-no in Jon's book. Having the Scarpelli gang interested in my whereabouts was creepy. I took the shower.

Jon wasn't home when I fell asleep and I didn't find him in my bed in the morning so either he had gone into work early or not come home at all.

Chapter Fourteen

I stopped at the donut drive-through before work so I arrived with jelly doughnuts for Mona, hoping they would get me some airport fares.

As I walked in, Mona snatched the box and replaced it with a fare slip.

"Mr. Pettibone needs a ride to the bank out on King Street near the construction site." An aging mini-mall was being rebuilt. The only upright structure was a branch of the local bank. Mr. Pettibone lived on Fruit Street at the edge of the commercial district. The bank he wanted a ride to was a good three miles from his house. I waited at the door while he tucked a blanket around his elderly wife.

"I'll be back real soon. I'll make it better, I promise." He kissed her cheek and followed me out. His hands were shaking as he pulled the hood of his sweatshirt over wispy white hair. The hand warmer pocket on the front bulged, giving him a potbelly. His eyes were clouded with age. His shirttail hung out and one shoe was untied.

"You want me to take you up to the Main Street branch? I can wait while you go in. Be quicker than going all the way to King."

"I got a friend out at the King Street branch," he mumbled, keeping his head down. "I gotta get some money to buy some medicine."

185

I eased up the hill through downtown. Traffic was heavy, the sidewalk teemed with pedestrians, and jaywalkers were rampant, each doing a self-righteous dance between the cars trying to negotiate downtown. Mr. Pettibone twitched in his seat.

"Can't you take a shortcut? If I were driving, I'd know a shortcut. And I'd be going faster. And I'd use the horn a lot. Maybe I should be a taxi driver."

And, thank God, you're not, I thought. I liked Mr. P, but he seemed really stressed today.

"I need to do the bank first, and then I got to go to the drugstore and get some medicine for my wife. I got the prescription right here." He pulled a piece of paper out of the pocket of his sweatshirt.

I stopped at a traffic light and looked at Mr. P. There was an odd-looking tuft of blond hair sticking out of his pocket. It was stiff and I couldn't figure out what he had stuffed in there.

"Maybe you could let me off at the bank and wait around the corner." His hands were shaky and in constant motion.

That sounded ominous. He stuffed the prescription back into the sweatshirt hand-warming pocket and a gun bounced out the other end onto the floor. He moved his foot over on top of it. And squashed it flat.

"Mr. P, what is going on?" I pulled around the corner, out of traffic and stopped.

"I told you, I gotta get some money for my wife's medicine."

"Do you have an account at the bank?"

He leaned over and picked up the plastic gun. He tried to bend it back into shape. "Not really," he said.

"But this medicine costs more than our rent. We never needed this stuff before."

"Don't you think someone at the bank might recognize you?"

"I got this." He pulled out a rubber Joan Rivers mask.

"Mr. Pettibone, you have trouble remembering to tie your shoes. You really think you can rob a bank with a flat plastic gun?"

"They'll never think an old geezer like me would do it. Can you wait around the corner while I do the job?"

"You don't have insurance, do you?"

"I got some life insurance. Took it out so my missus wouldn't hafta pay for my bein' put in the ground. But it's not enough to pay for the meds even if I somehow managed to die."

"Health insurance, Mr. P. Who pays for your doctor's visits?"

"Never went to the doctor before. The Missus had to go up to the hospital. They were real nice. Fixed her up with some medicine and told me to go get more. I tried to pay them, but they just kept handing me papers. Finally I gave up and left."

Bank robbery wouldn't exactly be a stable profession, but maybe better than Social Security or Medicare and a lot less paperwork. And then I thought about the real guns the police would use. Mr. Pettibone needed to dump the gun before he got shot, and he needed to get health insurance or medicare in case he got shot. I pulled into traffic and hung a left.

"Hey, this ain't the way to the bank."

187

"I'm taking you to get free medicine." I didn't know how to make the intricacies of the modern medical system clear to Mr. Pettibone, but I did know where to get him freebies. And I knew the people at the drop-in center/homeless shelter would get his paperwork done or know where to send him to get it done.

I parked in front of the ancient but beautifully rehabbed building that housed the emergency shelter in Northampton and, during off hours, the drop-in center. I pulled Mr. P out of the cab, shoving the plastic gun under the seat. I could flatten it more when I got back to Cool Rides. Then I could safely put it in the dumpster. Maybe I would cut it in half, just to be sure. We shuffled into the drop-in office.

"Meds," I said to the woman sitting next to the desk. "He has the script. He needs a note for the pharmacy."

She pulled out forms and started filling them in. She turned to me. "You need transport money?"

"Can you pay me, Mr. P?"

He looked at his untied shoes. The woman made out a check to Cool Rides. She turned to Mr. P.

"Take this to the downtown pharmacy. They'll charge it to us. This is a one-month supply. Come back here in a week and I'll have your medical card ready. Sign here." She pushed the paper over for his signature and handed me the check. It included a tip. God, I love this town.

After the pharmacy stop, I took Mr. P home. By the end of the week, he would know more about the services available to people in need than the governor, the mayor and any of the politicians who had passed legislation creating the services combined. The volunteers at the drop-in center knew the ropes. Northampton always took care of its people in need.

A vulnerable population attracted predators. The Scarpelli family provided the predators. How that predation was kept under control was the problem Jon and the rest of the Northampton police had to deal with daily.

Mr. P and his wife had survived on their own for a lifetime. They hadn't needed medical assistance or even housing assistance before. And that made me think about my trashed apartment and Susan Scarpelli and that made me remember she was still on the loose. I wondered if she was the one who had trashed my place. Old man Scarpelli was after the same disc. He might have searched but I might not even have known he'd been there.

Whoever did it had probably worn gloves and I lived in the Grand Central Station of fingerprints anyway. Belle's and my fingerprints would be the first ones to pop out of the system. Mine because Jon had busted me long ago and far away. Belle claimed she had never been busted. Did they print witnesses? Did I believe her?

I swung back by Cool Rides to see what Mona might have for me. Before I got out of the car, she had a fare slip in my hand.

I spent the day running kids to doctors' appointments and soccer practice, people loaded with electronics and oversize televisions from Wal-Mart to subsidized housing, mumbling dental patients, temporarily blind eye patients, and impatient college students who had forgotten the buses don't always run on time. Mona called on my way back from a junk food run for a local stoner.

"Annie needs to go to the liquor store. You're up." That was fine. I could get some beer to stock my apartment fridge while Annie got her sherry. I might not move back right away but I wanted to be prepared to receive guests on the off chance.

I picked Annie up at the retirement home. Her cocktail hour was notorious. But she never drank before five o'clock and never on Monday, just to make sure she could go a whole day without. Old-lady sherry was strong stuff.

"What time is it now?" said Annie as she got in the cab. "What day is it today? Is it five o'clock yet?"

"It's almost four o'clock and it's Tuesday. We'll have you home in time for cocktails." I parked in front of the liquor store and trailed in behind her. I headed to the beer aisle. She grabbed an extra-large shopping cart and forged her way to the sherry.

The beer aisle in a big liquor store overwhelmed me with the wonderful and exotic. I ended up with Budweiser. It was mostly for guests anyway. If they wanted exotic, they could BYOB.

I was staring at beer, blinded by the sheer variety, when I heard Annie's shrill and angry voice. Her eyesight was terrible and her hearing was worse. Sometimes she thought the clerk cheated on the change.

"And don't you ever butt ahead of me in line again, young man."

When I got to the counter, Annie was holding a monster sherry bottle by the neck. The clerk had his hands in the air and his mouth open. There was a body on the floor. Then I noticed the gun. I leaned over and pried it out of the body's hand. I laid it carefully on the counter. It wasn't plastic. The clerk lowered his hands and leaned over to see the body better.

"Golly, lady. Thanks."

"Well, I never. He was about to cut the queue. No one butts in front of me. I don't care what he needed. I had my sherry all set and he had no right."

I sighed. It had been a boring afternoon. I guess I was due for a duct-tape experience.

"Did you hit the alarm?" I asked the clerk.

"No, but jeez. The boss is going to be rip shit. We get charged for the alarm. Maybe I could just call the police business line." He looked at Annie and me for approval.

"Well, I don't think you need police for cutting the line. But whatever you think is best. Could we go now? Is it 5 o'clock yet?" Annie asked.

"It's always 5 o'clock somewhere, but we need to wait here a few more minutes."

I told the clerk to hold off while I speed-dialed Jon's cell phone and explained the situation. I held it away from my ear while he ranted about civilian involvement.

"Are we fighting?" I asked.

"No, I'm not close enough to fight. But I will be in five minutes. Will it make a difference if I say, don't move?"

I punched the phone off.

Annie said, "Just as long as we get home by 5 o'clock. What day is it? Is it Monday? I certainly hope not. I could really use a drink."

"It's getting closer to 5." And by the time she got back, it would be close enough.

Jon arrived, took a look at the guy and said, "Shit, that's Lenny Zipco."

"You know him?" I asked.

"He's a small-time heroin dealer out of Springfield. The supply lines must be in really bad shape if the dealers are holding up liquor stores."

"Maybe dealing heroin isn't scary enough for him," I said.

"Probably safer," Jon answered.

They finished loading the would-be robber into the patrol car, getting a statement from Annie who mostly addressed the bad manners of this younger generation, the clerk who commented on the sturdiness of the sherry bottle, and me, who had arrived after the fact. It was 4:30. Annie could have her drink as soon as she hit the retirement home.

Jon stared at me, eyes narrowed, scowling in frustration. "What part of don't move don't you understand?"

"I figured you'd be home late."

"Tonight, I'm going to cuff you to the bed."

Hmmmm.

He leaned over, brushed his lips past my forehead, and stalked out the door.

I was thinking about moving back to my apartment tonight. Maybe I could delay that until tomorrow or the next day...or the next.

I dropped Annie off at her condo in the retirement village. She offered me a nightcap. It was nowhere near night but respectable enough for cocktail hour. I declined but noticed several of her friends had gathered at her front door. I headed back to Cool Rides, leaving a roomful of elderly cocktail swigging ladies laughing about Annie's adventure.

Mona, Willie and Belle were playing cards when I trotted through the door. There was a stack of driver applications sitting on the table next to Mona. They looked untouched. We currently had four drivers if you counted Belle and Willie. We had five cars.

"Spit!" Willie laid down his cards with a grin. It looked like Belle had made the grade as a driver.

"So, how was your day?" I asked her.

"I think there's weirdness in the air today," she grumbled.

"Yeah? What happened?"

"The first fare was a mother and daughter fighting over cleaning guess whose room. Then a father and son arguing about school. Then a couple fighting over sex. She's screaming, he's yelling. All of a sudden, they start groping like friggin' porn stars. It's getting so hot I have to up the air conditioning. I made it to the house just before the zippers came down. He throws a 50 at me and they jump out like their pants are on fire. It was a 10-dollar fare."

"Are we going shoe shopping?"

For a minute, I thought Belle was blushing. With her color, it was hard to tell.

"Nah. After I dropped them off, I swung by the porn store and blew the tip on a new vibrator. I took a break after the next three fares in a row propositioned me. I need to go clothes shopping. Taxi driving and ho work need different duds."

"Maybe you need to cut the bling a little," I said. Her glittering spandex top caught sunlight coming in the window. I squinted at the blinding sparkle bouncing off her barely contained chest. "And maybe a higher neckline?"

I looked down at my plain T-shirt, faded jeans and worn sneakers. There had to be a middle ground that would de-bling Belle and re-bling me.

She picked up a few cards and laid them on the table. "See, I might have got you in the next hand," she said to Willie.

The landline started ringing. Mona picked it up. "Honey, it's for you. The lieutenant, I think."

Belle waved at the phone. "Say hi for me."

I stepped into the office and closed the door. "Hi, what's up?"

"I'm coming over to pick you and Belle up and take you to my house. I'll be there in 10 minutes. Don't move! I mean it, Honey."

"Wait," I squeaked. "I need to take a cab home with me tonight. I'm scheduled to work at 9 tomorrow. What's so important?"

"We'll talk when I get there." Click.

I hate being hung up on.

Chapter Fifteen

"What's the good cop say?" Belle was laying out a game of solitaire.

"If he's the good cop, who's the bad cop? And he'll be here in five minutes."

"And?"

"And we'll talk." I shrugged.

Jon pulled up in front of the garage in three minutes and came in.

"Honey, Belle." Jon nodded to us. "We need to talk."

"Uh-oh, he's got his cop face on. I really don't like that one," Belle said and moved a few cards around.

Me neither. It usually means my control buttons are about to get pushed.

"We found your friend Bozo, whose name, by the way, was Lester Cardozzo."

"Was?" I had a bad feeling suddenly.

"He was bailed out of our nice, secure, jail cell yesterday and was head down, feet up at a construction site in Springfield by morning. He was in the Porta Potti, shot in the back of the head. The other two have declined bail."

My stomach did a fast roll. I didn't like Bozo. He had put a gun in my face, kidnapped Belle and, I had no doubt, committed some very nasty crimes. Not a nice person. But he had become a passing acquaintance and I didn't know many people who had died violently and died young. I had seen too many dead people recently but he was the first one I had any personal contact with, however unsatisfactory it was. He wasn't much older than me. Some mother, somewhere, would grieve, maybe. I grabbed the table and shoved my chair back with a jerk.

Belle glanced up at my face, turned over the ace of spades with one hand and casually reached over and pushed my head down between my knees with the other.

Jon came around the table and put a hand on my back. "Breathe deep," he said. "So, I'm thinking either Scarpelli is cleaning house or Susan Young is in panic mode. The Springfield police are watching Scarpelli. A body in their jurisdiction, which Cardozzo was, convinced them to cooperate in the investigation." He paused. "His daughter is another question. We can't find her. You two will stay at my place until we do. She may be operating on her own. Right now, she's a person of interest in enough murders to bring her in for some questions." Jon rubbed my back.

None of this was a request. My defiant personality tapped me on one shoulder and whispered, "Make your own decisions." My manipulating side tapped the other shoulder and said, "You can use this situation!" Somewhere between my shoulder blades, caution raised its ugly head. There wasn't any room left for normal.

I straightened up slowly. "I'm okay now. Yeah, we could keep the sleepover going a while longer." I looked at Belle.

"Hey, having our own house cop around right now might be just dandy."

Jon narrowed his eyes at her and grunted.

Although my job required some independence, I knew when to pick my fights. Jon had to go to work tomorrow morning, too. I was sure he wasn't going to handcuff me to the bed unless he was in there with me. Even if he did, Belle was on my side, and between the two of us, we could defeat any serious restraints Jon had.

We trooped out to Jon's car. He got into the driver's side. I looked wistfully at my taxi. Mona needed drivers as much as drivers needed her. She would give me fares. Belle and I could stick together and be safe enough. At least from Susan Scarpelli. The rest of the crazies out there were a different problem.

We spent the evening eating more Chinese take-out and watching the comedy channel. I temporarily forgot my problems in the face of Stephen Colbert's brain-candy comedy.

Jon went back to work for a few hours and didn't get home until I was in bed and asleep. He left before I got up. Unless he had the time to check up on us, Belle and I were on our way uptown. We could snag coffee and a taxi.

It was a glorious summer day. We loaded up on caffeine and sugar and headed to Cool Rides.

Mona's eyes opened a little wider and her mouth puckered, but she handed me car keys and two slips. Both were local short hauls. They wouldn't pay much rent, but they might help Belle get a more appropriate wardrobe.

We took some teenagers to the tattoo parlor even though they already had tattoos covering arms, necks, and ankles and three piercings in each ear. One had a brand and the other had a distended earlobe, the latest fashion statement for the pierced and skin art crowd. Since we had an hour before the next pickup, we decided to go shopping. It was strange to shop and still keep an eye out for crazy Susan. I was imagining Susan as an insane, murdering monster, lurking behind a rack of brown, uniform style pants in Wal-Mart.

Belle was trying to imagine herself in anything besides spandex and glitter.

I handed her a pair of plain brown slacks. "Brown is the new black."

"Those look like shit," Belle said, holding up the pants.

"You haven't tried them on yet."

"No, I mean, they really look like poop. You could stain your pants and no one would notice."

"Maybe that's the advantage. To the brown."

"Yeah, with an aging population, incontinence won't show so much."

Belle finally found a white shirt that didn't hide her boobs, but they weren't overflowing either. And a pair of straight black pants toned down her silver 3-inch heels. Definitely de-blinged but not enough that she looked like she was attending church.

On the way out, we passed the shoe department. I stopped at a pair of gold sparkly stilettos with 6-inch spike heels. "How do you walk in those?" I ran a finger down the heel.

"Why would you walk in them? They're slut shoes. You don't walk in slut shoes."

"What do you do with them? Where could you wear them without tipping over?"

"Tipping over is the point. You wear those to bed, he's gonna stuff the cannoli with the best chocolate. Every box of those shoes should be required to contain a slew of condoms."

My gaze went back to the shoes. Sighing, I thought about Jon and then about control issues and cannoli stuffing.

I followed Belle to the car. We headed to Florence Heights for our next fare.

Florence Heights is the alternative to Hampshire Heights. The only height in most public housing is in the name, and this was no exception. Florence Heights is six miles from downtown if you have wings and travel in a straight line. There is no easy, direct driving route to Florence Heights. Most drivers avoid it for the same reasons they avoid Hamp Heights. No tips, long waits, possible violence.

Our guy lived three buildings from the main road. Because Florence Heights was more isolated than Hamp Heights, it had less highway trash in the landscape. The apartment we pulled up to actually had flowers planted by the door. Maybe the tenant did some gardening.

Maybe not, I thought as a muscular black guy with a shaved head came out. He had on blue jeans that fit with the waist...amazingly...at his waist. He was about 35 and wore a wife-beater T-shirt that showed off tattoos on both arms. One tat said "I'm in love" with no name, leaving his options open. The other said, "Here come de judge" and had a tiny scale under it. It wasn't clear whether the scale represented the weighing of justice or drugs.

Belle jumped out and opened the door for him, getting a good look at his package in the process.

"Thanks," he said, smiling. His teeth were way too good for Florence Heights. State-funded dental care was my guess.

He slid in and fastened his seat belt.

"So, where you goin'?" Belle asked.

"The courthouse."

"Ah, so, what's your name?"

"Carlton"

"I'm Belle, and this here's Honey. We be at your service and your means of transport for the afternoon. You just tell us what you need and we will make you happy."

I rolled my eyes and poked Belle in the thigh.

For the rest of the ride, Carlton and Belle exchanged stories about the two Heights, comparing living conditions, police attention and general mayhem. The consensus was they were pretty much the same. If you kept your head down and minded your own business, it wasn't bad. Public transportation was lousy from either.

When we got to the courthouse, Belle and I both got out, expecting someone to meet our fare...a lawyer or a cop...and pay the bill. The only person outside the courthouse entrance was the elderly door guard.

"Mornin', Judge Witherspoon," he greeted Carlton. "Been stayin' at your momma's house again, I see. How is that lovely lady?"

Belle looked at me.

Carlton winked at Belle. "Nice meeting you ladies," he said. "Hope we meet again, not in my courtroom, of course." He handed Belle thirty dollars. "Keep the change. The ride was a great way to start the morning."

"You have got to be kidding." Belle stared after him. "He don't look like any judge I've ever seen."

The guard sidled over to us. "I can always tell when he's visiting his mother. He dresses different. Likes to fit in, I guess. I sure do wish she'd move in with him. But she likes it there. One of the best judges I've seen on the bench in thirty years."

"There goes the judge," Belle grunted. "And I thought I could'a been in love."

"Wait a minute," I said, opening the driver's door. "You were interested when you thought he was a felon. Just because he went to law school and got educated, he's off limits?"

"Well, duh! It's not the college education. Hell, I got one of those. It's the law, as in which side he's on." Belle looked at me like I was beyond dumb.

"You've got an education? Like how much?"

"I did college. My degree is in government with a minor in social work. Came in handy in my previous line of employment. I knew which lines to cross from my government classes and how to cross them from my social work."

I wondered if the judge had assumed as much about Belle and me as we had about him? Big tip, so who cares? I disagreed, but I understood Belle's attitude. She assumed a judge would never be interested in a relationship with a former prostitute, so why waste her time on a relationship that would never

201

happen? It made me wonder if she was really sure she was done with her former life. But it was interesting to know she had a better formal education than I did.

Ten minutes later, we were back at Cool Rides to see what kind of people moving we needed to do.

Mona stuck her head out the door. "Don't bother to get out of the car. I got two more for you. One right now. One in an hour. Short hauls, no conflict, but you'll need to hustle." She handed us the yellow slips with names, locations, destinations and phone numbers.

The first pickup was uptown to the hospital. It was Spike. He was one of our regulars, and his eight-inch mohawk he dyed different colors, mood-dependent, had earned him the nickname. He dressed in black leather and chains and had multiple piercings in the visible parts of his body. I had heard rumors about the less obvious places for piercing but I never confirmed that those hidden parts of his body had holes as well. Visually, he was what you never want your daughter or your son to bring home. But the accessory that really stood out with Spike was the baby stroller. The stroller was filled with mini-Spike. An angel of a two-year-old boy with his hair mohawked, spiked and colored to match dad, accompanied Spike everywhere. Spike was a stay-at-home father, and a damn fine one.

He was taking his son to the free clinic at the hospital for a checkup which probably included shots of some sort.

We dropped them at the ER and off-loaded the stroller, the baby blankets, the pacifiers, the toys, the car seat and the diaper bag. We left them standing next to a pile of gear that would make a mountain climber happy.

"We'll wait for half an hour. If you get done by then, you get half-fare home. Otherwise, we have a pickup in an hour so we'll have to come back for you."

"Hey, that's great. We'll hustle, right, Samuel?" He leaned over and patted his son on the cheek. The angel giggled.

"Jeez, that is so cute." Belle watched him walk through the swinging doors.

We sat for about five minutes. That doesn't sound like very long but completely lacking entertainment for longer than five minutes was tough and very boring. We parked the car in the massive parking lot and began the wait.

"I'm hungry." Belle rolled down her window. "I wonder what they got for hospital food in there."

"Okey, dokey," I said. We went through the emergency room filled with screaming children, sniffling and coughing adults, probably a few plague victims, and found the breakfast café. We were the only customers.

We had settled into a booth with our tray of sugar-based food of indeterminate origin when a woman in a baggy flowered jumper, a big-brimmed straw hat and sunglasses slipped in next to me. She looked like Annie Hall doing Iowa farm girl. Right off the bus, waiting for the first pimp to commandeer her.

"Long time no see." She slid her glasses down her nose.

"Holy crap." Belle began to slide out of the booth.

It was Susan Young Scarpelli or whoever she was today.

Chapter Sixteen

"I wouldn't go anywhere." She lifted the matching jacket that covered the gun in her hand. And the ominous silencer on the end of it.

"You wouldn't dare shoot that in here. Besides, you'd ruin that cutesy-wootsy matching jacket." Belle's eyes cut to the empty counter. I had seen the clerk walk off with a plate of doughnuts for her own jean-tightening break.

"We're in a hospital. If I shoot you, you have a chance of survival. But I'm a good shot. Dead before you hit the floor. And, personally, I like the matching-jacket concept."

"Just what is it you want from us?" I tried to stall for time. Someone had to come into the coffee shop sooner or later. Sooner would be better although no one would mind seeing that jacket filled with holes.

"I need to clean up a few loose ends. You two are, like, a loose end. Who's going to take me seriously if I can't close the books on a two-bit taxi driver and a whore?"

"You should be in Mexico." Belle settled back on the bench.

"Don't push me. I need to be ruthless if I'm going to take over my father's organization. And I am going to take it. What I don't need is you two in my way. You were just a means to an end. And I need that disc back. Your boyfriend will hand it over when I offer to swap you for it."

"Since you shot Lester, I think the police might be more of a problem than we are." I crossed my arms and leaned back, too.

"Lester's dead? Well, I sure as hell didn't shoot him." Susan's face paled.

I looked at her for a few seconds. Some emotion flashed in her eyes. Pain? Anger, maybe. Or insanity. What kind of relationship had she had with Lester? And did I believe she didn't know what had happened to him? Maybe it was Daddy, cleaning house again. I doubted there was any evidence either way. If her expression was grief, it passed quickly.

"Shit," Susan muttered. "This is gonna be harder than I thought. The old geezer may have some balls left after all."

"Maybe Daddy is a wee bit pissed off." I bit into a cream doughnut. "Did you trash my apartment?" I didn't see Susan as a long-range planner and now she was becoming unpredictable. Her world had shrunk to include herself and herself. Anyone who didn't believe her reality was dismissed or eliminated. Belle and I fell into the latter category.

"Goddamn right I trashed it. We wanted that disc. It had good information I can't remember. And you idiots gave it to the police. I need it back."

"I think I'm being dissed." Belle looked at me. "Do you think I'm being dissed?"

"Hey, I'm not the idiot here," I said. "I'm not taking on your father, the crime boss in the area, trivial as that area is. I keep my head down and my nose clean. And is that the royal we?"

"Yeah," said Belle. "And I keep my head down. So maybe some self-examination type of stuff is in order for you, Susan."

"Oh, bugger off." Susan sounded stressed. "The police have zero on me. I didn't do Lester."

"Hey," said Belle. "What about you keeping me prisoner against my will? That's gotta be illegal somehow."

"Maybe I was held prisoner in my own house. Maybe those other two thugs were my father's. Yeah, that could play. Okay, I could go a different direction here. I could just get Daddy locked up. That would work for me. But I still need to do something about you two. You're a blot on my reputation and I need to swap you in for that disc."

I didn't think I'd ever been called a blot on someone's reputation. "You're on your own there. I don't think we can help you. The police don't deal with blackmail well."

"They will if little pieces of you start showing up in the right places, one finger from each of you should get some action," said Susan, showing the gun again. "You don't want me to start shooting off rounds in a hospital. I might hit someone besides you. So get your asses moving. We are so out of here."

"Can I ask you one more question?" I wanted to keep her where someone might notice us and provide a distraction.

"Jesus, you are a curious bitch. What now? The shoes?"

"Well, that, too." I paused. "Why did you shoot your husband in the butt, in the courthouse, in broad daylight?"

"Shit, what an asshole he was." Susan's ego was getting the better of her. She wanted to share. I was a good listener. "He was stepping out on me. I had to show him I could get to him anywhere, any time. I married him because he was working for my father. Who knew he was such an idiot? And such a dud in the sack?"

"Yeah," Belle said, "messing around on the boss's daughter? Dumbsville."

"Who cares about the boss? That was me he was fooling around on and my father-the-boss didn't give a shit. No way was that going to happen. He needed a lesson, big time. I'll get to Daddy dearest later." Susan grinned. It was scary.

"So, then you shot him dead? Seems like marriage counseling would have been easier." Where the hell was the waitress?

"I didn't shoot him dead. He stole a few millions of Daddy's money and was getting ready to skip town with the cash. That's a no-no in our family."

"Guess he didn't know the rules," said Belle. "Can I ask about Horace? I mean, he wasn't my favorite person, but he seemed loyal to the family. Why'd you shoot him?"

Susan looked exasperated. She sighed and moved the gun to a more visible position.

"You keep asking why I shot people. I hardly ever shoot anyone. I certainly didn't waste ammunition on Horace. Lester and someone were over there looking for the disc. We didn't want it to fall into the wrong hands. Of course, you idiots took care of that. Horace was an accident. He came flying through the window and Lester freaked and shot him. I personally would have tortured him and found the disc. But dumb Lester overreacted."

I would have hidden under the table before I would have shot anyone.

"But enough with the questions. Time to go." Susan waved her coat-covered arm toward the entrance.

"And just where are you taking us? Huh? You think you can just walk out of here with two respected members of the community and make them disappear?" said Belle.

"Who? A ho and a taxi driver? Like the community is really going to miss you. I can't even figure out why Willie gives a shit about you. Just hire new drivers. They must be a dime a dozen. But he cares, so here we are. And then there's that numb-nuts cop. I take off enough fingers and I'll get stupid Willie to cooperate and get the disc back."

Voicing my thoughts that a taxi driver or a prostitute was worth twice as much as a lawyer or a mob boss to any sane community seemed counterproductive under the circumstances. The conversation was getting weird, and Susan's motives resembled scrambled eggs, mixed up and well cooked. But she kept talking and, by the time she shut up we had an idea of where we all stood. She wanted to take over her daddy's business. To do that, she had decided to prove she could increase the moving of certain product up the interstate. To do that, she'd tried to recruit the Cool Rides Taxi Company. To do that, she had to put some pressure on Willie. We were her pressure. She also needed to know who in her father's organization would back her and who would stick with him. Horace had that information on the disc we had given to the police. No wonder she wanted to shoot us.

As I was trying to find good reasons for Susan not to shoot us, two ambulances roared up to the ER entrance, sirens blaring, brakes screeching. Susan looked at us and fired a round into the floor. The hospital staff was focused on incoming. No one even looked our way. Too much noise to sort out a gunshot with a silencer from the rest of the chaos.

"Come on, up and at 'em." Susan stood and stepped away from the booth. We all trooped out of the coffee shop and started toward the entrance to the building.

Just as we reached the automatic door, I heard a high-pitched wail and the pounding of many feet.

"Nooo shoots." Mini-Spike tore out the door, flying on spinning 2-year-old legs.

And hit Susan in the back of her knees with all the torque his chubby little body could muster. Susan flipped over backward. Her gun went skittering across the floor. Mini-Spike scrambled up and over her, stomping on her stomach, and headed for the door in a blur. Susan started to get up.

And big Spike tripped over her, kicking her in the ribs. He mumbled an apology, regained his footing and ran after his son. A nurse followed him and stepped on Susan's hand.

An orderly followed the nurse and connected with a foot.

When the parade had finally passed, Susan struggled to her feet. Belle was on her stomach in the vicinity where the gun had dropped. I suspected it might be under her spreading bosom.

"You," Susan hissed. "You I will deal with. One way or another, I'll finish this." And she staggered out the door.

My cell phone rang.

"Where the hell are you?"

"Hi, Jon."

"Honey, if I didn't fear for your life right now, I would strangle you. Where are you?"

"I'm at the hospital."

"What? What happened and what's the damage?"

"I'm fine. I was just delivering a fare."

Just then our fares came back in. Spike had his arms wrapped around a kicking, screaming, red-faced Mini-Spike. "He found out he had to get a shot. I guess he understands more of what we were saying than I thought. Hope your friend is okay." He slung the child over his shoulder, sack-style, and disappeared back into the ER.

I could hear Jon yelling at the other end of the phone.

"Are we having a fight? Because if we are, I need some comfort food. I have some doughnuts here, but I'm not sure it's enough. I think I need chocolate. And, by the way, Susan Scarpelli stopped by the hospital to say hi."

I could hear Jon sighing on the other end of the phone. "Do you need any help?"

"Not unless you want to corral a 2-year-old who just learned the word shot."

"Shot what? A 2-year-old shot someone?" His voice was rising again, by an octave or two.

"Shot, as in what the doctor gives you. We're headed back to Cool Rides as soon as Spike finishes getting Mini-Spike inspected."

"We need to talk. I need to know what Susan was doing at the hospital. We have a warrant out for her as a witness and person of interest."

"Yeah, we need to share information. And accommodations and stuff like that."

"Stuff?"

"I have another fare in 15 minutes. Gotta go." I flipped the phone closed.

"Is hot buns about to come roaring in with his bubble light screaming?"

"The bubble light doesn't scream. That's the siren." I slid down the wall until I was sitting next to Belle.

"I know that. I was speaking metaphorically."

"No, he's not. I don't think." And it was true. Right now, I couldn't think. I needed to get back to Cool Rides. Safe ground for me.

Belle stood up. She had Susan's gun in her hand. "Let's go." She tucked it in her oversized bag and offered me a hand up. "Here come Spike and Mini. We got another fare to pick up. Time's a-wasting."

We dropped Spike and Mini downtown. Mini had apparently made his peace with his father, or he had just worn himself out. His hair was flat. I wondered how long it would take Spike to redo the do on his son.

After we dropped the Spikes, Belle pulled out the next fare slip.

"Well, look at this. I know this woman. She's in the business."

"As in your ex business?"

211

"Yeah, she's a ho. Her client base is mainly in Springfield, but last I knew, she was building up a good local constituency. You know that 'buy local' ad campaign? She could be the poster girl for that."

"I'm not sure that's what they had in mind. Where are we picking her up?"

"Swing this chariot around to Crescent Street. She's meeting someone at The Street Café."

"Whoa, swank. Business must be good."

"Sweetie pie, that business is always good. But it can wear you out fast. I just outgrew it."

"Or maybe found out how scary it can be."

"Yeah, that too. Hey, you got any kind of self-defense in that undersize suitcase you carry?"

"Like?"

"Like gun, stun gun, pepper spray, big dildo?"

"Big what? How would a big dildo defend me?"

"Girl, use your imagination. How'd you get Bozo's attention when we were locked up at Susan's condo?"

"I grabbed his balls." Or something equally squishy.

"Exactly. Think how much more effective a big old dildo would have been. And then you could have whacked him over the head with it. And it still would have been perfectly good for later use."

File that one away for future defense. I didn't even own a dildo. Or a gun or a stun gun. I did have some pepper spray. "So, what have you got in your bag?" I asked Belle.

"What haven't I got? I got Susan's gun, which we never told the lieutenant about, right? And I got a bottle of hair spray." Belle dug around in her purse.

"And I got some pepper spray and a pair of brass knuckles. And a big ol' dildo."

"You have a dildo in there? No, you're kidding."

"Take a gander." And Belle pulled out the biggest penis I had ever seen not attached to a stud bull. It was encased in a clear plastic box lined with blue silk. I almost drove off the road.

"Stop distracting me. The original must have belonged to a horse."

"Yeah, it can make a strong man feel mighty inadequate. That's a good self-defense right there."

I slowed the cab and turned onto Crescent, a street lined with charming Victorians. Belle's friend walked with a stride that was graceful, commanding and feminine all at the same time. She was elegantly dressed in a silk suit that would have been at home on any CEO. The wardrobe was different from Belle's. It was obvious who was in charge in her client relationships. Could I take lessons? I really wanted to learn how to be in charge. If I would ever have a chance at running the Cool Rides Taxi Company, I would have to master that special skill. Also, if I ever wanted to survive a relationship with Jon.

"Honey, this is Charlotte. She graduated from Smith and decided to put her degree to work. There's nothing like good networking."

"Hey, Belle. I heard you hadn't been in circulation for a while. Sorry about Horace, I guess."

"Yeah, no one deserves to die early. But he came damn close to earning what he got. I got tired of the life. I'm giving cab driving a whirl."

"Whatever floats," Charlotte replied. She had a deep cultured voice. I could see her giving public-speaking lessons.

"Why do you figure she works as a prostitute?" I asked Belle after we dropped Charlotte off.

"Why not? Good as far as a job goes. Pays well. Flexible hours. I didn't mind it. I just got bored. And what with Horace eliminated from the management position, it seemed like a good time to let it go. Besides, in Charlotte's case, she had a lot to prove. Like that she likes being called 'she,' but 'she' isn't. And letting her off here reminds me it's lunchtime. I need more than doughnuts to sustain me."

"What do you mean, 'she' isn't? She isn't what?"

"She isn't a she. She has balls and a penis."

"No! She went to Smith College. She's a prostitute, for God's sake."

"God didn't have anything to do with it, and Smith doesn't require a DNA test. They just assume. And she's a damn fine ho with a specialized technique. Does some dominatrix stuff and lots of mouth-to-crotch resuscitation."

I thought about Charlotte and men and how many of her clients knew. Then I let it go. Belle was right. I needed fuel, too. "Okay, food."

"I hear a burger calling my name. And fries. And maybe a hot fudge sundae." Belle grinned. "Packard's?"

Packard's is a local bar that serves the ultimate hamburger. It's stuffed with jalapeño peppers which are stuffed with pepper jack cheese. Then it's dipped in a beer batter and deep-fried. It ain't rabbit food.

I called into Cool Rides to see if Mona had any pickups for us. She had an airport at 2 o'clock, so now was a good time for lunch.

At 1:30 we rolled into Cool Rides, stomachs sated and arteries clogged. The next two hours were an uneventful ride to the airport. Unless you count our fare being stopped and searched by the feds. But he had already paid and tipped, so it didn't count in my book. His book was probably different.

We got back to Cool Rides around 3:30. Mona gave us six more short hauls. By 5:30, Andrew had reported in. I was glad he was a night person. The ten o'clock train from New Haven was usually at least an hour late. To maintain our reputation for being on time and reliable, the driver went to Springfield at the scheduled time and sat for an hour. That meant getting home around midnight. Too late to start work at 9 the next morning. Andrew was somehow able to turn off his excessive energy and sleep while he waited. I needed to be in my own bed or, possibly, someone else's bed. But I needed a bed.

Belle and I headed back to Jon's house so Belle could cook. She wouldn't discuss details, but dinner was going to be made.

"I'm going to go next door and ask Lucille if she wants some dinner," I said. What I really meant was Belle hadn't made any dessert and I knew Lucille would have the sugar part of any meal covered. She handed me a full plate and we popped back to Jon's side.

Jon arrived at 6:30 to the smell of lemon chicken, herbed rice, and broccoli with hollandaise sauce. I'd set the table, which told me I was bordering on domestic. I wondered if Jon noticed and how he felt about having live-in help. He was comfortable enough to sit down and devour the food.

When we had finished and cleared, Jon leaned back in his chair and eyed me speculatively.

"We need to talk about the Scarpellis. Both of them." He tipped his chair down.

Belle rose and headed toward the bedrooms.

"You, too. Don't even think about skipping out tonight." He pointed at Belle.

Lucille smiled her usual beatific smile and sat with a sort of vacant look in her eyes. I was beginning to realize Lucille's facial expression and her brain activity were extremely separated. I suspected her mind was two steps ahead of mine at all times.

Belle returned to her chair and sat.

"I'm having trouble fitting some of the pieces of this father-daughter relationship together. I need to know more about what she said to you at the hospital."

I thought about her comments. Was she dealing with reality if she thought she could oust her father? He'd been in business a long time. Those kinds of loyalties weren't built fast or easily. Maybe she wanted an entry into the male-dominated hierarchy. Her father didn't seem overly concerned about the disc being in the hands of the police. The most it could do for the police was tell them who to watch, inside and outside the blue brotherhood. They couldn't bring it into a court of law. Anyone could have put it together for any reason.

Lucille refocused her eyeballs and turned to Jon. "What we have is three shootings: Horace, Susan's husband, and Lester Cardozzo. We have Honey's

216

apartment trashed. We have Belle kidnapped. We have a visit from Mr. Scarpelli. Maybe the motivations for the shootings are unrelated and the rest of the incidents are collateral damage to something we don't know about."

At the mention of Mr. Scarpelli, Jon frowned. He was still mad we'd let him into the house. I wasn't sure how I felt about being collateral damage.

"We have a confrontation with Susan and you have the disc," Lucille finished.

"I think we know why Susan shot her husband, the first time anyway," Belle said.

"And are we going to share this?" asked Jon.

"Keep your pants creased, pal. Yeah, we can share. Susan said her husband was stepping out on her. She didn't seem to like him anyway and he wasn't very good where it counted."

"Did she say whether she hired someone to kill him? As long as she was confessing to you, I mean," Jon asked politely.

I coughed. "She wanted him to know she could get to him anywhere, any time, so she picked the most public, secure place she could think of. It worked. He was terrified of her. He embezzled money from her father to get away. And ended up dead anyway. We know she didn't actually kill him. But Scarpelli Sr. couldn't have been happy about his money being embezzled," I added. "She also said Horace was shot by accident. That's what Belle's friend said. He went flying through the window when he tripped off a skateboard. Lester overreacted a bit and nailed him between the eyes."

Jon drummed his fingers on the table. "So, Lester's murder was, possibly, just house cleaning by Scarpelli. And, thank God, not in my jurisdiction."

Lucille said, "So that accounts for all the bodies. But why is Susan still threatening Belle and Honey? I think the taxi company is at the center of it. Susan didn't come after Belle until Belle started driving for Cool Rides. And they went after Honey before they went after Belle. So, the disc was only part of Susan's motivation."

"Maybe the disc was a fuckup by Susan. Whatever was on it pissed her father off. Now she's trying to redeem herself," I said, "and let's not forget she's crazy. Lucille is right. Susan said stuff about using Cool Rides. I think she and Daddy may have a difference of opinion over that. But it does seem she wants to take over the Scarpelli operations and Scarpelli Senior is resistant."

"We just have to find her," Jon said. "I got a search warrant for her office. That wasn't easy. Attorneys are more protected than a Wall Street banker. She may not have killed anyone yet, but I think she could get away with it if she decides to." He grimaced. "She seems to have lost her boundaries. We may be dealing with psychological issues that go beyond family fights. You and Belle need to take this more seriously."

I had passed beyond serious and advanced to hysteria mode, but my coping mechanism has always been to put on blinders and pretend to be normal. If Susan Scarpelli could walk into a courtroom and shoot someone, she could get to me whenever and wherever she wanted to. I sometimes felt like I had the street smarts of Bambi in the headlights. Susan hadn't had much luck yet, so maybe she was due.

"How does Scarpelli make a living?" Everyone looked at me blankly. "Everyone has to file a tax return. What's he claim as his income source?"

Jon grinned. "Porta Potties. He has some trucks and a bunch of shit houses. He moves them around to construction sites. The feds have looked at his books. Never found anything they could nail him for."

"What about that guy you busted at Salvo House? The one the senior citizen brigade wrapped up. They said he was driving Porta Potties with white powder."

"Corn starch. But we wanted him to answer a bunch of other questions, so thanks for loaning out your duct tape," said Jon.

"So, then, what's his real source of income?" I asked again.

"Transportation." Jon leaned back in his chair. "He owns the Route 91 corridor between Hartford, Connecticut, and the Canadian border. Northampton is a big stop because of the five colleges. He doesn't actually deal. He just transports and distributes it to the second-tier dealers."

"We have that in common. I'm in the transportation business, too. Just more legitimate. And limited to people." We all pondered that for a minute. "What's he use to move stuff now?"

"We've never been able to get a handle on it. Maybe his trucks, but we've used every excuse to stop and search and never found anything. No one ever volunteers for that duty. Moving shit in Porta Potties would make some sense. Might damage the product. Not that the crack heads would notice." Jon sighed. "I guess I better talk to Willie tomorrow. Lucille may be right. Scarpelli needs to expand, and Cool Rides would be better cover than any of the other companies because it's so squeaky clean. Did Willie ever mention any pressure being put on him?"

"Not to me, but Mona would be the one to ask. She and Willie are pretty tight. They share a lot," I said, glaring at Jon. "Susan sure thought she was putting pressure in the right place."

Jon looked at Belle. "What about the other cab company?"

"Lucky's Limo? All I ever did was get rides to Holyoke and Springfield. Sometimes with Horace. Sometimes not. They never stopped anywhere else when I was in the car."

"Did Horace stay with the car or get out with you?"

"He usually stayed with the car. They would just drop me off. I called for a pickup when I was done. I don't know where they went."

"So, we have a mobster who controls illegal goods on the interstate. There's family in-fighting about who's in charge and how to expand. We have a lot of threats against a taxi company traveling that interstate. And no proof of anything more sinister," said Lucille.

"Susan slapped me around. They took me against my will." Belle's voice went up a notch and her chin rose.

"They threatened me with a gun," I added.

"At least one of the guys who threatened you is dead. Safe to assume he was the one who shot Horace. He's not in my jurisdiction anyway. We're left with

Susan's husband. She's got an alibi. Daddy's cleaning up her mess." Jon drummed his fingers again. "What's on your agenda tomorrow?" He looked at me and then at Belle. Maybe he had finally given up on the control issue.

"I'm driving. Belle and I could still stick together. Cuts into the income, but we might both survive to spend it."

"Yeah, I'm up for that," said Belle.

We had lots of theories about the murders but no proof of anything there either. Talking to Mona and Willie might help. Northampton, apparently, had more drug problems than most of its well-heeled, well-educated and non-addict population realized. Mona found hypodermic needles in the flowerpots in front of the Cool Rides garage on a regular basis. I saw an occasional junkie nodding off uptown. Once in a while there was a drug-related death reported in the local news. But most of the drug problems had stayed to the south, in the larger cities. Drug use was moving north and the police wanted to know who was delivering it.

Lucille decided it was bedtime and went next door. Belle said she had a book and disappeared into the bedroom.

Jon's cell phone rang. "Stevens." He sighed into it. It had been a long day and his was probably about to get longer. "Yeah, okay." Police lieutenants had to be available for a lot of hours.

It was a domestic violence with a restraining order and a warrant out on the woman involved. She wouldn't leave her boyfriend's apartment and patrol had called for backup.

He rose and went to the door. "Don't wait up."

My existence was becoming emotionally taxing. Understanding Susan's psychotic reasoning was way beyond my capacity. My brain needed a rest. I headed for bed.

Chapter Seventeen

The next morning, I was considering my choices for breakfast when my cell phone rang.

"Where are you?!" Mona barked. "I got rides coming out my ears. It's almost nine o'clock!"

"I'm on my way." I glanced at the clock, which said eight-thirty. I guessed time was relative.

Belle was leaning against one of the cabs when I arrived at work. "We got a special for the airport. That means both of us. You can ride shotgun and do the special part since my driving is so much better and you look like you might've gone shoe shopping to put a smile like that on your face.

"Hunh," I muttered but I was feeling good about having my apartment back, and I hadn't had a fight with Jon in almost twenty-four hours.

"Who's the special?"

"Elvira Snodhour. Lucille told her about our service and also told her, and I quote, 'you've got more money than God, Allah, and Buddha combined so don't be such a tightwad.' She doesn't usually use us but the cheap guys don't do the special consideration and she says she's getting too damn old to roll a wheelchair through crowded airports herself. She can't run over enough toes and her new cane is heavier because they don't make them the way they used to, so whacking shins has become burdensome from many viewpoints. Lucille told all this to Mona and said

223

that 'Miss Snodhour could be difficult.' You get to push this happy camper through security."

"I could drive, you could do the pushing," I said.

"Nah, you're too happy to drive. I'm still grumpy. Anyone cuts me off, I'll just run them into a bridge. Mrs. Elvira Snodhour will bring you back into reality. You'll be grumpy by the time we get back."

"Oh joy," I slid into the passenger seat.

We picked up Elvira at the retirement home in the independent living section. I found her in the lobby acting like an angry potentate about to lop off some unlucky peon's head. Squat and round with short white hair and an eternal frown on her wrinkled face, she looked like Buddha in need of lots of cosmetic surgery.

The receptionist came out, clearly relieved. "Oh, I am so glad you're here. She came down early to wait for you. I know what was wrong with last night's dinner, this morning's breakfast, her children, her siblings, every employer she ever had, and then she started on national politics."

I pushed Elvira out to the cab, helped her into the back and checked her seat belt. I jogged the wheelchair to the lobby.

"Good luck and have a happy ride," said the receptionist, smiling grimly.

I trotted out, buckled in, and gave Belle the thumbs up.

The complaints started before I got my seatbelt fastened. "And don't expect any tip. It's highway robbery to take advantage of an old lady. Just because we aren't as smart as a telephone these days doesn't mean we're stupid. And after I pay all those income taxes there's nothing left to pay for this stuff. You young people just don't know how to work these days. And you have no respect."

It was going to be a long ride.

"And you better not be like that other company. They stop everywhere and pick up anybody. I refuse to tolerate other passengers."

I sank down in my seat, hoping if she didn't see me she might stop complaining. Belle was ignoring her because Belle was plugged into her music.

"I will never use that company again."

She ranted the entire forty-five-minute trip. She criticized the airlines as I pushed her to security. She didn't like their taste in carpet, paint or interior decoration and she especially didn't like their taste in wheelchairs.

"Cheap and slapped together. It's a wonder it doesn't fall apart under me."

By the time I left her in the waiting area, I was looking around for something to whine about myself.

When I got back to the car, Belle unplugged herself from the music.

"Holy cow, shoot me now before I turn into her," she said. "I need some comfort food."

"I thought you were in music land and couldn't hear her."

"Honey, God could hear that woman and God is a long way away. And, did I mention, I need comfort food?"

We got back on the highway and Belle pulled in behind a truck keeping an even sixty-five miles an hour. We had seen three radar traps on the way down, so we were minding our manners. I was dreaming of all kinds of junk food when a late model Corvette screamed by. It was arrest red and had to be doing ninety. The cops would be busy chasing that Vette and wouldn't even notice us.

"There's my rabbit," said Belle and picked up the pace to seventy-five. Any experienced driver looked for a distraction for the speed traps. Belle was picking up the lingo of professional driving.

Sure enough, just before the Northampton exit, we saw the blue lights flashing and the Corvette's driver was scrambling to talk the cop out of a whopper of a ticket. We tootled by at seventy and pulled off the interstate. Anyone buying a car in that color shouldn't have broken the law or, at least, should have had a savings account dedicated to speeding tickets.

"The wolf got your rabbit." I grinned.

"Yeah, and I need donut holes. That way I can eat more and not get so full." We swung by the drive-through at Dunkin' Donuts and arrived at Cool Rides with a box full of holes. Mona popped a chocolate one in her mouth as the phone rang.

"Fool Rudes," she mumbled with a mouth full of comfort. She grabbed a bottle of water and swallowed hard. "Where are you and where would you like to be," she sang out, her mouth sort of empty.

"I'd like to leave a message for Belle." We could all hear the voice on the other end of the phone.

"This isn't a message service, it's a taxi company. Perhaps I can be of assistance." Mona was using her best I'm in charge here voice.

"This is Judge Witherspoon. I'd just like to leave my personal phone number for her to call." The voice matched Mona's in charge attitude.

"Oh, well, I'll be happy to pass that along to her," Mona said as Belle backed out the office door. Mona jotted down a number and tore off the paper. She hung up and we followed Belle outside.

"So, what's this about?" asked Mona.

"He's just some guy we picked up and brought to the courthouse. I assumed he was there as a defendant." She looked at me. "And don't act as if you weren't thinking the same."

"I know who Judge Witherspoon is!" Mona gave us both a withering look. Mona knew everyone and everything that ever happened in town. And what she didn't know she would soon. "Why does he want to talk to you? And why do you get his personal number?"

"We sort of hit it off during the ride. Then I learned he's a judge."

"What's wrong with being a judge?" asked Mona. "And with an ass like he's got, who cares?"

"I care. He's in law enforcement." Belle glanced at me. I thought about Jon who was about as in law enforcement as anyone could be. "And I'm not. In fact, I might describe myself as non-judgmental. And since judgmental is written into his job description, I don't see we have much in common."

I wondered how Mona knew about the judge's ass. I agreed about its fine form, but he is a judge and those robes hide a lot. I understood Belle's attitude. Jon and I would have the same problem. His attitude was if it was against the law, don't do it. I felt like there were so many laws that if I obeyed them all I wouldn't get out of bed in the morning. It was an ongoing source of disagreement.

"We got rides." She pointed to Belle. "Enough for you too, and I still think you should call the judge."

Belle held out her hand. "Just give me the ride."

Mona slapped paper into each of our hands. I noticed she had added the paper with the Judge's phone number to Belle's who stared at it for a moment before cramming it in her pocket. We compared rides to make sure we didn't want to swap. Belle got three college kids to the train station and I got a doctor's appointment for Mary, wheelchair needed. That meant I would take the Cool Rides collapsible chair which fit in the back of our cars. Most of the cab companies had their own wheelchairs to avoid transporting the heavier ones most people have for personal use. There are some private vans that strap down the heavier ones, but they require a ramp and hard lifting. The elder van had a hydraulic lift that was the envy of everyone. But that was taxpayer funded. So, off I went with our dinky, light-weight chair. Belle grinned and took off after the college kids hoping to be the next generation of world leaders.

When I got to Mary's house, she was waiting in her own wheelchair in the garage. We swapped chairs. I loaded her up and pushed her personal chair back into her garage. What Belle hadn't noticed and I hadn't mentioned was that the appointment was in Brattleboro, Vermont, my second favorite small town.

"I am so glad you do this. The van that takes my big chair makes about a million stops. They load up those big wheelchairs and then they unload them. I never know when I'm going to get where I'm going," Mary said as she fastened her seat belt, checked that the car had airbags and cautioned me to obey the speed limit.

I spent the afternoon in Brattleboro which was known for its artsy downtown and shared the dubious distinction with Northampton of being another major stop on the drug running corridor.

It was mid-afternoon when I got back to Cool Rides. Belle was sitting in a lawn chair in front of the garage windows, sunning herself.

"No rides for at least a half-hour," she said. "So you have time to share about how it's going with Lieutenant cutesy-wootsy. Do we need to go shopping?"

"Lucille kind of went shopping for me," I mumbled, not sure if I wanted to explain the super-sized, extra-sensitive, non-allergenic, scented, ultra-stimulating, ribbed condoms. I wasn't sure if I would ever use them.

"Does she have the same taste in under-garments as she has in dresses? 'Cause if she does, you need my help more than I thought."

"Nope. She told me peeling away layers is good foreplay but you better have a great last layer and you better deliver when that's gone."

"Shoes are the last layer. I know you have some good ones, but a new pair never hurts. There are things a woman can never have too much of, and shoes would be one of those. And undergarments, and handbags, and cute little jackets. I need to shop!"

"Yeah, I could use a new pair of slut shoes." I had a feeling Belle and I were on similar wavelengths in this conversation, so I dragged another chair over and sat with my face in the sun. I wanted to look healthy when I died of skin cancer.

"And about Mr. Hot-buns." Belle shifted so she could see my face and detect any half-truths, exaggerations or outright lies.

Mona came out before I had a chance to say much.

"Last ride for you. Two students to the mall and back. That's all I got."

"Hey, we can go together and peruse the smutty shoe selection and the never-there underwear while we wait for the kiddies to do whatever their daddy's dime allows. Smutty and tacky are a great combination." Belle held her foot in the air.

"Victoria's Secret. I rest my case." I looked down my shirt front and sighed.

"He who counts likes it." Belle grinned.

She was right about that but, judging from recent overnights at Jon's house, it was going to be a miracle if we got as far as using Lucille's gift. Not for lack of effort, my love life with Jon had been more wishful thinking and fantasy about what might happen than any actual happening. As far as we had gone was intense and exciting but the main event had yet to happen.

I bought a matching teddy and thong in silver glitter anyway. We hit the shoe selection and found four-inch spike-heel closed-toe glitz bombs to match. I would have bought the open-toes but by this time a pedicure wasn't in the budget.

The next morning I got to work without having used any of my shopping loot.

"You're up." Mona handed me a slip. "Get the battery pack out of the garage. This guy needs a ride to his dead car and wants us to get it started. Pick up in Hamp Heights."

"Where's the car and what do I charge for the jump?"

"In the lot behind the movie theater. Hit him for an extra ten." Mona paused. "You do know how to hook up a battery pack, right?"

"Well, um." I had used jumper cables but never a battery pack. "Is it the same as jumper cables?"

Belle wandered over from parking her new to her Mini Cooper.

"Come on, I know how to use that. When I lived in Maine, we used to bring the pack in every night in the winter. Then we'd start five cars in the morning. I also know how to hotwire." She turned to Mona. "You got a run for me or you want me to take Ms. Helpless here to jump the car?"

"Go ahead. But come right back. No shoe shopping, or if you do, my size is seven," she said.

We got to Hampshire Heights and found the address. It was the worst of the worst. The kid who came out was barely driving age. His pants were the hang low style, wife-beater tee shirt, oversized, untied shoes, baseball hat sideways, jacket open and off the shoulder. His face was in eternal scowl mode and he had a tattoo of a car on his shoulder. He was the poster boy for Gang Bangers Are Us. I hoped he had a driver's license and then reminded myself it wasn't my business.

I collected twenty dollars for the ride and jump and we headed to the mega movie complex at the local mall. He and Belle chatted about living in the Heights.

Belle shared a couple of war stories and had the kid laughing in five minutes.

When we got there, he didn't seem to remember where the car was parked. I could understand that. I spent the better part of two hours finding a car the first time I was in a mega-parking facility.

"Just drive around for a while. I'll find it." He was fidgeting and beads of sweat popped out on his forehead.

We went up and down a few rows and he finally pointed at a brand-new evil looking black Corvette.

"That's your car!?" Belle leaned out the window, gawking.

"What, you think just 'cause I live at the Heights I can't have a good car?"

"Kid, there is no way on God's earth we are jumping that car for you. I don't think you can get inside anyway. You got a key?"

"I'm gonna get something. I told them I would get something." The kid seemed to deflate now that he was confronted with the reality of grand theft auto.

"Told who?"

"The Car Studs. They jack cars."

"And you want to be in with them?"

"Hey, man, that's who's there. It ain't like I got a big choice. Jackin' cars is safer than runnin' drugs. A lot of guys start by selling, then they do the product and then 'BOOM' they're dead. I'd rather do cars. You ever seen Gone in Sixty Seconds? I could be Nicolas Cage."

"Okay, I'm taking you home," I said.

"What!? Hey, Mama, what you doin'? I need to get goin' here."

"Which you can do. Just not on my watch."

"I could teach him how to hot wire it. Then he gets to make up his own mind, take responsibility for himself," Belle added helpfully.

"Hey, yo' sista, you know how to get me that car? Turn around. We can make this happen. I am so up for takin' responsibility for me."

"Jesus, Belle!"

"Or we could take him to the Counseling Center."

Belle and I had made the acquaintance of a shrink when he went to Holyoke to meet a client and came back to find all the wheels and tires removed from his car. We were the only cab company who would come get him. And we only did that because there were two of us and he paid accordingly. He worked in a private agency specializing in guiding at risk teens away from the gangs and crews.

I was deciding whether this kid had enough potential to dump him on our favorite shrink when Belle muttered, "Or I could jack the car for him."

We all sat and stared at the mega-car. I had to admit if any car in the entire lot was worth the effort, it would be that one. Probably well insured too. I found myself having less sympathy for the owner of the excessively macho, expensive car than I did for the kid who was trying to keep his head above the gang structure provided by his situation.

"Okay, okay. Counsel Center it is. You're in luck," I addressed the kid. And drove him to see the first psychiatrist of his short car-jacking career. There was some resistance when we got there but Belle grabbed his ear when he jumped out of the car. She could go from complete relaxation to high speed in the time it took me to open my eyes. She had him inside the Center before he could figure out what the alternatives were. She came back out in five minutes with a big smile on her face.

"That is one fine looking shrink," she said and plopped herself on the passenger seat. "Almost makes me want to be neurotic. Back to home base."

"As if," I laughed. Belle was one of the most stable people I knew. Despite her background, she could deal with social situations that made me cringe.

"Wait a minute! Does this mean you would date a shrink but not a judge? What's wrong with a judge that isn't just as wrong with a shrink?"

"Hey, I just said he's hot. And a judge is a whole lot closer to the law than a shrink and you know how I feel about the law. Besides, I'm as well adjusted as they come, so I never said I wanted to screw him."

"Well, Adjusted is our middle name."

"Adjusted R Us?"

"If I were any more stable my feet would be glued to the floor."

We were laughing enough to threaten my undies when we pulled into Cool Rides.

Mona met us in the parking lot. "Lucille to the Senior Center, students to class because they missed the bus because their roomie was talking on her phone because, because. I could tell you their life history." And she handed us each a fare slip.

Lucille was finishing her gun cleaning project and putting it all away when I got there. There was a platter of fresh cookies and bags of cookies to take to the Senior Center. I assumed the plate was for immediate consumption so I took one for each hand. Chocolate chip-walnut-oatmeal, and chocolate-macadamia nut-cranberry. I made sure I finished them before I got in the car. I did need my hands free for driving. Maybe not as bad as texting and driving, but Lucille's cookies defined distraction.

"How is young Jonny?"

Even though the houses shared an inside wall, Jon's bedroom was buffered by the guest bedrooms so I didn't think Lucille could hear any noise that might send her diving for her vibrator...on the off chance such noises would ever get produced.

"Oh, he's doing fine. He still hasn't figured out how Mr. Scarpelli is transporting his drugs up the interstate and that's making him crazy.

"I thought that horrid other taxi company was involved in drug transport."

"Lucky Limo? The cops watched all the livery or taxi license plates for a while but they couldn't find anything. So, it's back to square one."

"Perhaps that was all in Ms. Scarpelli/Young's chaotic imagination."

I dropped Lucille at the Senior Center laden with cookies, brass knuckles and all the accouterments needed for senior bridge games. She had, fortunately, left her Glock at home.

I went back to see if Belle had returned from taking the talking heads to class and to find out if she had used the judge's personal phone number.

When I pulled in, the Judge was there, leaning against his car. Belle was standing nearby, apparently pretending he wasn't there. When I opened the door, he shook his head, waved to me, got in his car and left.

"That was interesting," I said.

"Yeah, whatever." Belle clearly didn't want to discuss it. I decided to ask her for some advice about my relationship with Jon. If that didn't open her up, nothing would.

"So, Jon likes silver glitz." I started cautiously. "At least he says he does, but I'm still working on that."

"Huhn," Belle grunted, knowing exactly what I was doing.

"I'm trying to decide where to go from here."

Silence.

"Okay, I give up." I started to walk into the office.

"I just don't see him as friend material. He's gonna want commitment and all that shit. I'm not cut out for that. Especially if he finds out what my past life entailed."

"So, tell him. If he still wants to be friends, great. It'll keep you off jury duty anytime he's the judge. You do remember my relationship with Jon started when he busted me."

"That no jury duty thing is a nice silver lining. And speaking about silver and Jon, what, exactly, did he do to prove how much he likes silver glitz?"

Oh good, back on track.

"More than you're letting his judgeship do. The question is, why do we pick men that see commitment as a way of life? I think Jon and the judge probably agree on that. And you and I probably agree even more. No commitment, no responsibility, life is free, the way it's meant to be."

"Yeah, it's a myth that men play around more than women. And then some stupid woman said 'men will be men' and now we have to prove 'women will be women' and screw whatever we want."

"Wow, the judge really put you in a mood."

"Damn right." Belle huffed, fluffed her hair and stalked inside.

I followed, feeling like she was at least in a better mood than she had been when the judge left. Maybe Mona would have a few good rides.

She did. Each of us got two rides to the airport, numerous deliveries of people to doctor's appointments, and I finished the day with Lucille going home from the Senior Center.

I was still early on in my relationship with Jon so, even though I had a key, I knocked as I opened the door to his house. He was already home, watching the local news on his big screen TV. I stood next to him and realized the news was about Jon. He had stopped a heroin overdose because he carried Narcan. Someone with a smart phone got lucky and filmed Jon as he administered the drug. It was a touching moment and the department would get lots of mileage out of it.

Jon off buttoned the TV, sank down on the couch, stared at the blank screen.

"If I hadn't had that stuff on me, he would have died. He was only fourteen years old."

I sat next to him and leaned my head on his shoulder.

"Will the department start issuing it?"

"I'll sure as hell strongly recommended it."

We sat for a few minutes. Then Jon put his arms around me. He sank into the couch and just held me. I put my arm across his body and hugged.

He kissed the top of my head. "Until they legalize this stuff and put it under a doctor's care, we need to find the transport. We need to fucking bust Scarpelli's operation."

"I'll keep my ears open."

"No! Stay away from Scarpelli. I don't want to worry about you. He won't go after you again. And the other transport companies know we're keeping an eye on them. He's using something else." Jon held me a little tighter.

I knew, but didn't say, that his protective attitude would NOT affect the way I lived my life or worked my job. My ears were always open. It's a necessary personality trait for a taxi driver.

By ten o'clock we finished pizza, watched two mind numbing comedy shows and were both yawning. It had been a long day for both of us.

Jon took my hand and led me to the bedroom, making it clear where I was spending the night. I put on an oversized tee shirt since I didn't get the Vicki's Secret vibe from Jon tonight. When we got in bed, Jon just pulled me to him, wrapped his arms around me and dozed off. Sometimes sex is a good antidote to death, sometimes not. Fortunately for Jon, the kid hadn't died, but he was still in an off mood.

Jon left early the next morning. He would have lots of paperwork about the near-death overdose. And I knew he would pay the kid a visit. At eight o'clock I got up and hit the shower. I was running early and the smell of fresh coffee drifted over from Lucille's part of the house. I decided to see if she had breakfast cookies as well. That would mean oatmeal, hopefully with chocolate chips.

I knocked and heard her sing out, "Coming." She threw the lock and opened the door a crack. "Oh, Honey, I have cookies so do come in. But I won't be going to the Senior Center for a while yet." She had a smile that made me suspicious, and she was still in her bathrobe.

Then I smelled bacon. Lucille never cooked bacon.

I stepped inside and started toward the kitchen. I stopped so suddenly Lucille bumped into me. There was a man sipping coffee at the table. He was somewhere in his seventies, thick white hair, slim build, sparkling blue eyes...in a word, quite the hunk.

"Honey, this is Arnie Delisle. Arnie, Honey Walker. She drives the Cool Rides taxi. Do have some cookies, dear." She motioned to the plate on the counter. "Or would you rather join us for breakfast?"

"Breakfast?" I croaked out. "I better get to work. Call us when you need us." I retreated out the door and rushed to my taxi. "Need to get to Belle, need to get to Belle," I muttered under my breath. For all Lucille's talk about sex and how to accomplish it, I had never seen her the morning after and I had never met the object of the evening before. I felt like a kid who just realized my existence proves my parents had sex. Belle, whose experience was as vast as the Rocky Mountains compared to my little hills, could tell me I was overreacting. And how old was he? And what were his intentions? And, most important, should I tell Jon?

I pulled into Cool Rides and sighed with relief when I saw Belle's Mini Cooper. I hustled inside, took a deep breath and began to feel silly. I would mention the existence of Arnie in an offhand way and see how Belle reacted.

"Hey," I said to Mona. "We got anything special this morning?"

"Not until ten o'clock. Then I got two airports, one for each of you."

Belle wandered back outside. Her radar must have picked up my mood and she wanted to know details.

"Okay, spit it out," she said when I joined her.

"This is weird. Well, maybe I'm weird."

"You're definitely weird and, right now, wired. What did the sweet Lieutenant do to you?"

"It's Lucille. She's got a boyfriend!"

"Only one?"

"I mean, I went over this morning and he was having breakfast with her. She was cooking bacon. In her bathrobe."

"Bacon...sounds serious. What's he look like?"

"A hunk. Well, a seventy something hunk."

"Good for Lucille, a younger man, or maybe an older one. I've never established a firm age for Lucille. Anyway, a young stud. I like it."

"Why do I feel like I walked in on my parents? And, you're right, I'm not sure he's a younger man. Lucille has never revealed her age to me either." I sighed.

"Just make sure his intentions are dishonorable and ask if he has a supply of condoms. And, yeah, Lucy could be anywhere over sixty, maybe even fifty-five if I squint. She does keep herself well."

"Lucille has plenty of condoms. She wouldn't need to tap anyone else's supply."

"What's his name?" Belle assumed I had taken the time to get some information. She was right but not nearly enough.

"Arnie Delisle."

"You're kidding. Lucille Ball and Desi Arnaz, Lucille and Arnie?"

"Oh, yeah, I didn't think about that." I giggled.

We were about to stop the giggles and start the real conversation when Mona came out with fare slips.

"You got Sister Mary Claire," she said, handing me the slip. "She's flying to New York to meet with her publisher."

"You got Mrs. Witherspoon who is going to visit her sister in Baltimore." She handed Belle the slip.

"What!? Give the judge's mother to Honey. I'll take the Sister Mary Claire. I'll even drive her to New York. Did you tell her I could do that?"

"Mrs. W is a long-time customer and she requested you. Probably wants to see why her son is in such a lousy mood these days. Because somebody won't even go have a cup of freakin' coffee with the man. Anyway, what she wants, she gets." Mona glowered and Belle knew there was no arguing. Okay with me. I loved driving Sister Mary Claire. I gave Belle a finger wave and drove off.

Chapter Eighteen

Sister Mary Claire was dressed in a light blue civilian power suit and waiting in front of one of the few Catholic churches left in town. With a shrinking population and four churches the congregations had combined to support the one building the Springfield diocese deemed to be the chosen one. The other buildings were up for sale. But with a new Pope the Sister had high hopes. She was busily raising money for her church's many projects. She worked with the homeless, the poor, sick children, poor children, the poor elderly, the sick elderly and any other group of disadvantaged and disenfranchised souls that would have her. She raised money, lots of it, for her various charities in a most unique and discreet manner.

Sister Mary Claire wrote porn. Sometimes she wrote erotica. But mostly she said she didn't have time to make up plots and characters required by erotica. Straight out porn took no time and paid well. All proceeds went to charity. Her vow of poverty was as intact as her vow of chastity which, according to the Sister, was never in doubt. Most of the world assumed the cute short stories she occasionally published were the source of her cash flow. But the taxi driver always knows the truth. Put two people in a car together for any length of time and talk happens. I had become Sister's confessor; my taxi, the confessional. And I kept the secrets to myself. I had, in the privacy of my apartment, proof-read some of the Sister's material. Wowza! Even in the porn industry, there are standards and spell check doesn't catch everything. So the Sister had a problem finding people to help with the proofing. Discretion was extremely important. I was one of her privileged beta readers. God! I loved my job.

I would enjoy the ride to the airport and then I could listen to what happened between Belle and Mrs. Witherspoon when I got back.

The Sister got in the front seat. That meant she wanted to talk. If she had chosen the back seat, she was in work mode, would have her laptop out and would not want to be disturbed. The ride to the airport was too short for writing mode.

"I need a name," she said without any lead in.

"Whose name do you need?"

"The hunk. And he needs to be virile but mature enough to have outgrown his stupid days. Successful and really hot in bed. Has to know what a female orgasm is and how to coax it out of a woman of any age and experience. Got it?"

"Oh, yeah." I thought immediately about Jon but decided not to suggest it. My experience to date was limited to foreplay but I was certain Jon was going to fill my fantasies just fine. I might be the Sister's confessor, but she didn't fill the confessor role for me. Belle was as close to having a confessor as I came.

"Right now, I'm just looking for the name. I've got the character, but names are important. I think this may be a romance. I'm running the possibility by my publisher. That's why we're having a face to face. I need to convince him I can do plot and character more effectively than one needs in pornography."

"Sister, you work with a lot of people in harsh circumstances, right?"

"Oh, yes. Part of my calling."

"Why don't you write about them? A love conquers all sort of theme?"

Dead silence filled the car. I hoped I hadn't crossed some sort of line. Could she really put her separate lives in closed compartments and never let them cross over?

Suddenly Sister Mary Claire turned to me. "Oh, my Lord! The Holy Father must have sent you to me today. How could I have not thought of that? I know exactly what I can write. Oh, I am so excited. I still need a name."

"How about Captain America's alter ego? He's real popular right now."

"Captain who?"

"Steve Rogers. He's a comic book character who goes around saving the world."

"That's a good name. Short, easily remembered."

We still had a half hour to go before we got to the airport, but the sister leaned her head back and closed her eyes.

"I must think for a few moments. Will you wake me when we get to the off-ramp?"

"No problem." I smiled.

As I helped Sister out of the cab and unloaded her carry-on, she handed me her charge card. "Please add a thirty-dollar tip."

"Whoa, are you sure?"

"Honey, this concept is going to sell like hotcakes. I just know it. I'll tell you all about it when you pick me up."

I ran the charge card through my phone attachment and handed it back to her, hoping she wasn't being too optimistic. When she had disappeared into the terminal I spotted Belle pulling in behind me with Mrs. Witherspoon.

"Now, my dear, I have never had such a pleasant ride to the airport. You be sure to put that tip on there," she said, handing over her charge card. I grinned and waited so we could caravan back.

We did a sedate seventy until we got off the highway. I let my mind wander to Jon's problem about how the drugs were being moved on this road I was traveling. We pulled up in front of Cool Rides together. Belle came over and opened my door for me.

"Those slut shoes are real close to my closet. That woman knows how to tip."

"Geez, Sister Mary Claire too. Shopping tonight. Maybe I'll pay the rent too." I grinned and worked hard not to giggle.

"I saw some purple pumps, ankle strap, only a three-inch heel, dual purpose. I can wear them to choir practice. I need those shoes!" Belle fist pumped the air.

"New undies for me," I sighed happily.

"Yeah, gotta have something for the hot Lieutenant to take off your overheated bod." Belle beamed.

"Uh, huh." I smirked.

We went inside to tell Mona how much we loved her.

"Next rides are at twelve thirty so you should take an early lunch." Mona held up two fare slips. "I take it you're willing to take Mrs. W wherever she wants to go. I'll put you down for her pick-up. Same for you and the Sister?" Mona looked to me.

"You betcha! How many colors of thongs do they make and how do you wear them outside the bedroom?" I asked to the room in general. I wondered if Mona ever wore thongs.

"You don't," said Belle. "Let's do lunch. Call if you need us." She saluted Mona and we trooped out the door.

"So, I take it the judge wasn't discussed." I tried to match Belle's stride.

"Hell, no. His mama is a lady of big brain. She knows when to let it rest. Unlike other people I might know. We talked accessories. Shoes, bags, scarves, the woman knows her fashion."

"Okay, fine," I grumped.

"Pizza, pizza?" Belle sashayed up the hill to Main Street. I really needed her to teach me how to walk. I flumped after her.

The crowd at the counter of Pizza Palace was three deep and long. We were working our way forward when we heard a commotion behind us. Reverend Slime, one of the local street dealers, staggered forward, knocking his way through the crowd.

"Gimme the key to the can. I gotta take a shit fast!" he yelled at the kid behind the counter. He jittered around, eyes bouncing from wall to ceiling and back.

"Oh joy!" muttered Belle, "Now we all get to eat with that image in our mental makeup."

I stared morosely at the display of pizza. Eating suddenly became less important. But my stomach won out over the gross Rev. Slime and I ordered a slice of black bean avocado with lots of other stuff on it.

Rev. Slime pushed his way back through the line to the men's room. He had some trouble inserting the key but, finally, got it open and lurched inside.

We all knew Rev. Slime not because he was a taxi customer but because he was the dealer for the street people and downtown teenage population. He had big expensive cars and gold chains around his neck. He also had a sign that said "Minister" that he placed on the dash of those expensive cars in the hopes that he might avoid a parking ticket. It never worked and he was on a first name basis with the parking clerks. His car had been booted more than once. Recently he had started using his product and wasn't looking good. The police watched him but hadn't been able to bust him. He was a complete reprobate but a smart one. They couldn't catch him actually doing any of the deals we all knew he did. He specialized in schizophrenic cocaine addicts and runaway teens. They made terrible witnesses.

We finally got food, slid into a booth unfortunately near the men's room, and ate in record time. Then we started on dessert. Normally we wouldn't do dessert after pizza, but the Palace was having a special on organic chocolate covered bacon. What could be more nutritious and healthy? Belle was sucking on the last bite when someone yelled out, "He's been in there too long. Gimme the damn key."

Someone came out from behind the counter with the spare key. He knocked on the door. No answer so he unlocked the door. Regrettably we had a perfect sight line to the toilet. Rev. Slime had used a bit too much of his product, pitched forward off the commode, bashed his face and left a pool of blood on the floor. A trail of slimy brown followed him from the seat to his ass. His pants were around his knees and a needle flopped out of his arm.

"Shit!" whispered the counter kid. "Call 911!!" he screamed, backing out of the closet sized space. My phone was on the table in front of me so I made the call but I noticed at least five other people with cell phones out. The dispatch console must have lit up like a fireworks factory hit by lightning.

In less than two minutes we heard sirens and in three minutes the EMT was through the door. He knelt next to Slime's body, feeling for a pulse.

"Bring the stretcher," he spoke into his shoulder radio. "And a body bag. No hurry."

"That's not good," said Belle. I wasn't so sure she was right but I kept silent. If someone had to go, at least it wasn't one of the teenagers he sold his lethal product to.

Fifteen minutes later we walked down the hill, listening to the siren wail its way up to the hospital. We knew The Reverend Mr. Slime would be declared DOA, Jon would hear about it immediately, and it would be all over the front page in the morning. The police would be frustrated about their inability to find Scarpelli's transportation lines. Not many people would grieve the loss of Rev. Slime. He would be replaced as a retailer of fine drugs fast enough that his customers would only suffer a short and temporary bout of hysteria. But now I had seen first-hand how messy an overdose could be. No one deserved that.

Belle and I spent the rest of the day running short hauls to court dates, lawyer dates, and a few report-for-incarceration dates. We even had a few doctor dates. By the end of our shifts we were ready to crash. Belle headed for her newly rented apartment and I walked over to Jon's house. Belle offered me a ride but I needed to be alone and quiet for a few minutes. I really didn't like Mr. Slime but I had made the mistake of naming him. So his death was a shock. The walk to Jon's house was all of ten minutes but it put me in a better mood.

Jon, on the other hand, was still in his frenzy of having been presented with another heroin overdose. He was pacing around the house, muttering to himself when I walked in.

He turned when I opened the door and stared blankly at me. Then he wrapped me in his arms and held me for a long minute.

"I'm sorry you had to witness that mess," he whispered.

"I'm okay. I didn't really know him very well. He was a slimy guy. We called him Rev. Slime."

Jon leaned back from his embrace. "Not to his face, I hope."

"No, I never talked to him and he never used a taxi because he had those big cars. I did watch him sell to someone who should not have had more medication than his doctor gave him. You do know that was his specialty? That and kids."

"Yeah, we knew. We just wanted to find out who supplied him before we busted his ass."

"I guess no one deserves to die young." But if anyone did, I thought, it would have been Rev. Slime. I kept that to myself.

Jon dropped his arms but held onto my hand. "I picked up Italian take-out on the way home. I guess we should eat." We sat and watched the mind-numbing account of the afternoon events on the local news. Apparently, several of the cell phones I saw weren't being used to phone 911. The short film clips of Rev. Slime's body being hauled away made the evening news. By the time we had worked our way through the Comedy Channel for a few hours, we were both giving in to the exhaustion of a long day.

We sat on the couch for a little longer and held each other. Death made both of us need some live physical contact without any sex involved. We fell asleep wrapped around each other.

That attitude lasted until sometime in the wee hours of the morning when I woke up to something long and hard resting between us. Unfortunately for Jon's erection, it was his cell phone that interrupted our sleep. He groaned and rolled off the bed. I knew he wouldn't be back for hours, so I rolled the other direction and went back to sleep. The next thing I remembered was the smell of fresh coffee brewing. I found him in the kitchen looking far too awake for someone who had been up since four in the morning.

Jon gave me a ride to work and followed me in the door.

Mona handed me a ten-dollar bill, pointed to one of the cabs and said, "Lucille, an emergency. Arnie forgot to pick up condoms. Go by Quik Shop and pick up a package of large and take them over to her house. Don't stop, do not collect two hundred dollars, and don't land on boardwalk. She seems to be in a hurry."

Jon rolled his eyes. "Jesus! I don't want to hear any more. I'm at work now." And he shoved out the door.

Welcome to my world, Jon. We deliver whatever you need—people, toilet paper, condoms. My guess was he knew about Arnie, had probably even met him, but didn't want to think about Lucille pounding the mattress.

"Go!" said Mona, and I hustled off on my mission. I got to the grocery store where you could buy a lot more than groceries. The condoms were prominently displayed by the pharmacy counter. There were different sizes, materials, colors, smells, shapes and probably some other possibilities I missed. Strangely, I had never purchased condoms. I certainly had no idea what size Arnie might be or what color Lucille might like. I had never asked, in the course of conversation: "So what's your favorite color in condoms?" I finally grabbed the regular large pack, dashed to check-out and left the store more aware of the difficult decisions men have to make.

When I got to Lucille's house and rang the bell, I heard the locks throw, slide and finally click back. Lucille peeked out.

"Oh, thank God. I was running out of ways to keep it on track and upright. At our age, it can be difficult. And we don't really need the glove, but it's just so much fun to slide the little...well, big,

251

actually...maybe enormous is more accurate...onto that oversized dong. And I do always practice safe sex."

Lucille slammed the door and I heard her footsteps retreat at a rapid pace. I realized she had been wearing an identical silver sparkle teddy to mine. I hadn't been able to see Lucille's bottom half so the thong was still a mystery. This had been my first fare of the day so Arnie had spent the night again.

I drove slowly back to Cool Rides, thinking about growing old. Lucille seemed to be in the peak of health for someone of elderly but unknown age. But what happened when your body or mind failed you? This was one of the few times I had heard Lucille make a reference to aging and it was in reference to her favorite topic—sex. How did she deal with what I'm told by the media is a significant loss of sexual activity over the age of fifty? Would Jon still find me interesting when I'm sixty-four? More important, of course, is whether I will find him interesting. A good topic for woman talk. I decided to ask Belle what she thought. Then I mentally kicked myself. I was thinking thirty plus, big plus, years in the future. Would Jon still be around, would the world still exist or would the comet finally have found our blue planet and decided it was time to start the long process of evolution over again?

Asking Belle had to wait until afternoon because Mona came out with fare slips before I even got out of the car. Five local fares, all with their own wheelchairs, light weight and collapsible. I could do one right after the other and do enough lifting that I wouldn't dream of joining a gym. Even the light weight chairs needed to be wrestled into the back of the car. A lot of our clients and the population in general use wheelchairs, walkers, canes, or some sort of assistance staying upright and mobile.

Belle had snagged a run to Logan Airport in Boston. Those shoes would be hers before the gold lamé thong would be part of my bedroom wardrobe. Short hauls were always interesting and usually fun but they didn't pay the bills and they rarely tipped. When Belle finally returned, she was moaning about the Mass Pike traffic. It was so bad she had to stop at one of the mega-malls just off the highway which just happened to be having a huge shoe sale which just happened to have lots of shoes in her size.

"Being a lady of height, I have size 10 feet. My size goes on sale first."

I thought Mona might be angry that Belle had stopped on company time and in a company vehicle but Belle pulled out a pair of red suede ankle boots in, of course, Mona's size, which proved Belle had a well-developed sense of survival. She handed me a pair of red thongs with a big black arrow pointing down.

"I'm sure your Lieutenant knows the right direction, but it never hurts to reinforce it," she said.

Then she pulled out the five boxes of shoes that were clearly marked size 10.

Chapter Nineteen

We had finished admiring Belle's shopping spree when the phone rang.

"Ride up," said Mona, as she practiced walking in her new boots. They had only two-inch heels but required practice for someone who habitually wore sneakers. Mona handed me the fare slip absently as she marveled at how her feet had been transformed.

"It's Mary Clarkson. She has her own travel chair but you'll need to help her inside. She'll call for a pick-up when she's done," Mona said distractedly. Now I knew what to do when Mona needed a mood change.

Mary was sitting in her travel chair in the driveway. She was bubbling with excitement by the time I got her and the chair into the car.

"I'm going to a 'people in chairs' convention. I get to see new products and talk to other people who are mobility challenged. It's going to be so much fun."

We got to the hotel where the mini convention was being held and there was a woman madly wheeling her chair around the parking lot pointing people in five different directions. She screeched to a stop at the passenger side of the taxi and handed Mary a sheet of instructions and a ribbon.

"Get yourself seated and then they'll park your chair in the room to the right of the door where you go in. Here's a colored ribbon to help you identify it when you come out."

"Oh, nice, I get a purple ribbon." Mary smiled.

I got her situated and pushed her travel chair into the storage room. It was a parking lot for every color, shape, and size of wheelchair, travel chair, cane, crutches, and other devices to help the mobility challenged. I left her chair in the sea of equipment that helps people from point A to point B, its purple ribbon prominently displayed. I noticed, however, at least ten other purple ribbons. Not being a mobility-challenged person, I had never noticed the subtle differences in the modes of transport before. I was amazed at the variety. Mary's was pretty standard. No embellishments other than the ribbon. Using regular chairs at the tables was the difference between four people at a table and six. Wheelchairs take up a lot of space, so those who could, occupied regular chairs.

Traffic brought me to a standstill on the way back and when I got to the garage, Mary had just called. Sometimes it's easier to stay put.

When I got back to Cool Rides it was end of shift and Belle had already left. I knew Jon was working late so I decided to spend the night at my apartment. I read the first hundred pages of Fifty Shades of Grey and decided everyone was a little kinky but some people had lots of money and their kinky was more easily practiced. I fell asleep dreaming of thwacking Jon with a riding crop as I rode him like a pony. I always wanted a pony.

The next morning, I arrived at work in time for coffee which Mona had made with a new coffee maker we had all chipped in for when we realized it was cheaper than the five dollars we were spending each morning on the way to work. I sat long enough to get comfortable with coffee and the newspaper. Just as I got to the most important part of the paper, the comics, Mona came out of her lair with a fare slip.

"You need to go get Lucille. She's at the hospital recovery unit."

"She okay?"

"Oh yeah, it's Arnie. He broke his leg. Fortunately, after they finished using the condoms you took her. He was walking down the sidewalk. My suspicion is his mind was filled with other wonders and walking wasn't one of them."

"Do I need to take the wheelchair?"

"Nope, Arnie is under house arrest for a few days before he can come home and Miss Lucille sure as hell doesn't need a wheelchair. She'd probably pop a wheelie. She's gonna want you to take her back and forth to visit Arnie for a while, so plan on that. Maybe take the car home or to Jon's house, or wherever tonight."

When I got to the recovery unit, which was essentially a nursing home, Lucille was outside waiting for me. Arnie's fall had taken place before Lucille had a chance to get fully dressed. She was in a pair of dark slacks and a long shirt. Her usual dress mode of old lady flower print dress had disappeared. And she was without her sensible shoes! She was wearing low-heeled slut shoes. Slut shoes don't have to have six-inch spike heels. Hers were open toed, red satin with black beads. She dressed differently when Arnie was around and looked ten years younger. There was a hint of darkness on her eyelid and, oh Lord, was that mascara? I was trying to decide whether this was a good development in Lucille's life when she yanked open the door and plopped herself onto the front passenger seat.

"This is becoming a very long one-night stand and somewhat inconvenient. I told him I'd come back for a visit later tonight as I do feel a bit responsible for all this. I'll expect you to pick me up at six and I'll call when I need you to return for me."

Wow! I had never heard Lucille complain about a one-night stand before. I wasn't really sure she had any...either one-night stands or complaints. If she did, she was very discreet about both.

"I can do that."

"Very well. But the only way this will be worth the effort is if I get an after-dinner aperitif, if you understand me."

Uh, oh. I definitely understood Lucille. Public places suited her fine when it came to sex. I wondered if Arnie felt the same and if it might be difficult for him to perform adequately under such circumstances.

"You might want to give him a few days to recover. Having a leg break must be traumatic. And the nursing home must have some rules. Like a lights-out time, no visitors after nine?"

"If he has trouble getting it up, he can use other parts of his body. He may not be the smartest penis to pop but he does know how to use all of his attributes. Although, I must admit, conversation is a bit of a chore. He is willing to experiment and that's a positive. I'll expect you at six. We should be done before nine, but I'll call, so keep the phone on. And you might want to stay at Jonny's house tonight."

Lucille was a little flustered and her speech was sort of run-on. I kept quiet and let her ramble about

Arnie on the way home. I found out he had fallen out of bed rather than walking down the sidewalk. Getting him respectably dressed had been almost impossible but they both thought it for the best that he be fully clothed when the ambulance arrived.

"Arnie has a high pain threshold and that's a point in his favor. We even got him as far as the living room before the medics saw him. Still, I think he isn't long-term for me. But tonight would be a nice good-bye," said Lucille.

After I dropped her at home, presumably to recover from her long night and longer morning, I headed back to Cool Rides. It was an uneventful day unless you count the garbage truck blowing up and catching fire on the interstate. But it was behind me as I made my airport run so it didn't impede my progress. It made lots of explosive noises which followed us down the road, but my customer made the flight no problem with some good stories about her narrow escape from being covered with flying debris.

When I got back Mona had me haul a big screen TV from Walmart to a "single room occupancy" rooming house. The TV would take up the entire single room. The new owner of the TV said it was better than listening to anyone else who lived in the adjoining single rooms. I helped him carry the TV inside and it sounded like the war of the new technology. If his neighbor had a loud TV, he needed one louder.

"If we're watching the same show, I just turn off my sound. His fills in fine. But I need to override him sometimes."

I got back to Cool Rides at five o'clock and told Mona I would take Lucille to the nursing home and then leave the phone on in case she wanted a ride home. When I picked her up, it looked like she might spend the night since she was still dressed in her slacks, top and, most importantly, her fabulous shoes.

I dropped her off, drove back to Jon's house and fell asleep in front of Jon's big screen TV. I woke up at seven the next morning in Jon's bed. No sign of Jon. No calls from Lucille. I hoped she had enjoyed the evening without being arrested. I especially hoped the absence of both Jon and Lucille wasn't related. Jon had been home because I was in his bed and I hadn't put myself there. I showered, dressed. No word from Lucille, so I drove to Cool Rides to start my day.

By the middle of the day, I had run two people to the big international airport and picked up two more from the mini local airport which was too small to land planes bigger than ten passengers. No Lear jets, which was unfortunate, as people using one might have yielded some large tips. But anyone flying in their own plane for convenience had the bucks to tip well. By five o'clock I was beginning to wonder what had happened to Lucille. Mona hadn't heard from her.

A few minutes later Belle drove in.

"Hey, you want to go to a nursing home?" I asked as she extracted herself from the car.

"I've had a rough day, but I don't think I look that bad."

"To visit Arnie and see what's happened to Lucille. You look fine. What's been rough about your day?"

"Whoa, slow down. Arnie is in a nursing home?"

I realized Belle hadn't been around yesterday when Mona sent me off to fetch Lucille from and then back to the nursing home.

"He fell out of Lucille's bed and broke his leg. He's at the recovery home. But we haven't heard from Lucille since I dropped her off there for dinner last night. I thought I'd check it out, see how Arnie is doing."

"Yeah, okay, I'm in. Might as well see where I'll be in forty years, plus or minus."

We took Belle's Mini Cooper since she always wanted to drive it. If Lucille needed a ride it had four seats, sort of. We could cram me in the back and Lucille, who was less flexible, would get shotgun.

When we arrived at the nursing home the parking lot was almost full. Belle found a space between two large vans and pulled the Mini in. It instantly became invisible. We walked up the long and sloped sidewalk to the automatic doors. They slid silently open, triggered by some unseen infrared beam.

I approached the reception desk. "We're looking for Arnie Delisle. He broke his leg yesterday."

The woman behind the desk had poufy hair and a shirt that was a little too tight across a large chest. She pulled a pencil out of her hair and ran it down the list of new arrivals.

"Room 104. Down the hallway on the left." She went back to reading her soap opera magazine.

We found room 104 and knocked softly.

"About time! Get in here, where you been?" The voice was male and demanding.

I poked my head around the corner. Arnie was in bed. The bed next to his was empty.

"Oh, I thought you were Lucille. She left...let's see...sometime last night, for Christ's sake. I thought she'd run out on me. She was supposed to find a wheelchair to take me outside. Don't know where the hell she went," he whined.

"Hi Arnie, I'm Honey, Lucille's driver. We met before. This is Belle. She works for the cab company too."

"I know who you are. I just want to know where Lucille is. She walked out on me. I really need to see the sun just for a few minutes," he continued to complain.

"We could do that," I said and looked questioningly at Belle.

"Sure, why not? You go get the chair, I'll keep Mr. Cheerful here company," Bell said and winked.

I walked to the reception desk and inquired where I might find a spare wheelchair.

"There's a whole room full of them." She pointed. "Two doors after where you came out. Take any one. But be careful of the door. It locks from the outside. If it closes behind you, you're in there until someone misses you. Which may be never."

I trotted down the hall, opened the door, being careful to brace it with my foot, and snagged the first chair from a sea of identical transports. I was wrestling it clear of the door and into the hallway when another wheelchair shot out behind me and down the corridor.

I caught a fleeting glimpse of spinning wheels, white hair, and trailing duct tape as Lucille tore off toward the front door. She blasted by an orderly who had shoved an empty chair up the sidewalk and was heading back to storage. He yelled at her to stop, turned to pursue and decided he stood a better chance of catching her if he used the chair he was pushing. Wheelchairs can really travel, so unless you were a marathon runner, which this guy clearly wasn't, it was faster by chair than by foot. I jumped into the one I was holding, and we formed a careening caravan barreling toward the entrance. Lucille approached the automatic door as someone was coming in. The door was open and she zinged through. It started to close just as the orderly screeched into it. It bounced against him once and slid back. I was right behind him. We both sailed outside. He stopped short in front of me and jumped out. I collided with his chair and got dumped on my butt. The empty chair crashed into the stone wall that lined the sidewalk and exploded into pieces of metal tubing.

Lucille was nowhere to be seen.

"What's going on and why does that woman have duct tape on her wrists? Why was she in the storage room?" I was yelling at the orderly as I pulled my cell phone out of my pocket. I pushed Jon's number on speed contacts just as the guy dove for my phone.

"Give me the fuckin' phone, lady. You ain't callin' no one. You and your friend need to go somewhere far away!" And he grabbed my arm. We danced in a circle and I kicked him in the shins. I tried for a knee to the balls, but he was on top of that possibility and turned away too quickly for a good shot. I could hear Jon's voice yelling, but I was too busy fending off the crazy orderly to do more than scream, "Lucille, nursing home!" I tried to yell more but one of his extra-large hands got caught in my mouth.

The wild man almost had my phone pried out of my hand when I saw six feet of glittering red spandex flying down the sidewalk. Belle collided with my attacker and they landed hard on the cement. Belle was on top. I heard a whoosh of air as the orderly lost his breath to six feet and one hundred and seventy pounds of angry female.

"Hunh! I can't leave you alone for ten seconds without some asshole busting your butt. What the hell's going on? And I saw Lucille in some big hurry heading out the door with duct tape on her mouth and hanging off her arms and legs and ankles. She may have to go shoe shopping 'cause duct tape doesn't mix with fine footwear. And who is this guy I'm sitting on?"

I looked around for Lucille and spotted the broken wheelchair scattered in front of the stone wall. There were plastic packets of white stuff scattered around next to the pieces of tube that made up the chair.

Chapter Twenty

Jon was at the head of the pack when he arrived surprisingly quickly with two patrol cars following. He stopped at the base of the sidewalk and the patrol cars pulled in behind. His backup jumped out with weapons drawn. Belle was still sitting on the slowly recovering orderly. I was holding my cell phone and looking down at the remains of the busted wheelchair. Jon came striding toward me, a grim expression on his face. At least I was his first concern.

"Are you okay?" He grabbed my shoulders and studied my face.

"I'm fine, but Lucille may need some help."

"What the fuck is going on here?" Then Jon saw the little white packets. "Holy shit!" He knelt down and examined the broken pieces and the plastic baggies. "So that's how they're doing it. I wonder if Scarpelli is involved at all. Maybe he really did retire." Jon was mumbling to himself.

He turned to one of his officers. "Cuff him," he said, pointing to the orderly. "Mirandize him."

Belle had removed herself from the proximity of so many blue uniforms and was hanging out farther down in the parking area. I looked at her and realized Lucille had joined the party. She was standing behind the wheelchair she had used to escape in, and the chair was behind Belle. She still had the duct tape over her

264

mouth. I could see removing it might be like pulling a super strength band-aid off an open wound on a pissed-off pussycat.

"Umph!" said Lucille as loudly as the situation allowed.

Belle opened her oversized bag, which she had held onto during the entire episode with the orderly. She rooted around inside and came up with a travel size bottle of baby oil. "Hold still," she told Lucille. She put a drop of oil on the edge of the tape and slowly worked it off. When she had less than a quarter inch to go, she gave it a yank and Lucille squeaked.

"Kill that man. Give me a gun. Someone give me a gun!" Lucille took a step toward the officers holding the cuffed orderly. Both of them stepped back. Belle grabbed Lucille's arm.

"Slow down lady. I need input. What the hell happened to you?"

"I would like to know that also. Have you been missing?" Jon had figured out the transport of heroin up the interstate, but he didn't understand what Lucille was doing here, why she had duct tape on her mouth, was in a wheelchair, or why Belle and I were rounding up the crooks for him. I wasn't very clear on any of that myself.

"And what the hell are you wearing?" He shook his head. I realized Lucille was wearing her bling shoes. Jon may never have seen her in them because they were for specialized use in Lucille's seduction arsenal to which Jon might not be privy.

Lucille raised her chin, pulled herself up straight and said, "I think we should all go home and take a little rest. I will explain as much as I know later."

"How about you talk to me now?" Jon scowled.

"I've been up all night. That orderly locked me in a room and threatened me. That's all I'm saying until I have regrouped. It's enough to hold him." And Lucille marched off in the direction of Belle's car.

Belle and I followed and I scrunched myself into the back seat while Lucille gracefully lowered herself in front. The patrol officers started stringing crime scene tape. One of them escorted the prisoner to a squad car and took off. I agreed to come to the station the next day with Lucille and Belle and explain what part of the apparent transport operation we had actually witnessed. Jon agreed Lucille needed a rest after her ordeal. Arnie was going to have to wait to see the sun.

঺৵৵

The story still dominated the news two days later. Ten employees of the nursing home had been arrested in connection with the smuggling and retail distribution of heroin from New York to the Canadian border. They would take empty wheelchairs down to whichever source city they were using and return with chairs stuffed with heroin, making numerous stops along the way. The first orderly arrested turned state's evidence so the entire network began to crumble. Mr. Scarpelli was not named as a conspirator. In fact, his name never came up at all. That made me wonder how delusional his daughter might be and how far she would travel on her fantasy. Or did she know all about the wheelchair distribution network and want to take on the competition as well as her father? Susan had disappeared so no one had any answers about her intentions. The busting of the competition could encourage her or discourage her, depending on how rational her thoughts were at any given moment.

I decided to keep her in the back of my head but not let her dominate my life the way she had been for the last few weeks.

I was sitting at Lucille's kitchen table munching my breakfast cookie. Lucille had decided to break it off with Arnie, and I was scheduled to take her to the nursing home. He was probably ready to leave since the facility was scrambling to replace most of its staff and the service couldn't have been very good.

"He's okay in the sack but he complains too much. He was fine for a one-night stand, until he tried to actually stand." Lucille was packing her purse for a trip to the Senior Center after seeing Arnie. I noticed her checkbook and her brass knuckles going in and assumed she was entered in a bridge competition.

When we got to Arnie's room, there was a middle-age man standing next to the bed. Arnie was up and dressed and his bag was packed.

"Uh, hi, Lucille. This here is my son from Cincinnati. I've decided to move back. It's too crazy here. The orderlies look like zombies. I'll miss a few of my friends." He winked at Lucille and I wondered if he remembered what their relationship was.

Back in the car Lucille breathed a sigh that sounded like relief to me.

"Now he can complain to someone else. I haven't been dumped too many times in my life, but I'm glad this was one of them. Take me to the Senior Center. I need to go hunting."

Chapter Twenty-One

The next morning, I woke up at Jon's house. It was 8 o'clock. Time to hustle. I was guzzling coffee when Belle wandered in. She had spent the night while she waited on a bed delivery to her new apartment.

"You check in with Mona yet to see what's up this morning?"

"Nope." I handed her the cell phone. She punched in the short code for Cool Rides, number 1, and handed it back.

Mona answered. She mumbled two words and I groaned.

"We have to pick up Denise. She wants a ride from her place in the Meadows," I said. Belle had met Denise once and I had described some of the adventures I had had picking her up.

Denise was one of our occasional regulars and she had been homeless for as long as I had known her. She called every two to four weeks wanting a ride to one of the cheap motels out on the old highway. There were three of these and she could always count on one of them to have a room available. None of the upscale, in-town hotels would take her. Most were too expensive anyway. We all kind of liked Denise. She tipped well and was always entertaining. It was just that we had to drive with all the windows down and the air conditioning on full blast, and we had to detail the car when we got back to the garage. We still ended

268

up using one of those sprays that smell marginally better than a dead ashtray.

The Meadows was a section of Northampton made up mostly of farms, forest and the Connecticut River. It also contained the small airport and the three-county fairgrounds. There were a few houses in the Meadows, but the city planner, in a fit of "not in my back yard-ism," passed rules forbidding any new building in the area. The result was a large piece of land unpopulated by permanent structures. It provided ideal spaces for wildlife, drug deals, drunk college students, and a camping site for the homeless population convenient to downtown and all their sources of income. Street begging was Denise's favorite source of cash flow. She lived with her brother and another man in a tent with an ancient propane stove inside and a campfire outside. It was the campfire and lack of a bathing facility that made us air out the cab after a Denise ride.

"She wants to be picked up at 9." Belle poured coffee.

At a quarter to 9, Belle and I loaded ourselves into the cab. Jon had gone to work before either of us got up, and Lucille must have been busy. No wonderous odors wafted out that might make it worth breaking down her door, so we headed to the Meadows.

Denise's castle of the moment was an old Army tent. It could house six people, so room wasn't an issue. Privacy was. The outhouse and general wash-up was several acres of woods behind the tent and the Connecticut River. Once a month, Denise would save up enough dimes, nickels and quarters for a hot bath and a real bed.

We pulled up on the dirt road about fifty feet from the tent and honked the horn. This would have been considered bad manners with any other fare. We always walked to the door and knocked. If that failed to get them out, we called on the cell phone. Denise didn't always have a cell phone and, when she did, it wasn't always charged. She would arrange her rides the day before, when she was in town working the sidewalks. Given the lack of privacy, we never approached the tent or the area around it. I had done that once. I found her brother sitting with his back against a tree, five feet from the tent. He was bare-assed and taking a giant dump. He grinned and waved his penis at me. I retreated to the taxi and sat with all the doors locked until Denise came out.

Apparently the morning toiletries were over. Denise trotted down the path to the road and slid into the back seat.

"Forward, James, or make that Jamette." Denise was looking chipper and wide awake. Her hair was combed, and she was, shockingly, wearing mascara.

"Got myself married last night," she said without any lead-up to the story. "The old man, well the new old man, is already out at the North Prince Motel. Hitched a ride there with one of the farmers. I told him I'd join him once I got my face done."

"You look lovely, Denise," Belle said.

"Yeah, well, ever the blushing bride. I need to get away from the brother for a while. He's such a prick. I tried to get the cops to haul his ass. There's a warrant out. But they could care less about that shit."

"What's the warrant for?" I asked, getting sucked into the story.

270

"Oh, just 30 days for an open container."

"That's probably not a priority for the police. They have a lot on their minds these days." Like a few murders and an uptick in the heroin supply, which would now be a downtick—for a short period of time. Northampton had become a small town with big city problems.

"I coulda told them about the murder," Denise mused. "But I called the FBI instead. They told me to call the staties."

"Did you?" I glanced over my shoulder at her, wondering if Denise could have seen one of the murders on Jon's agenda. Or if she was talking about one of the other homeless folks who might have crossed her brother once too often. Would anyone in authority in Northampton notice if a member of its homeless population suddenly didn't show up for work? Given Denise's source of income, most of the population of Northampton probably wished she would miss a day at work.

"Nah, I got bored with it. He wasn't worth the trouble. Anyway, now I got my honey to keep me busy."

"Yeah, guys'll do that to you," Belle said, looking at me.

Denise, oblivious to Belle and me, continued her train of thought.

"I thought they might want to know he murdered a guy and dumped him in the Ashfield Lake. Wrapped him right up in one of my best blankets. Stones, bungee cords and—plop—right in the lake. Yup."

"Did you see this happen?" I asked, wondering how much was true and how much was an attempt to get rid of her brother. Sibling rivalries, one never knew. Functional family is an oxymoron.

"Well, duh. Of course I saw it. Bodies sure do look white when they're dead."

"Denise, maybe you should tell the Ashfield police, or maybe someone right here in Northampton."

"Nah, they all think I'm crazy. 'Sides, I don't bother them, they don't bother me."

"But you did call the FBI."

"Did I say that? Well, maybe I did, maybe I didn't."

I gave up questioning. I could tell Jon what she said. Leave the ball in his court. I had enough on my mind. Like, where was Susan? The Springfield police hadn't turned her up at Daddy's house. Unless Daddy had thrown her out or worse. But she was his sole heir. Even if she was a woman, she was a Scarpelli woman. How much did family mean to the old man? Was he sure she really was his family?

We pulled up in front of the North Prince Motel. There were only two other cars parked in front of rooms, so there was plenty of space for Denise and her new "husband," but I told her I would wait while she talked to the front desk. Sometimes, if they were mostly rented or if they had had a good week, they would turn her away. Whether they let her rent a room depended on how much they needed her cash. They would have a major cleanup after she left. Denise pulled a wad of money out of her loose pants pockets and peeled off a twenty- dollar bill.

"Keep the change. Do I know how to tip or what?" She must have had five hundred dollars in the wad. It was a ten-dollar fare.

Belle got out of the car. "Must have had too much coffee. I'll be right back." She went into the lobby to find the restroom. Denise followed her in.

I sighed and slouched in the seat. I yawned. I stretched. I closed my eyes and felt the warmth of the sun on my face. I decided to call Jon and mention what Denise had told me. Or, if I were honest, just to hear his voice. Speed dial is great. I pushed the number button for Jon, put the phone on speaker mode, and slid it into the center console.

"Stevens."

"Hi, lieutenant of the cute butt."

"I sure hope this is Reverend Mother Mary from my high school days."

"We're about to head back to Cool Rides. We just dropped Denise off at the North Prince Motel. I have a good story about that. I thought I might pass it on to the police." I gave him the short version. He groaned and said he'd pass it on to the State Police since he couldn't be sure it was in his jurisdiction, and he hoped to hell it wasn't. I heard a click and I leaned back to enjoy more sunshine.

When the car door opened, I pushed myself up to a sitting position, opening my eyes as I reached to turn the key...and saw Susan sitting in the passenger seat with a very large gun. She certainly had a good supply of those ugly pieces of metal. It answered the question about where she was and how delusional she had become. She wasn't looking good. The power suit of our first encounter was gone. She still had on the baggy clothes from the hospital. They had a few tears and smears of dirt down the front. Her short hair was getting frizzy and tangled and her eyes had dark circles under them. She looked as wild and crazy as she was.

"Hi, Honey, I'm back. And, by the way, Belle has been detained. This was not the smartest place to come. Amazing how easy it is to get crazy people to be sane for just long enough to do what you've paid them to do."

"You bribed Denise?" That was about as low as Susan had gone so far. Denise was crazy and unpredictable. But so was Susan. She had clearly lost the power of logical thought.

"I gave her and her new idiot a wedding present of a big fat roll of cash. It was the least I could do."

"So, now what? You want to make your bones on me?"

"Oh, Honey, you've been watching too many Godfather movies. Anyway, bones or no bones, I'm not going to shoot you dead and dump you in a nice, smelly toilet, if that's what you're worried about. And I promise I won't put a dead horse in your bed. Come to think of it, that might be an improvement for you." I didn't like the detail she provided. Lester Cardozzo had been dumped in a toilet. And Jon was almost in my bed.

"Then what the hell is going on? What are you trying to do?" I asked.

"I'm just trying to finish up. The board of directors assigned me a project, and I need to make a completed presentation next week."

"A project? I'm a project?" I answered dumbly.

"Yeah. I'm supposed to enhance the possibilities of transportation along the 91-interstate corridor between Hartford and the northern border of Vermont.

We reached maximum capacity with our current carriers and then your idiot cops busted them. We need to expand, and Cool Rides is the ideal expansion associate. But we need some cooperation here, and Willie isn't providing it. Are you getting my drift here?"

"You want me to convince him to join your project."

"You are so perceptive. You might make partner yet. Belle is just going to sit tight with my friend in there while you and I go for a ride."

Leaning forward, I gave my brain a silent pep talk and started the car. Don't panic. Stay calm until you can't.

"Where to?"

"Cool Rides, of course."

"What are you going to do when we get there?" I hadn't expected her to go into such a public place.

"I'm going to give Willie a contract. Then I'm going to call my friend in there." She waved her hand at the motel office. "I'll tell him to chop off one of those beautifully manicured fingers Belle loves so well. Every hour until the contract gets signed, he'll get another finger. Special delivery, by taxi." Susan started laughing and I realized her tenuous hold on reality had disappeared. Unfortunately, the gun she was holding was very real.

I gurgled and took off.

Traffic on the strip was heavy and we hit every red light. There was a fender bender in front of one of the strip malls and both parties were out and screaming with traffic inching around their wildly waving arms. Half an hour later we pulled up at Cool Rides. There were no cars in front of the garage, and the office seemed quiet. There should have been phones ringing, music blasting, tools clanking in the garage. I knew this, but Susan didn't have the rhythm of the company hardwired into her brain.

I grabbed my phone and shoved it in my pocket. Cool Rides runs on cell phones so the drivers take them everywhere. If you were sitting on the toilet, the phone sat next to you. You never, ever left them in the car.

I got out cautiously. Susan looked at me. "I've got a very large gun under this coat, Honey, and I'll use it. Probably on Willie first. He's been such a pain in the ass. Maybe that would be most efficient. So, behave yourself."

I raised my hands over my head and turned to the office door.

"Oh please, enough with the theatrics. This is a fucking business meeting, not the final episode of The Sopranos. Just walk in like you're checking for another fare."

I lowered my hands and tried to see what was going on inside the building. Not much, as near as I could tell.

Mona was in the office cubicle, her head bent over papers on the desk. Willie was probably in the garage. I was on high alert, adrenaline pumping, absorbing details I'd never noticed. The unisex bathroom door was cracked open. The door from the office/waiting area to the garage was the same. There was silence from the garage.

Susan walked us to the office and spotted Mona. "Go find Willie, or Mona will lose a kneecap," she said into my ear.

"So, where's Willie?" I tried to lean casually against the door.

"Garage," Mona replied without looking up.

Susan gestured me in that direction with the coat. I would never think of jackets as just an accessory again.

Willie came in from the garage, looked up and saw Susan. His expression changed, and a wave of hatred I had never seen before crossed his face as he walked toward us.

"Susan," he said, "I thought we agreed you wouldn't come around here again."

"Aren't you cute today? We didn't agree. That's the problem here. We need to agree I'm not going to change the shape of Honey's face. Or Mona's knees. Or Belle's hands. Or just put a fucking hole in your head. We need an understanding."

Willie looked around. "Where is Belle?"

"Oh, Belle's hands are in good hands. They have a big ax." She paused. "So, let's negotiate."

"Just what is it you want from Cool Rides?" Willie was talking too loudly.

"I need you to service whatever I want transported up the interstate corridor. I need your assurance you understand exactly what the consequences will be if you say no again. And our business needs 50 percent of your business. You will be paid extremely well."

Willie shifted his weight forward. Mona rolled her chair closer to the desk. I stood like a stone. Although the "paid extremely well" had not escaped my notice.

"What part does your father play in this?" Willie asked.

"Ah, dear old Dad. No ambition. You could run a truck through his company and he wouldn't notice. It needs new blood. That would be me."

"Why not just increase his truck fleet? Use them." Willie had raised his voice.

"Too obvious. They get searched every time they take a load of shit somewhere."

"Why me? Why not Lennie's limo or Larry's or Lulu's or whatever the hell it is?"

Susan looked at him like he was the stupidest person on earth. "Because, Mr. Country Hick, they are at capacity. We load them up any more and somebody is going to notice. I can't believe they haven't been busted yet. Nope, Cool Rides is the cleanest operation around. And with the other competition gone, thank you so much," she said, turning to me. "It's just perfect for our expansion plans. Now sign the damn contract." She pulled a single sheet of paper from her jacket and placed it on the table.

I couldn't believe Susan thought a contract signed under this kind of duress was going to change her family or business status. She might have to kidnap one of us permanently to make this work. Maybe she assumed none of us would go to the police. Maybe this was all in her head and Daddy had no expansion plans at all. So many maybes, so little sanity.

"Does the other cab company have a contract?" I asked. "Luther's or Lars' or Lola's or whatever? Because, if they do, I want to see it. I mean, just how much is this worth to you? What are you giving them?

278

I think Cool Rides should at least be at the same rate. Don't you, Mona? Willie?"

I was stalling for time, and Susan knew it. But her ego, or her insanity, was in charge. "I'm a lawyer, for Christ's sake. You think I don't know how to write a contract?"

"Yeah, but do the drivers get danger wages?" I was keeping her going as long as I could which wasn't all that hard since she seemed to want to be the center of attention.

"The biggest danger right now is I might blow some vital piece of your body off. Willie, sign on the line." She extended a well-chewed fingernail toward the piece of paper.

Just then the phone rang. "Pick it up. And put it on speaker. You're not taking any fares right now."

Mona punched the speaker button and lifted the receiver. "Cool Rides."

"Yo, Cool Rides yourself. You tell Miss Lawyer woman she is not long for this world. I don't take kindly to threats against my wonderful fingers. I got a full-scale mani/pedi two days ago."

Susan turned a shade of red. "What the fuck? Let me talk to Benji."

"Your goons? Oh, they are so tied up right now. And their ability to converse with you is limited. They got some gray sticky stuff all over their faces...and other parts of their bodies."

"Belle, I have a gun here. And I have Honey and Mona and Willie. So don't be fucking stupid. I will reconfigure someone's body here."

I caught a movement in my peripheral vision. Jon's face emerged from the shadow of the bathroom door. I could see his gun in his hand.

I started to cough, grabbed my chest and staggered closer to Susan. She moved between me and the door.

"Don't think I won't shoot, Honey. I'd love to see you with one less appendage." Her back was to the bathroom now. Jon cracked the door open another few inches. He slipped out behind Susan. Mona and Willie didn't react and I understood why the office was so quiet. I had never closed down my cell phone. Jon had heard all of Susan's rant. We carefully kept our eyes focused on Susan.

Belle's voice echoed back into the office. It seemed too loud in the silence. "I don't give a crap what you do there. I'll find you and your life will be hell. No one messes with my new nails."

Jon was behind Susan. He raised his gun and pressed it against Susan's neck. Willie and Mona fell to the floor. My hand reached out, all by itself, in slow motion, and slapped Susan's gun. It flew in a graceful arc out the office door, landed with a thud and shot out the front window. Pebbles of glass flew in every direction, catching the sunlight and making a beautiful waterfall. My autopilot went out and I slumped down next to Mona. By the time I peeked over the desk, Jon was snapping handcuffs on a screeching Susan.

"You fucking asshole. I'm Susan Scarpelli. No one messes with a Scarpelli. My father will cut you up into little pieces. The Connecticut River will be polluted with your body parts for years. I'll carve your dick off and cook it for dinner." She struggled in Jon's grip.

He calmly pulled her arms higher behind her back.

"I will get you. Sometime, somewhere, when you aren't looking for it, I will shove a stick of dynamite so far up your ass your testicles will come out your nose." I had to give Miss Scarpelli credit for creative threats.

Seconds later, four uniformed officers were dragging a kicking, screaming Susan to a squad car. I stood up, grabbed Jon by the ears and kissed him on the mouth as hard as I could. He slid an arm behind my back and the kiss got a lot more interesting. When he stopped, I did a little dance and raised my fists above my head. I wasn't sure if the dance was about Susan being hauled away or about the kiss. Either way, my body needed to dance.

Mr. Scarpelli might be very relieved Susan was not in circulation anymore. What Susan might be able to do from a jail cell was questionable, especially if Daddy wasn't inclined to help.

&⚬&

Jon, Willie, Mona and I were sitting in the Cool Rides waiting room letting our adrenaline fade when Belle leaped out of an Uber car and stormed inside. "What the hell happened here? I need input. I need data. I need all the stuff. What did you do with the bitch? I'm gonna rip her fingers off."

"Hi, Belle. Good to see you again." Jon smiled his thousand-watt smile.

"Good to see me, my ass. I thought driving a taxi would be safe. After life in the business. Being a ho is easy compared to this shit."

"Yeah, but this is more fun," I said. "How is the North Prince?"

"The North Prince still has most of their fingers and toes. Barely. They may never get a manicure again, though."

Jon smiled. "Plenty of uniforms out there?"

"Oh, yeah, like they were lots of help. Excitement was all over by the time they got there. Next time send them a little earlier." She plopped herself down next to Willie. "What kind of pizza we havin'?"

Susan had, apparently, neglected to figure in size and street smarts when she hired the North Prince staff to subdue Belle who had read the situation when she walked in the door. She had Benji on his back with a gun in his face before he could even point the gun Susan had given him in the right direction. To his credit, Susan had shown him a fake police ID and told him he would be aiding the cause of peace and love if he locked Belle in the back room. I doubt her fingers were in any danger, certainly not from Benji. But when he mentioned Susan's plan, Belle immediately duct-taped him to the reception desk. He didn't understand that torture isn't standard police procedure in this country. He was confessing to crimes that hadn't been committed or possibly even thought about yet. Belle had been trying to shut him up when the police cars arrived.

Chapter Twenty-Two

Three long days later, I was sitting at my tiny kitchen table, watching football on my tiny TV set, eating a large bowl of popcorn. I was admiring butts and tats and maybe some of the strategy of the complex NFL playbooks. All three days had been spent filling out paperwork, sitting in interviews with the feds, and flopping exhausted into bed at night. My bed. I had officially moved back into my apartment, but Jon had a better (by a lot) TV. And he had pizza and beer. And he had himself. Belle had met a friend from the days of her previous profession and decided to go over for some reminiscing. I didn't think Jon would tolerate a night of girlie talk about Belle's good old days. She smirked when she told me she would spend the night there. But I was ready for some down time. Being in my own space felt good.

Susan's lawyer convinced a judge to declare her unfit for trial. The feds had busted her on charges beyond my understanding. Threatening a police officer was at the bottom of the long list of charges. Somewhere below that was her intimidation of Cool Rides and its drivers. No surprise there. Her father hadn't objected to the declaration of unfitness. It would make it almost impossible to trace any of the intimidation stuff back to him. He had probably paid off the judge to agree that she was nuts but, realistically, he probably didn't have to. She tried to be

283

her own lawyer, but the same judge declared her unfit for that too. She hadn't actually done any hard-core violence to anyone except shooting her husband's butt. Since he was beyond pressing charges and Susan was officially crazy, she would spend a long time in the state mental hospital. Everyone agreed Lester Cardozzo had accidentally killed Horace. The real pisser in all this was that I never found out about the red shoes. Susan will probably go to her grave without revealing that source. And it's depressing but unlikely there was any change in the flow of drugs up the interstate corridor. Cool Rides Cabs wouldn't contribute to the distribution effort, but that probably wouldn't slow it down much. The other cab companies might find themselves getting pulled over more often. Where there was market, there would be a supply, but our company wouldn't be part of the system. And I felt like I was one step closer to knowing what the problems of running a small business were and how to deal with them. That meant I was closer to making Willie an offer for a bigger share of the responsibility and the ownership. I may become a normal, more or less successful business person someday. I may even live up to my potential.

Of course, there was no evidence anywhere about who might have killed Lester Cardozzo. The police bought into the idea that Lester had provided them with the other bodies and his wasn't in Jon's jurisdiction, so who cared? Belle had declined to testify about her kidnapping. She still couldn't tolerate being in a room with uniformed police, and a courtroom was beyond her without some heavy motivation. She put up with Jon only because he had a great kitchen, a big-screen TV and a free bedroom. Jon's biggest frustration was the police still hadn't figured out if Scarpelli was participating in the movement of heroin. The boys in blue had glued themselves to every one of Scarpelli's trucks and to most of the taxi companies but had no evidence of product coming north other than the wheelchair gang, and they hadn't mentioned Scarpelli. But that was a problem for another day. Susan was safely under the care of some unfortunate psychiatrist and probably half-a-dozen social workers. I sure hoped she didn't decide to play sane for long enough to get out of the locked facility. I had seen her in action, and she could be very convincing. After all, she played the legal system for a fool for a long time.

I spent the night in my private space doing my private things, thinking private thoughts, just being alone for a change, and in charge. The next morning was filled with sunshine. I reported for work and had a blessedly normal day helping the Cool Rides Company – my company, well a little bit anyway – recover from the Susan trauma.

࿇

By evening Jon and I were sitting on his couch watching a baseball game. We had been talking about the smugglers, but Jon wasn't too forthcoming about an on-going case and I was more preoccupied with whether Belle was going to accept an invitation to coffee from Judge Witherspoon. We had fallen into a blissful silence when Jon's cell phone rang. He looked at the caller ID and grunted. I think it was an unknown number. He punched it onto speakerphone so he could concentrate on the game while whatever solicitation droned on.

"Lieutenant Stevens?"

"Who is this?"

"This is Antoni Scarpelli. I'd like to arrange a meeting with you if you could be so kind."

"When, where, and why?" Jon stood up and walked away. I could still sort of hear what Scarpelli was saying. That was because I got up and followed Jon. If my taxi company was involved, I thought I had a right to know.

"Anytime, at your house. I would like to discuss Miss Lucille."

"What the fuck? What have you done to her?" Jon signaled me to call Lucille.

She picked up on the second ring.

"Well, of course I'm fine. Why wouldn't I be? I hope you aren't thinking that idiot Arnie upset me. Thank you for inquiring but I'm in excellent health, both mental and physical." I rung off with Lucille, shrugged my shoulders to Jon indicating Lucille was okay.

"Where are you right now?" Jon asked Scarpelli.

"Outside your house."

Jon grabbed me and shoved me toward the bedroom. I jerked my arm free and went behind the kitchen breakfast counter. I wasn't about to miss this conversation. Jon scowled at me but I crossed my arms over my chest and stayed put. He pulled his gun out of the closet lock box and tucked it in the back of his jeans.

"What the hell, come right in, but leave the weapons and the bodyguard outside," Jon muttered into the phone and moved to the window to watch the old man get out of the car. His driver helped him to the door. "Well, fuck, it can't get any stranger," said Jon as he opened the door.

"You—" he pointed a finger at the bodyguard "—stay outside. It's okay, Harry. He's a cop but I think he might be one of the honest ones."

And one of the well-armed ones, too, I thought but I didn't say out loud.

Mr. Scarpelli came in and Jon shut the door. He flipped the locks even though Harry could have broken down that door or just about any door short of a jail cell given enough motivation.

Scarpelli shuffled to the kitchen table, pulled out a chair and sat down.

"By all means, have a seat," Jon said and sat opposite him. I decided to stay behind the counter where I could duck out of the line of fire.

"So, now you've found out I'm not in the transportation business. If you'd asked, I might have steered you in the right direction. But that's all done and over and I'm enjoying my retirement."

"So, who killed Horace and your son-in-law and Lester Cardozzo? You have a lot of bodies floating around for not being involved." Jon looked grim. I didn't think he believed Scarpelli's profession of innocence.

"Ah, Horace. Poor man, he was an accident. Lester was always a little trigger happy. And my dear daughter, who, by the way, isn't actually my daughter as I was incarcerated at the time of her conception. Her husband? Well, Lester had developed a bit of a crush on Susan and he was eliminating the competition as well as grabbing a substantial amount of my money while doing so. And Lester, he was a message to Susan from the competition. You might question them, since you have them all in custody, about murder as well as transport of illegal substances." Scarpelli smiled softly. "But that's not why I'm here. I don't need to tell you any of this. I'm just trying to explain to you that I am an honest businessman."

That sounded like Jon knew more than I did about Scarpelli's business involvements. I hate when someone knows more than me about what I want to know about. And, given my interactions with the Scarpelli family, I should be at the top of the knowledge pyramid.

"Just the Port-a-Potties? That's your sole source of income?" Jon looked skeptical.

"Well, I do have some investments. The stock market is up at the moment and I have some very profitable pizza restaurants. They are completely legal. You should try some of my pizza sometime. I'll be happy to host you and your lovely lady." Scarpelli winked at me.

"And what do you want from me?" Jon said impatiently.

"Your blessing."

"My what!?"

"To see Miss Lucille. I've been alone for a long time. She is quite a woman and I would like to see her. Given our last interaction, I deemed it wise to assure you my intentions are honorable in all ways."

"You want to date Lucille?" Jon almost choked on the words.

"Yes, I find her very attractive."

288

"You do know she's former FBI?"

"Of course, I vetted her very carefully before I came to you. I know a great deal about her. I feel we may be compatible in many more ways than you might expect, on many levels."

I hoped his vetting included gun permit applications because Lucille was probably better armed than any of his bodyguards and most small nations.

"I'm not giving anyone my blessing. I, however, won't shoot you. I'll leave that up to Lucille. What she does with you is her business. I would ask you not to come to my house again. You can meet her anywhere she agrees to."

"I'm just a lonely old man, Lieutenant. I hope in the future we can come to a better understanding. In the meantime, thank you for agreeing not to shoot me."

"You have a lot to answer for in my book, Mr. Scarpelli. I'll need to think a long time and do some of my own vetting before I let you come here again."

"Ah, yes, I suppose the police consider me a 'made man.' I never was very good at pulling the trigger. I found it much more satisfying to live by my wits."

"You'll need them if you start seeing Lucille." Jon stood up and it was clear the conversation was over.

"Thank you and nice to see you again, Miss Walker."

Yeah, I thought. Maybe we can double date for pizza sometime.

Jon held the door and the bodyguard helped Mr. Scarpelli down the walkway and into the car. Scarpelli mentioned he would send Miss Lucille flowers and call her later in the week.

"Are you going to tell her?" I stood next to Jon as we watched the old man being helped into the car by his bodyguard.

"Nope."

"I'm picking her up in the morning."

"Honey, leave it alone. Lucille can handle herself."

"Jon, he's a lonely old man. Lucille is an interesting woman. They might get along."

"Not for us to decide. If it happens, it happens. Don't push it." Jon was on edge, but so was I. He had treated an old man rather harshly, in my opinion. And he was in the dog house because he knew more about Scarpelli's business than I did.

"Romance isn't one of your strong suits, is it?"

"Nope."

I glared at him, "There are things a woman should know. Lucille should have some warning."

Jon shook his head. "She'll find out when she finds out."

I narrowed my eyes. This was one point on which we might never agree, but I didn't have to accept his attitude this time. I stalked around the counter, snatched my oversized purse and headed to the door.

"Honey, don't...shit!" I heard Jon curse as I slammed the door. Then I remembered I hadn't brought the cab to Jon's house with me.

I fished in my bag and pulled out my smart phone. I punched in Belle's speed number. Cool Rides was number one, Jon was two, Belle was three. I might need to reverse those two.

"Yo, sup?" Her voice soothed my ruffled psyche.
"Men are assholes!"
"Un hunh. What are you gonna do?"
"Bitch session, and I need a ride home!"
"On my way."

Chapter Twenty-Three

Belle hung out at my apartment late into the night and we decided men were one of those commodities we couldn't live without but we couldn't shoot so we just would continue to manipulate them into doing what we thought they should do. I would tell Lucille about Antoni Scarpelli's intentions when I picked her up in the morning.

When I had explained the night before, Lucille scowled and said he would have to be awfully good in the sack to overcome his drawbacks. I thought about that and decided Jon had enough good attributes to overcome any drawbacks he might have in the romance department.

The result was that I was in Jon's house, on Jon's oversized sofa, watching football on Jon's huge TV and admiring more male butts two days later.

When the score was lopsided enough to stop watching, Jon picked up the pizza box and beer bottles. I grabbed the dirty paper towels and followed him to the kitchen. After depositing the garbage on the counter, he turned around. The towels fluttered to the floor.

We made our way backward, kissing and groping, to the bedroom. My pulse rate was higher than when Susan had held a gun to my head. I guess that sums up Jon's effect on me. We stumbled through the bedroom door and were rolling around on the bed when bells started ringing.

The earth might have been moving, too, but it wasn't Jon's technique ringing the bells. There are a handful of people who always answer their cell phones. Doctors, firefighters, police, moms. And, unfortunately, Cool Rides taxi drivers. Our phones were screaming for attention separately, together.

We both punched our phones open. We both heard "Get your ass in here now."

ॐॐ

Three hours later I staggered into Jon's house. It felt like I had transported the entire Smith College field hockey team home. Oh yeah, because I had. Their bus had broken down and Cool Rides had to send its entire fleet of cars to gather them up and bring them across the river. But the tip had been enormous and Cool Rides now had an in with the person at the College who arranged special transportation. That was good networking and I felt like I had helped my company with a step up the transport ladder.

I tossed my keys onto the counter. There was a large gift box lying there with a pink bow and a card. Of course, I had to read the card. Maybe it was for me. How would I know if I didn't read it?

"Good luck!" It read. No name, no signature. It might have been for me. Just as I was thinking about opening it, Jon walked in.

"Where did that come from?" He eyed the box.

"I don't know. I just got here. It was on the counter when I walked in." I put my hand out to pull the bow.

"No, wait," said Jon. "You didn't bring it, and I sure as hell didn't leave it here." He circled it. "Did you touch it?" He looked at me.

"I read the card."

"What's it say?"

"Good luck."

"I'm calling the bomb squad." Jon pulled out his phone. "Too much stuff has happened in the last three days. If Scarpelli isn't feeling like revenge, Susan sure as hell is. And I don't know what kind of contacts she has."

I backed up a few steps while Jon punched numbers into his phone. "No sirens," he said as he ended the conversation. "Why wake up the neighborhood?" he grumbled. "Let's go outside and wait."

Five minutes later a big truck lumbered up and three men in space suits jumped out. A squad car with two more uniforms followed. Jon pointed over his shoulder at the house.

"It's on the kitchen counter."

The first space suit through the door left it open, so of course we had to watch, from a substantial distance. They approached the box from three sides, passed a variety of gizmos over it and around it. They pushed it gently with a short rod and finally lifted it with a pair of long metal tongs and headed for the door. Nothing happened. We backed up as the space suit walked, gingerly, to the controlled environment next to the truck. He deposited the box on the metal table. Space suit two slipped a rod under the box lid. He flipped it backward to reveal the tissue paper within. He slowly pushed back the fluffy pinkness and raised it to reveal something very small. The one with the tongs snatched the object inside the box and held it aloft for all of us to consider. Should we run for cover? It was pink, silky, slinky and barely there. The space suit was holding a thong in one hand and dangling a matching teddy on the end of the rod. I could feel the grins starting. As one, they flipped back their helmets, their gazes left the box and they focused on Lieutenant Jon Stevens.

"Guess we can leave this for you, Lieutenant, sweetie. It looks a little small, though." The one who had opened the box slid off his space helmet.

"We don't get this good a call very often. Thanks, handsome." He addressed this to Jon whose face had shut down into a blank expression. The suit put the offending clothing back, and one of the uniforms came over and picked up the box and bows. He strolled slowly over to Jon and made a show of handing it over, tissue, bow and contents. The suits and uniforms returned to their vehicles. I could hear giggling.

"Who the hell would send me that?" Jon growled, stepping back into the hallway.

I was wondering the same thing when Lucille stuck her head in the doorway and sang out, "Is everyone okay, Jonny?"

Ah, the light dawns. The bomb squad pulled away from the curb and made its dignified and slow trip, followed by the uniforms in their patrol cars, down the street. Life on Lincoln Avenue would resume its sedate pace. Jon would eventually live down the incident at cop central, but it would take some time.

"I hope the gift works for you. I got one like it and it was just what I needed." Lucille smiled her angelic best.

Jon grunted and closed the door in her face.

He walked over with the now-infamous box. He lifted the offending garments out and held them up. He turned around and looked at me.

"Put it on," he ordered.

It took me ten minutes to strip, fluff my hair, slip into the barely-there outfit and slide on the four-inch spike-heeled, open-toe, silver sequined slut shoes that I had in my big bag.

It took Jon ten seconds to take it off me. He left the slut shoes in place.

Read on for an excerpt
from Honey Walker's next adventure:

Sky High Taxi

by

Harriet Rogers

Chapter One

"Gak!" I shrieked when a body launched headfirst through the window of my cab. It was the passenger side and he would have been my first fare of the day if he had chosen to enter feet first. Now there appeared to be a bullet hole in him and I wasn't sure about his life status. My name is Honey Walker. I drive for Cool Rides Taxi in Northampton, Massachusetts. Questionable bodies are not an everyday event.

I was planning to run him to the Amtrak station in Springfield, twenty minutes south of town. He had a paper bag, a bad haircut, paste white skin and clothes that didn't fit. A red jacket with Bill's Bar BQ and Tropical Fish embroidered across the front was loose over a stained white tee shirt. His pants were electric blue with a gold stripe. They were held up with a scarred leather belt with an off kilter cheap chrome buckle. The outfit screamed *Goodwill*. I wondered if he had chosen the red, white and blue color scheme or if it was just at the top of the free box. He leaned forward to say something. I heard a loud pop; he flopped through the open window and my brain recognized the sound as a gunshot.

A cabbie's job is to deliver the client safely, collect the fare money and, hopefully, a tip. Since I hadn't delivered and he hadn't paid, I was 0 for 2—3 if you consider the tip. I heard another gunshot and a paint chip flew off the hood of my cab. I grabbed the top half of the passenger by his frayed collar and mashed my right foot to the floor. The cab rocketed forward with the bottom half of the passenger flapping like a demented flag. The safest place I could think of was around the corner. I tightened my grip to finger numbing white, flew through a stop sign and screeched to a halt in front of the police station. It's a small town.

Two cops standing in front of the station grabbed their radios when they saw my cab with the bottom half of a limp body hanging out the window. The blood dripping down the side of the cab might have affected their reaction time. One cop pried my fingers off the fare's jacket as an ambulance rolled around the corner.

The EMT jumped out, put a finger to my fare's now even whiter throat and yelled, "I got a pulse!"

The ambulance went into full scream mode and screeched off with my fare. The other cop removed my white knuckles from the steering wheel. My heart was hammering, and I was gulping air like a beached goldfish.

In milliseconds I was inside cop central, in an interrogation room. My fare was on his way to the hospital or the morgue. I didn't know which.

The cops seized my taxi. The contents of the almost passenger's paper bag had scattered across the front seat. Lots of prescription pill bottles. He must have had some serious health issues. Now they were either more serious or didn't exist at all.

I sat for at least a million hours waiting for someone to use the interrogation room to interrogate me. There were a few donut crumbs and paper cups on the table. It was obvious what they usually used it for.

When a cop finally came through the door, it was Jon. Police Lieutenant Jon Stevens is a close personal friend. Really, really close. He didn't look happy and I was pretty sure it wasn't because his sex life was lacking.

"We need to talk." He leaned against the door frame with his arms crossed over his chest. He frowned at me. Even unhappy, all six feet of him looked outrageously good. He also looked very much in charge. Right now, that meant in charge of me. I'm not good at authority stuff. When pushed, I tend to push back. Jon looked ready to push. He also looked ready to pull his hair out in frustration.

Jon is six inches taller than me and too good-looking for his own good—or for mine. His dark blue eyes can turn from deep pools of seduction to cop flat way too fast. Lately he's been in a good mood because the city built a new police station. The old building, often referred to as a rat maze, is being turned into a parking garage. So Jon's big blue eyes have been more involved in seduction and less in cop mode. That's good for me.

At five foot six inches with curly blond hair, blue eyes and a cute turned-up nose, I'm the all-American girl next door. That is, if you live in the fifties and next door to Ozzie and Harriet.

"All you do is drive a taxi, for Christ's sake! How do all these bodies find you?"

"At least I delivered it to your door. And speaking of 'it,' did 'it' go to the hospital or the morgue?" My heart rate finally slowed to that of a hummingbird. I could talk instead of babble. I was sitting on my hands because they were shaking, and I didn't want Jon to see them.

"Hospital. Last I heard he's getting bullets removed from his body."

"So, you have some forensic evidence. All those pill bottles must tell you something. And the blood? Maybe you could wash it off my car before I take it back to the Cool Rides garage. Mona's gonna be pissed. And I didn't get paid and there might be a dent on the hood of the car. I am so toast."

Mona is our dispatcher and general guardian of the cars.

"Uh huh. You ever pick him up before? Where were you taking him?"

"No, and to the Springfield Amtrak."

"You pick up a lot of people. Any idea where he was headed on the train?"

"No, and him, I would remember. His haircut was bad, his clothes didn't fit, and he looked like he hadn't seen the sun in a long time."

"He hadn't. He just got out of county."

"County? As in jail county?"

"Uh huh."

"Then I would guess you knew I hadn't picked him up before."

"Yup."

"You are such a cop." I didn't use the word as a compliment. Jon didn't take the bait. But my hands were finally steady.

"Yup."

"So, can I have my car back?"

"Yeah. We took the bag and bottles and some blood samples. You can run it through the car wash." He grinned. "Good luck with Mona."

Jon knew the Cool Rides staff and he knew Mona would notice the ding in the hood no matter how clean I got the car. And she would be livid.

I snuck the car back to the garage, snatched the hose and scrubbed every inch clean. The missing paint chip on the hood stood out like a zit on a teenager's nose. I knew it would be fixed by the next day. Willie, the majority owner of Cool Rides, and Mona kept the cars immaculate.

I was getting ready to face the wrath of Mona when my cell rang.

"Lucille to the senior center." It was Mona. She was too busy to come out of the office.

"Okay. I'm on it." I rolled the hose back, hopped in the car and flew out of the parking lot. I was happy to put off the inevitable disapproval when Mona saw the tiny little almost non-existent bullet bing in the hood. I'm good at postponing confrontation. Jon would tell Willie anyway. Why aggravate anyone sooner?

When I got to Lucille's house, she was busy. But I smelled fresh-baked cookies, so I didn't mind.

I sat at the kitchen table and watched as Lucille tucked a curl of grey hair behind her ear. She pushed an arthritic finger around her kitchen junk drawer, rummaging through cracked rubber bands, unbent paper clips, dried-out stamps, a 9mm Glock, ammunition and silencer. She stroked the barrel of the Glock, expertly attached the silencer, shoved bullets into the handle grip and chambered a round. I bit into

302

a chocolate chunk macadamia nut cookie, closing my eyes in bliss.

Lucille padded to the window. A rabbit hopped across the lawn. It twitched a tiny pink nose, sniffing for danger, and inched toward the garden. Lucille opened the window silently and steadied her hand on the sill. I glanced at the cookies on the plate in front of me and watched the rabbit lift its white cottontail. It left a brown pearl of excrement on the lawn. An incriminating piece of lettuce hung from its mouth. Visions of blood-drenched vegetables danced in my head. I decided not to eat lettuce if Lucille ever offered it and took another cookie off the plate. Chocolate chip walnut.

"Lucille?"

"Shh."

"Lucille! Don't…"

"Shh!" She repeated with the authority of age and experience.

I took a bite of cookie.

There was a loud pop and a chunk of grass and dirt exploded an inch from rabbit stew. The brown fluff launched itself straight up and hit the grass like a ground ball drilling through the center fielder's stomach. It didn't stop running until it was three houses down.

"Oh, good." Lucille removed the silencer. "That's Marion's yard. She loves animals. It's never good to disturb the neighbors." She smiled, popped the ammo out and returned gun, bullets, and silencer to the drawer. "So, what do you think?" She gestured at the cookie that was halfway to my mouth.

"You missed," I gurgled.

"You don't like it?"

"The rabbit."

"Well, I didn't want to kill the misguided creature." She looked indignant and swished her flower-print dress as she turned to me. "And I never miss." She sighed. "Will the cookies help me get lucky with the new geezer wheezer at the senior center? And just to be clear, torturing old ladies is that rabbit's favorite pastime."

"He's gay," I stated.

"The rabbit? And how would you know?"

"The Senior Center," I replied calmly.

"Honey, dear, you aren't keeping up, unless you're talking about the rabbit, and I wouldn't know about his orientation. We've had several new arrivals and I need to stake my claim soon or that awful Henrietta will scoop them up. Now focus. The cookies?"

My conversations with Lucille were rarely focused and usually disjointed. I was trying to think in a straight line. Lucille preferred triangles, stars, hexagons or anything that gave her brain lots of room to wander.

We first met when I drove her to the airport on her way to scatter her husband's ashes. Most of him made it through security and onto the airplane. There was a leak in the box and a little bit of him ended up in the giant ride-around airport vacuum. Some went up the nose of a drug-sniffing beagle. But that was months ago. Lucille was ready to move on with her love life. She looks like Betty White and acts like Clint Eastwood. Sometimes she seems a little vague, but I happen to know she has a steel-trap mind and is a great shot with a big gun. Rumor has it she used to work for the FBI.

Lucille pays the fare in cash, but she tips in homemade cookies. The object of her cookies and her affection is any unattached male over the age of sixty who knows that oral sex is a two-way street. She lives in a two-family Victorian side by side. Her landlord, who lives on the other side, is the same police Lieutenant Jon Stevens from my recent interview at the cop house.

Lucille rarely worries about who's in charge of her relationships since it is always her. I don't have the same luxury. Jon is an authoritative kind of guy and I'm an anti-authoritative kind of woman.

Lucille tossed her handbag onto the counter. It landed with an ominous thud. "Let's make sure I have everything we need."

Using the pronoun "we" allowed her to add to the bag's contents. She rooted around in the cavernous interior, pulling out two paperbacks. One looked like a steamy romance. The other was a copy of War and Peace.

"Excellent examples of fine literature. I never know what kind of mood I might be in." She held up the heavier book. "I've been trying to get through this since I was in high school."

She fished out lipstick, a nail file, and a box of condoms, followed by a purple vibrator.

"Oh, I sincerely hope I need those," she said, pointing to the condoms. "But not that." She slid the vibrator into the kitchen drawer next to the Glock. I had a brief mental image of the Glock with a condom stretched snugly over the muzzle.

She pulled out a Swiss army knife with more attachments than my email. "Not for bridge." She tossed it back to the junk drawer. "Hmm." She held up dental floss.

I shrugged. "If Julia Roberts needed it in Pretty Woman, why not?"

Lucille dropped it into a pocket and pulled out a roll of toilet paper.

"Is the supply at the senior center inadequate?" I asked.

She smiled and tossed it in the direction of the bathroom. Assorted pens, pencils and note pads were tucked inside and zipped closed. Sunglasses, reading glasses, long-distance glasses, back-up glasses, matches, a flashlight. The last went back into the drawer. Her wallet, checkbook and passport went into a side pocket.

"Now, do you think I need any more defensive weapons? I'll leave the Glock at home, but possibly the brass knuckles? The checkbook in case I lose the bridge game. The passport in case I need to leave the country. And it's a good I.D. More intimidating than a driver's license."

"Lucille, you're going to play bridge. None of the players are less than seventy years old. Where will you use the condoms? They don't even have beds in the senior center." I ignored the brass knuckles. Seniors are serious about their bridge games.

"Honey, you have no imagination. Haven't you ever done it in a dressing room?" Lucille's eyes misted. "I remember one time in New York. We were in Saks Fifth Avenue…"

"Time to go."

306

"Of course, these days, what with all the meds floating around, you never know when they might get it up. Too many pain killers, not enough Viagra."

Too much information, I thought as I hastily scooped everything into the oversized purse, sensing the beginning of one of our disjointed conversations. I hustled out the door.

Lucille followed reluctantly, glancing around for something more to cram into the bag.

A simple trip to the senior center probably wouldn't cause any problems between me and Jon. On the rare occasions that our professions overlapped, the results weren't pretty. A taxi is a magnet for people in a hurry. Sometimes they are more anxious to get away from somewhere than to go to somewhere. That may involve police cars in an equal hurry. We get calls from cop central telling us to please not pick up anyone in specific areas. It usually means that the anyone they are talking about is an escaped prisoner or may have just held up the local bank. Small town bank robbers are not known for their long-range plans and they occasionally forget about get-away transportation. More than one has called a cab to take them to and from a robbery. I once got the call from the cops right after I had picked up a scruffy looking character in the vicinity they were worried about. I told them to patch me through to Lt. Jon Stevens, pulled around the corner to the police station and told my fare to get out. There were three uniforms waiting.

But probably not at the senior center. My biggest ambition is to live a life free of drama, filled with music and flowers everywhere. Taxi driving has the music if I put a disc in the player. And flowers, like my life, grow wild. Unfortunately, in the two years I've been driving, the taxi has also had a high level of drama.

Still, before this morning, I hadn't seen Jon for a few days. And, to paraphrase Three Dog Night, one is a lonely number. I wouldn't mind seeing him in a more intimate setting, although Lucille might have encouraged me to seduce him on the table in the interrogation room.

We got to the senior center in five minutes. Lucille got out and heaved her bag with everything that a long-march army would ever want over her shoulder, staggered up the sidewalk and disappeared into the gathering of elders.

I headed back to the Cool Rides garage to see what Mona had on my agenda. Mona is slightly over five feet tall and guards the taxis like a pit bull. She keeps the drivers focused and on target. We always need new drivers. Some drivers, especially guys, have trouble with her dictatorial approach. I went inside to the office, hoping she might not notice the bullet bing.

"You got a train station, prepaid charge card. Kid's name is Terry," Mona growled and handed me a fare slip.

"I'm on it." I trotted back outside.

The slip gave me name, address, cell phone, time of pick-up and address of drop-off. Pickup was right away. The train station was twenty minutes down the interstate. I hustled just in case one of those pesky big rigs had turned over in the middle of the highway. Exiting the highway sent me through the nicer part of Springfield until I turned the corner to the train station. About a decade ago the station moved from a glorious

Grand Central style building to a depressing pre-fab box attached to the front of a wall made of pyramid size stones. Around the corner is one of the biggest strip clubs in the city. It's a tough part of town. Rumor is that the old station is going to be rebuilt. In the meantime, taxi drivers try not to linger.

I pulled into a space near a fire hydrant but far enough from it that if the giant stones caught fire, I wouldn't be in the way. There were no cars parked behind me. A big black caddy with tinted windows was three spaces ahead. Most of the passengers had hurriedly dispersed. Two people were left. One was a gangly sleepy-eyed teenager with too-big jeans. He was good-looking but had a veneer of grime, like he had been living on the street for a while. A big guy in a suit loomed over the kid, blocking the route to my cab. The suit's body type reminded me of a TV show I had seen about mountain gorillas—big upper body, long arms and really short legs. The teen looked stoned. But he was my fare. I needed to distract the ape in a suit and grab my passenger before he turned into a stain on the sidewalk.

"You owe me, fucking lowlife punk. Those were to sell." The suit was loud and pissed. He had an odd lisp and a nasal tone, like maybe someone had knocked out one of his front teeth and flattened his nose. I lowered both windows on the driver's side. The ape man grabbed the kid, lifting him off the ground. He shoved him against the wall and whispered something in his ear.

"Hey, someone call a cab?" I yelled.

The big guy turned and slid his right hand under his jacket. I've watched Lucille practice drawing her weapon at the shooting range. I recognized the move. But he let go of the kid when he went for his gun. In a split second the kid was on the ground and running. Luckily I had lowered the windows because the kid dove through the back one. I felt him hit the seat. The big guy was slower with his big bulk and short legs, but he was still only two steps behind. He thrust a huge arm through my open window. His other hand waved a gun. Up close and personal he smelled like a vat of mint julep. Too much aftershave. My eyes watered.

"Shit!" I yelped.

About the Author:

When Harriet Rogers was fourteen, she picked tobacco and didn't learn to smoke for three years. When she was seventeen, she picked oranges in Israel and had Ben-Gurion's revenge for a month. When she was nineteen, she worked the night shift at the Oxford pickle factory and couldn't have relish on her hot dogs for five years. She spent ten years getting through three years of college and, while she still doesn't have any letters after her name, she can say "shit" in five languages.

She has some 2nd and 3rd place ribbons from horseback riding...and a bad back, knee and elbow from the same.

When she was driving a taxi, she started a ten-book series about a taxi driver. *Small Town Taxi* is the first book in this series.

Her mission is to make people laugh. Laughter is the soul of the human machine.